Savage Apocalypse
Book One:
The Cry Of The Dead

By Scott Dokey

This book is dedicated to my daughter, Kaylee, whose radiant smile and contagious laughter lift me up even in the darkest of times.

CHAPTER 1

The cries of the dead were the only sounds that slithered through the air, a cacophony of despair that strangled any remaining hope. The apocalypse was no longer a looming threat; it had arrived, and it was all-consuming. Aldin screamed as the beast closed in on her, a cry that echoed into the void, unheard and unheeded. It was a sound of primal terror, the kind that grips your heart and squeezes until every beat feels like it could be your last. This was no ordinary beast; it was a creature born from the ashes of a once-gentle world, twisted into something unrecognizable by the hellish forces unleashed upon Terran 5. A world now in the throes of death.

The creature regarded her with its single, gleaming eye, the other a hollow, black socket. The flesh of its face had been stripped away, revealing the bare bone beneath, a grotesque mask of death. Through its mangled maw, a guttural growl rumbled, the sound of a nightmare made flesh. As it lunged, Aldin couldn't help but feel a pang of sorrow for the beast. It was a Derian, one of the gentle giants who once roamed the planet with serene grace. Now it was a monstrosity, driven by an insatiable hunger.

Aldin closed her eyes, bracing for the end. She could almost feel the beast's rancid breath, could almost hear the tearing of flesh, the crunch of bone. But then, a sound—a crack that split the air. She opened her eyes, expecting to see the beast's jaws closing in, but found it sprawled at her feet, a hole in its head and black blood pooling around her.

Ridley was standing there with a blaster in her hand and a crooked smile on her face.

"You came back for me?" Aldin's voice trembled.

"I almost didn't," Ridley replied, her tall, lanky form a silhouette against the dying light.

The words cut deeper than any wound the beast could have inflicted. Aldin's eyes misted over as she looked at Ridley, hoping against hope that there was still something left between them. She dropped her head, turning away from the only person she had ever truly loved. "Why did you?" she asked, her voice barely a whisper.

Ridley was silent for a moment, searching for words that no longer came easily. Finally, she said, "I couldn't just leave you out here to die."

"Why not? Everyone else did."

"What did you expect, Aldin? Look around you! All of this is your fault!"

The truth of it stung, a knife twisting in her gut. She hadn't meant for this to happen. She had only wanted to create a world free of pain. But her earnestness had unleashed a force that had torn the world apart, dragging it down into a spiral of death and destruction.

The apocalypse was here, and there was no escaping it. Not for her. Not for anyone. As she stood there, staring at the ruin she had wrought, Aldin realized that in the end, it didn't matter what her intentions had been. All that mattered was the devastation left in their wake.

***

Systemic Youth Hemorrhagic Fever, SYHF-20—so named for its ruthless assault on children with compromised immune systems—had reaped a grim harvest over the years. Thousands of little lives were snuffed out, including Aldin's brother, Seth, taken when he was just four. That memory, as sharp and unyielding as a serrated blade, drove Aldin. She had sworn to hunt down this invisible beast and end its reign of terror.

But the beast was elusive. Despite their technological marvels, the Intergalactic Scientific Assembly—ISA for short—had yet to create a cure. Undeterred, Aldin poured her soul into the fight, toiling to the point of exhaustion, until her vision blurred and her body begged for rest. Her unrelenting determination earned her a coveted position as a research scientist at Startac Labs, the crown jewel of Terran 5.

As Aldin approached the facility on her first day, her heart pounded with a mixture of excitement and dread born from the enormous amount of responsibility now thrust upon her. This moment was a crystallized dream from her youth, now finally within her grasp. She stepped into the grand edifice, her eyes drinking in the sight of the large replica of the first quantum field generator, and the complex formula that Jaxon Startac had devised.

She was memorizing the formula when she met Jensen, and the air seemed to chill instantly. Short and scowling, with a face set in a perpetual pout, his words cut deeper than any scalpel. "Don't pretend you can grasp the complexities of that formula," he sneered.

Aldin's mouth went dry, her voice stolen by the sheer audacity of his rudeness. Jensen's eyes bore into her, dissecting her without mercy. "I assume you're Aldin?" His voice dripped with disdain. "Follow me. I'll show you to your lab, though I doubt you'll last long enough to make it your own."

"What do you mean by that?" Aldin asked, her voice a fragile thing on the brink of shattering.

"Simply put, most new recruits find the demands here beyond their capabilities. They frequently leave after a short time for easier endeavors. I suspect you'll follow the same path."

Aldin's spine stiffened. Her eyes narrowed, her tone turning to steel. "But you don't know anything about me."

Jensen's lip curled in a sneer. "I know enough."

He turned sharply and passed through the nearby door, not waiting for her to follow. She barely slipped through the opening before it closed behind her, the heavy click of it echoing loudly in her ears.

The hallway beyond was lined with doors, each one leading to a lab dedicated to the study of different wildlife species, all for the advancement of medicine.

Jensen halted at one of the doors halfway down the hall. "Wait here," he barked before he disappeared into the room beyond.

He returned moments later with a lab coat and a key-card. "Your lab is next to my office." He said smugly. "Just know that I'll be watching you closely." With that, he spun around and left her standing there, her mind a whirlpool of doubt.

What have I gotten myself into? she wondered, trying to steady herself. Jensen's harshness had left her shaken, questioning whether she'd made the right decision in coming there.

Slowly, she trudged down the hall to the next door. But as soon as she stepped inside the lab, her trepidation melted away. It was like stepping into a wonderland. Her eyes widened in awe as she wandered among the workstations. A soft squeal of delight escaped her when she saw the compact particle accelerator in one corner, and another at the sight of the quantum generator across the room.

A voice startled her from her reverie. "It looks like you approve?"

Aldin turned to see two women in lab coats, both older, both identical. Their hair was streaked with gray and white, and they wore matching smiles.

"Yes, it's wonderful. Everything I've dreamed of. Though the head scientist doesn't seem thrilled with my presence."

"Jensen?" The woman on the left said, her tone gentle. "Don't take it personally. He's tough and direct, but he's a genius. Just socially... challenged."

Aldin chuckled, feeling a bit of the tension ease. "I'm Aldin."

The woman on the left smiled. "I'm Chastine, and this is my twin, Chantel."

"Welcome," Chantel added.

"I've never met twins before," Aldin said, fascinated. "Are you both senior scientists?"

Both women nodded in unison.

"I'll probably be calling on you a lot, if that's alright."

"Of course," Chastine replied. "Our lab is just down the hall, across from Jensen's office."

"Jensen certainly likes to be in the center of everything, doesn't he?" Aldin remarked.

"That he does," Chantel said with a knowing smile.

The twins turned and left, leaving Aldin to explore her new domain. The first hum of the particle accelerator was music to her ears, and soon, she was lost in the intricate dance of quantum mechanics and algorithms.

With the vast resources the lab provided, Aldin found

herself completely immersed in her work, more so than ever before. She dove into her experiments with a fervor that bordered on mania, but no matter how many times she tried, the results were always the same. Failure.

Yet she knew she was close. She could feel it, a tingling sensation just beneath her skin, as if the answer was whispering to her from the shadows of her mind. Then the floor dropped out from beneath her. She was ordered to halt her research. The command came from Jensen, citing out-of-control expenditures and a lack of conclusive results.

For a long moment, she sat at her workstation, teetering on the edge of tears. The sterile white of the lab walls seemed to close in around her, mocking her with their unyielding brightness. Then a chirp from her console broke the silence. She took a deep breath, steeling herself before pressing the button to receive the transmission. An instant later, a hologram flickered into existence before her. It was Tanith, a medic at Startac's Seascape facility.

"Aldin, I'm glad you're there. I have something you might be interested in," he said.

"Tanith! It's been a long time. What do you have?"

"We have a patient currently in recovery from the SYHF virus who has volunteered to donate a series of antibodies for scientific study. Given your extensive research into the virus, I thought of you first."

"You mean the research that has led me to a dead end repeatedly?"

Tanith chuckled, a low, rumbling sound. "If I know you, you won't give up until you find a cure."

Aldin grew somber, the weight of her failures pressing down on her shoulders. "I can't give up, Tanith. Too many have died from this terrible scourge. But Jensen shut me down. He's blocked me from working on the virus. If I defy him, I'll be forced out of the facility."

"That doesn't make any sense. You're one of the most gifted scientists there."

"It doesn't matter."

"Okay. I don't want to get you in any trouble. I'll see who else I can find," Tanith said.

He was just about to disconnect when Aldin stopped him. "Wait! Can you get them to me so he wouldn't find out?"

Tanith's holographic form shimmered, his eyes narrowing slightly. "Of course. I can be very discreet."

"Thank you," she said, the words barely more than a whisper.

The hologram disappeared, leaving Aldin alone in the oppressive silence of the lab. She wondered if she'd just made the biggest mistake of her career, or if this desperate gamble would finally lead her to the breakthrough she so desperately needed. The shadows seemed to shift around her, the air growing colder, as if the ghosts of those lost to the virus were watching, waiting, and hoping she would succeed.

Aldin spent the next few days in a haze of anticipation and anxiety. Every hum of the building's auxiliary systems, every soft murmur of her colleagues in the hallway made her jump. She continued with her other projects, all the while her mind racing with thoughts of how Tanith might get the samples to her.

Late one evening, as the lab was shrouded in silence, Aldin received an encrypted message on her personal device. It was a series of coordinates near an old storage facility at the edge of the research complex. She glanced around the empty lab, her heart pounding, then quickly gathered her things and left.

Under the cover of darkness, Aldin made her way to the designated location. The storage facility was a small and worn-out structure, long abandoned and seldom visited. Her breath was shallow, her nerves frayed as she waited in the shadows.

The night air was cool and still, the only sounds drifting through the air were the faint hum of distant machinery. The moon hung high in the night sky, casting a pale glow over the scene, but the facility remained cloaked in darkness.

As the night deepened, a shadow detached itself from the darkness near the building. Tanith stepped into the dim light of a distant spotlight, a small, unassuming case in his hand. A tall and lanky man, he moved with the confidence of someone who had done this many times before, his movements fluid and silent.

"Aldin," he whispered, his voice barely audible. He handed her the case, his eyes scanning the surroundings for any sign of movement. "Inside, you'll find the samples you need. Be careful."

She took the case in her hand, her fingers trembling slightly. The weight of it felt both reassuring and terrifying. "Thank you, Tanith. I don't know how to repay you."

He smiled, a brief flash of warmth in the cold night. "Just find the cure, Aldin. That's all the repayment I need."

With that, he melted back into the shadows, leaving Aldin alone with her precious cargo. She hurried back to her lab, every step filled with a mix of fear and hope. The path seemed longer in the darkness, each echo of her footsteps a reminder of the risk she was taking.

Once inside the safety of her lab, she locked the door and opened the case. The vials of antibodies glinted under the sterile lab lights, each one a beacon of possibility.

The cool, antiseptic smell of the lab was comforting now, almost like a second skin. Aldin moved methodically, her thoughts focused and clear. She couldn't help but glance at the door every now and then, half-expecting Jensen to burst in and end it all. But the minutes ticked by, turning into hours, and the night remained undisturbed.

Finally, as the first hints of dawn began to creep through the high, narrow windows, she held up the final vial. The liquid inside shimmered faintly, a promise of salvation. Her heart hammered in her chest as she prepared the sample for testing, every motion precise and deliberate.

The machines hummed to life, analyzing the sample with speed and accuracy. Aldin watched the readouts with bated breath, her fingers drumming a nervously on the counter.

A beep broke the silence, a single, solitary note that signaled the end of the test. Aldin stared at the screen, her eyes widening as the results flashed up. Positive. The antibodies were viable.

Aldin sank to her knees, her eyes filling with tears. It wasn't the end, not by a long shot, but it was the breakthrough she needed. And it had all hinged on a shadowy meeting under the cover of darkness, a desperate gamble that had paid off.

As she rose and began to prepare her report, she knew she would have to tread carefully. Jensen wouldn't take kindly to being defied, and there would be questions. But for now, in the stillness of the early morning, Aldin allowed herself a moment of triumph. She had taken the first step toward a cure. And nothing, not even the specter of Jensen's wrath, could take that away from her.

CHAPTER 2

A holographic 3-D module of the SYHF virus hovered above the table in the center of the lab, casting eerie, pulsating shadows on the sleek metallic surfaces. The intricate structure of the virus rotated slowly, each spike and node a grim reminder of the deadly pathogen she was up against. In a nearby airtight chamber, a live test subject injected with the antibodies lay restrained within the particle accelerator, which hummed steadily, its sound a constant, almost soothing backdrop to Aldin's frenetic activity at the complex series of computer workstations.

Her fingers flew over the keyboard, executing a series of complex commands on one of the terminals. The screens flickered with lines of code and graphs that monitored the test subject's vitals and the antibody's interaction with the virus. Aldin turned to watch the effects on the holographic model, her heart pounding in her chest. For a brief, tantalizing moment, hope filled her eyes as the simulation indicated initial success. The virus appeared to waver, its formidable structure weakening.

Then, without warning, the model flickered and reverted, the virus stabilizing and overcoming the antibodies. The hopeful spark in Aldin's eyes extinguished as quickly as it had ignited. She slammed her fist down on the counter with a force that sent a sharp pain up her arm. "I'm never going to figure this out!" she shouted, her voice echoing off the lab's cold, unfeeling walls.

Images of her little brother, Seth, lying inches from death in a sterile hospital bed, filled her mind. His skin, once vibrant and full of life, had turned pale and clammy, his breaths shallow and labored. It was an image that had woken her from sleep trembling more times than she could remember. Tears welled up in her eyes, blurring her vision. "I'm sorry, Seth," she cried softly, her voice breaking.

She allowed herself a few minutes of reflection, standing motionless in the dim light of the lab. Her shoulders slumped under the weight of her failure, her mind teetering on the edge of despair. But then, with a deep, shuddering breath, she straightened up, pulling her shoulders back. Determination hardened her features as she returned to the workstations, her movements precise and deliberate.

She launched into another round of tests, each one a desperate attempt to find the elusive breakthrough. The minutes turned into hours, the lab's sterile environment amplifying the passage of time. Each test ended with the same result: failure. The particle accelerator's hum seemed to grow louder, mocking her relentless efforts.

Her body began to betray her. Exhaustion crept in, blurring her vision and making her legs feel like lead. She forced herself to keep going, her hands trembling as she typed. The room around her started to spin, the edges of her vision darkening. She stumbled, her legs wobbly and unsteady. Desperation clawed at her mind as she fought to stay conscious, but her body couldn't take any more.

The lab swayed around her, the holographic virus model

spinning wildly as if it too was caught in her descent. Her knees buckled, and she fell to the floor with a heavy thud. The cold metal was unforgiving against her skin. The last thing she saw before everything went dark was the haunting image of the virus floating above her, mocking her.

***

The soft whirring of the machinery morphed into a metallic clang that shattered Aldin's sleep and sent her heart pounding in her chest. She shot to her knees, smoke snaking through the room like a hungry serpent. Panic gripped her as her eyes locked onto the particle accelerator, now glowing with a dangerous heat.

Her breath caught in her throat, and she lunged for the controls, desperate to power down the machine. Too late. The explosion that followed was a beast untamed, roaring through the lab with a fury that hurled Aldin across the room. Shrapnel and radiation laced the air, a deadly cocktail of destruction. She crashed into the far wall and slumped to the hard floor. Darkness swallowed the room, an eerie silence lingering before the backup power grudgingly flickered to life. Safety protocols kicked in, and the extinguishing systems hissed into action, battling the blaze that threatened to consume everything.

Aldin lay sprawled on the floor, eyes wide with fear. Her lab was a graveyard of equipment, sparks of electricity dancing in the air like tiny, vengeful specters. Ridley burst into the room, her face a mask of terror. Her eyes scanned the wreckage, locking onto Aldin's prone form, fearing the worst. Relief flooded through her when she saw Aldin struggle to her feet.

"Aldin!" Ridley's voice was a lifeline. "What happened?

Are you okay?"

"I don't know," Aldin's voice wavered as she gripped a nearby desk, trying to anchor herself in the chaos.

A voice, cold and dripping with malice, cut through the tension. "I'll tell you what happened."

Mishka, the head of security, sauntered into the room, her venomous gaze fixed on Aldin. "Your girlfriend fell asleep with the particle accelerator on."

Ridley's eyes widened in shock. "Is that true, Aldin?"

Silence was Aldin's only answer, her eyes dropping to the floor.

"Don't worry, Ridley," Mishka sneered. "We have it all on surveillance. I'll launch a complete investigation into her negligence immediately."

Ridley moved toward Mishka, but two security officers stepped forward, hands hovering over their blasters. The tension was a living thing, thick and suffocating.

"This is not the time, Mishka!" Jensen's voice sliced through the potential conflict, as he and a slew of facility personnel entered the lab. "We'll sort this out later."

Aldin flinched at Jensen's words. His contempt for her was legendary, a dark cloud that had often made her consider abandoning her work. But she had always held on, driven by a purpose that now seemed hopeless in the face of her latest failure.

Jensen's glare was withering. "Unless you can explain yourself, you sorry excuse for a scientist, your time here is over."

Aldin's voice trembled. "Look, Jensen, I'm close. I can feel it," she pleaded.

Jensen's rage was a storm. "You were working on the SYHF virus again? You were ordered to stay away from that! Your reckless disregard for authority has endangered us all!"

Realization hit Aldin like a physical blow. The virus! It had been inside the particle accelerator when it exploded. Her fear was cut short by a sudden clamor from a nearby lab, a horrifying blend of metal crashing and animals screeching.

"Check it out," Jensen ordered Mishka.

With a final scowl at Aldin, Mishka led the other officers toward the noise. "You too, Ridley. Up front, now!"

Ridley's anger flared, but she knew better than to defy Mishka. "I'll be back," she promised Aldin, her voice a low growl.

Aldin nodded weakly, the weight of her mistakes crashing down around her. Everything she'd worked for was slipping away, piece by piece, moment by moment.

Once the security team had left, Jensen turned to Aldin, a stern expression covering his face. His eyes were cold and hard as he looked at her. "I'm placing you on administrative leave, effective immediately, pending an investigation. You will not be allowed anywhere near this facility until the investigation is complete. Is that understood?"

Aldin didn't need to answer, compliance was a foregone conclusion, and Jensen knew it.

Suddenly, a chorus of wails echoed through the lab, a chilling symphony of pain and death. The sound was a horrifying screech that sent shivers down everyone's spine.

Blaster shots rang out, a desperate volley of light and sound, followed by the approach of footsteps. The steps faltered near the doorway, and a rookie guard named Jasper staggered into view. He collapsed forward, his upper torso sprawled in the doorway, his face and hands marked with savage claw wounds. Blood pooled beneath him, dark and relentless.

"Help me," he gasped, his voice a whisper of agony. Something yanked him back into the hall, his final scream echoing down the corridor.

For a moment, the scientists were paralyzed by shock. Then Jensen sprang into action, slamming a button on the wall that sent the door sliding shut.

"What are you doing?" Aldin cried. "There are still people out there!"

"The security team can handle themselves," Jensen replied in an icy tone. "That's what they're trained for. But you're welcome to join them if you'd like."

Loud pounding on the other side of the door made everyone jump. Aldin glanced at the monitor and saw Ridley, pounding feverishly to be let inside.

"Open the door!" Ridley shouted. "Don't leave us out here, Jensen!"

Aldin reached for the button, but Jensen grabbed her wrist.

"Don't you dare," he hissed.

"But we can't leave them out there!" she pleaded.

"We can, and we will."

Jensen ushered the rest of the scientists toward the back of the lab. "We'll go out the rear door and head down the maintenance corridor to the main lobby."

Aldin felt a wave of helplessness wash over her, tears streaming down her face. The thought of losing Ridley was unbearable.

"Where do you think you're going?" Jensen sneered as she tried to join the others. "You're not coming with us."

"But... what am I supposed to do?" Aldin's voice cracked.

"I don't care. Whatever's happening out there is your fault. There must be consequences."

Before she could respond, Jensen led the scientists through the rear door and promptly sealed it behind him. A second later, Aldin heard a decisive click. She was locked in, alone with her fear and the sound of her own breaking heart.

Ridley hesitated, her footsteps echoing down the dimly lit corridor. The flickering overhead lights cast elongated shadows on the walls, and the air smelled of dampness and decay. Mishka led the way, her eyes darting nervously from side to side. Ridley's mind raced, every thought a desperate plea for Aldin's safety. She couldn't bear the idea of leaving her behind with Jensen, that cold-hearted bastard who reveled in others' suffering. Jensen's contempt was palpable, aimed at anyone who dared challenge his authority. Yet, his utter disdain for Aldin was on a completely different level—a deep-seated venomous hatred that exceeded anything she had witnessed before.

Mishka's attitude didn't help matters. Their shared history, a tangled web of secrets and betrayal, weighed heavily on Ridley's shoulders. She wished Mishka would let go of the past, move on, but stubbornness clung to her like a curse. It was what had torn them apart in the first place—the relentless grip of old wounds and unforgiven mistakes. Ridley had felt like a prisoner, her faults held against her, extinguishing any chance of redemption.

As they approached the door leading to the gene therapy

labs, a cacophony of animal cries assaulted their ears. The source lay beyond that threshold—a place of twisted experiments and forbidden knowledge. Metal bars clanged, enclosures strained, and the air hummed with tension. Ridley's blaster hung heavy at her side.

"That doesn't sound good," she muttered, her gaze fixed on the door.

Mishka's eyes narrowed. "Everyone be ready."

But Kalen, the fresh-faced recruit who had joined their squad only days ago, had already pressed the button to open the door. Mishka's warning came too late. The creature lunged—a Malrun, once a harmless pet for many Terrans, now a twisted abomination. Its claws tore into Kalen's flesh, gouging at his eyes. The savage fangs clamped onto his neck, ripping his throat out in a spray of blood.

Kalen fell, life slipping through his fingers. The Malrun stood atop him, a grotesque parody of dominance. Its white fur was stained crimson, black ichor dripping from its mouth. Madness gleamed in its eyes as it prepared for another attack.

Ridley raised her blaster, firing at the creature and sending it crashing into the wall. For a moment it remained motionless, then they watched in horror a second later as the Malrun struggled to stand back up with a large blaster hole in its chest. Mishka responded with a blast of her own that hit the creature in its head, silencing it for good.

The other animals in the lab wailed—a chorus of mourning and fury. Ridley quickly pressed the button to close the door, but one creature slipped through—an agile primate, alternating between scampering on four legs and two—a gurgled grunting issuing from the beast as it flew through the door just before it slammed shut.

Ridley caught a brief glimpse of the chaos unfolding inside the lab, and watched in that split-second, like a slow-motion video stream, as a maddened horde of creatures rushed toward them, while others scampered up into the ceiling, or into the far corners of the room and disappeared, each one bearing the unmistakable signs of death. *This is bad!* she thought. *Real bad!* The chaos inside unfolded like a nightmare: creatures converging, shadows dancing, death lurking in every corner.

She barely had time to dodge away from the Pentu's attack, her boots skidding on the bloody floor. The beast lunged, its decaying claws scraping the air where she'd stood a heartbeat earlier. The walls of the dimly lit corridor seemed to close in, suffocating her.

When the Pentu turned its decaying head, its eyes locked onto hers. Its teeth, yellowed and jagged, snapped together in an angry snarl. But it wasn't rage that fueled those gnashing jaws; it was hunger. A desperate, primal need for sustenance. The beast's only driving force as it readied itself for another attack.

Jasper, the youngest member of the security team, fired a blaster shot. The weapon's hum echoed through the corridor, but the Pentu merely staggered, even though a wide swath of flesh opened up along its back, spraying black blood against the walls. The creature turned, revealing patches along its body where the flesh had fallen away, exposing bone and tissue. Its internal organs pulsed with a grotesque rhythm, like a symphony of decay.

"This thing should be dead!" Ridley's voice trembled, her eyes wide as the beast advanced toward Jasper.

Mishka fired her blaster, the shots hitting the Pentu without effect. The creature ignored her, its focus unwavering. Jasper fired again, but panic had set in. He spun, blaster trembling in his grip, and fled down the corridor. His screams echoed, ricocheting off the walls as he fired blindly over his shoulder.

The Pentu pursued after him, defying its decayed state. It moved faster than physics allowed, driven by an insatiable hunger. Jasper neared the lab, desperation etched on his face. Safety was within reach, but the beast leaped, its weight crashing down on him. Bones cracked, and Jasper crumpled to the floor.

The Pentu's claws tore at his back, and its teeth sank into his shoulder. Flesh ripped away, blood gushing. Jasper's scream echoed, filling the corridor. Blood pooled around him, a crimson tide. If he didn't bleed out first, he'd drown in it—the final offering to the insatiable hunger of the beast.

Using his last ounce of will, Jasper pushed his body up, the pain radiating through every sinew. The Pentu, a grotesque fusion of nightmare and flesh, clung to him like a leech. Its claws dug into his shoulder, and its breath, foul and rancid, washed over him. Jasper's blaster lay inches away, its cold metal promising salvation.

The beast rose, its eyes twin pits of malevolence. Jasper's fingers closed around the blaster's grip, trembling with exhaustion. He aimed at the creature's chest, the barrel steady despite his trembling limbs. The shot echoed through the dimly lit corridor, and the Pentu staggered backward. For a moment, Jasper dared to hope it was dead, that he'd vanquished the abomination. But deep within, he knew better.

As Jasper struggled to his feet, the world swaying around him, he glimpsed the lab door ahead. Salvation lay there, behind the reinforced steel. He stumbled, each step an agony, his vision narrowing to a tunnel of pain.

Death's door loomed, its threshold beckoning. The huddled scientists inside—their faces etched with terror—were his last hope.

The Pentu lunged, its claws slashing. Jasper's legs gave way, and he fell forward, his body teetering on the precipice. "Help me," Jasper croaked.

The Pentu's grip tightened, and it yanked him backward. The impact against the corridor wall was brutal, and Jasper's head exploded in a burst of agony, spraying blood and brain matter as darkness claimed him.

Ridley and Mishka turned the corner just in time to see Jasper's body collapse, lifeless, onto the cold floor, as the Pentu feasted on his insides with a ravenous desperation that echoed the growls of the damned. It tore through flesh and bone eagerly, seeking to sate an unending hunger that death itself could not quell.

Unloading their weapons into the beast did nothing; it was as if the laser fire were mere whispers against a storm. But when the creature, soaked in the crimson of Jasper's life, turned its gaze toward them, Mishka found her mark. A single shot to the head, and the Pentu dropped to the floor. This time, dead for good.

Immediately, the clamor inside the gene therapy lab grew loud enough that it echoed around them with an all-encompassing roar. Above them, they heard claws scratching feverishly at the metal ducts, searching for a way to get at them.

Ridley and Mishka looked at each other in terror. They knew it was only a matter of time before the sheer force of the horde in the lab would force the door open and release the nightmares inside. They raced toward the door, only to have it slam shut a moment before.

"It's Jensen," Mishka spat, venom in her voice. "He's saving his skin at our expense."

Ridley's fists hammered against the door, a futile gesture against the steel barrier. "Jensen!" she screamed, her voice a raw edge of panic and betrayal. "Open up! You can't do this!"

But the door remained indifferent, and Mishka's words cut through Ridley's pleas. "Forget it. We both know Jensen's a coward who only cares about himself. We need to find another way."

Ridley's heart ached to leave, to abandon hope, but Mishka was already moving, her command irrefutable. With a heavy heart, Ridley cast a last glance at the screen, saying a silent prayer that Aldin would see her, before she turned to follow.

The corridor offered no solace, only reminders of the nightmare they now lived in. Mishka paused by the Pentu's corpse, her eyes narrowing at the sight of a black ichor that snaked away from the body, a sinister trail that vanished into the shadows.

Ridley recoiled from the sight. "How can something like that keep moving? You shot it, and it just kept coming. It wouldn't die!"

Mishka's gaze lingered on the fallen monster. "Because it was already dead," she murmured, a chill settling in her voice. She stood, facing Ridley with a grave certainty. "And it's all because of your girlfriend."

Ridley's denial was instant and fierce. "That's insane!"

"Is it?" Mishka countered. "She was experimenting with a deadly virus inside a particle accelerator that exploded. Who knows what horrors the radiation unleashed?"

The argument was drowned out by the crescendo of cries and the pounding at the lab door—a cacophony that underscored the danger they faced.

Mishka was already moving, her resolve unshakable. "Believe what you will, but I'm not waiting for death to come knocking."

With reluctance shadowing her every step, Ridley followed. The sight of Kalen's body, the remnants of the undead beast, and the ominous black ooze that seeped from it filled her with a dread so profound, she knew in her bones that the worst was yet to come.

CHAPTER 4

The main lobby of Startac Labs buzzed with life, as visitors and guests mingled with scientists, marveling at the state-of-the-art exhibits in the museum section. The sleek, modern architecture of the building, with its towering glass windows and pristine marble floors, was a technological marvel. Holographic displays showcased breakthroughs in genetic engineering, while interactive panels allowed guests to explore the diverse wildlife that inhabited the planet.

Dr. Helena stood near a display case, explaining the latest developments in viral research to a small group of intrigued visitors. Her eyes sparkled with excitement as she spoke, her passion for science evident in every word.

"How do you maintain safety in the lab when you're working with these different viruses?" asked a young man, his voice filled with curiosity and a hint of concern.

Elena smiled reassuringly. "A lot of the specimens we use have been engineered to be harmless to Terrans. Our main focus is on how it affects certain animal populations, particularly those that are endangered. The goal is to find ways to boost their immune systems and increase their chances of survival."

A middle-aged woman with a camera leaned in closer. "How do you manage to alter the virus without it becoming dangerous?"

Elena gestured to a nearby holographic display that showed a detailed model of a specific virus. "We use a combination of genetic editing and advanced computational models to predict and control the virus's behavior. It's a meticulous process, but it allows us to ensure safety at every step."

"These animals you work with, do they ever show adverse reactions?" a teenage girl asked.

Nguyen nodded thoughtfully. "Sometimes they do, which is why we have rigorous testing protocols in place. We monitor their health closely and make adjustments as needed. Our goal is always to minimize any negative impact and maximize the benefits."

A man in his early thirties raised his hand. "Excuse me, Dr. Helena. Can you explain the difference between viruses that affect animals and those that affect people? How do you ensure cross-species safety?"

Helena nodded, welcoming the question. "That's a great question. Viruses are incredibly specific about their hosts. They have evolved to infect particular species by targeting specific receptors on the host cells."

Dr. Nguyen, standing beside her, added, "However, there are always exceptions. That's why we have stringent protocols to prevent any possibility of cross-species transmission. We use biocontainment facilities, genetic safeguards, and continuous monitoring to ensure that our research poses no risk to Terrans."

"But what if a virus were to mutate?" the man persisted. "Is there a risk it could jump to Terrans?"

Helena's expression grew serious. "In theory, yes. That's

why our work is so crucial. By understanding these viruses at a molecular level, we can anticipate potential mutations and develop countermeasures. Our goal is to stay several steps ahead of any possible threat."

Beside her, Nguyen adjusted his glasses, answering questions about the genetic modifications used in their experiments.

"What about the SYHF virus?" another woman asked. "All of us have been touched by this terrible scourge in one way or another. Since this facility is considered the leader in research on the virus, can you tell us about any recent breakthroughs regarding the search for a cure?"

Nguyen replied, "I agree that the tragedy of the SYHF virus has had a devastating effect on families for eons. Here at Startac, we have placed the search for a cure as the highest priority, and have the leading scientist in the field working diligently on it day and night. We feel like a cure is indeed, close at hand."

***

Trenton leaned against the wall near the entrance keeping a watchful eye on the growing crowd as visitors continued to file in for the annual recruitment event. Children laughed as they ran around the lobby, interacting with holographic projections of extinct creatures, while their parents chatted with the scientists regarding the specifics of academia.

A group of schoolchildren gathered around a display showing a holographic projection of a long-extinct predator. One boy, his eyes wide with wonder, pointed at the creature. "Is that real? Did it really exist?"

Helena chuckled, kneeling down to the boy's level. "Yes, it did. This is a reconstruction based on fossil records and genetic data. Isn't it amazing to see how creatures from the past looked and moved?"

"Can you bring them back to life?" another child asked, her eyes sparkling with excitement.

"Not exactly," Helena said with a warm smile. "But we can learn a lot from them, and sometimes we can use what we learn to help living animals today."

Suddenly, a low rumble echoed through the lobby, causing the ground to tremble. The holographic displays flickered, and a murmur of confusion rippled through the crowd. Helena exchanged a concerned glance with Nguyen.

"Was that an earthquake?" a visitor asked, looking around nervously.

Before anyone could answer, a deafening explosion shook the building. The floor buckled, and a shock-wave of heat and debris swept through the lobby. Screams filled the air as people were thrown off their feet. Glass shattered, and the once serene environment descended into chaos.

Helena scrambled to her feet, her ears ringing. She looked around in horror as a thick cloud of smoke billowed from the direction of the research labs. Panic surged through the crowd as the emergency alarms blared, their shrill cries adding to the pandemonium.

"Everyone, stay calm!" Trenton shouted, his voice cutting through the chaos. "Head to the emergency exits in an orderly fashion!"

But his words were drowned out by another sound—a deep, guttural growl that sent a chill down Helena's spine. She turned towards the source, her heart pounding.

Emerging from the smoke, a grotesque creature stumbled into the lobby. It had once been a majestic Kambura, a large feline whose ability to withstand various neurotoxins had caused it to become the subject of numerous studies. Now its body was a twisted parody of life, with large patches of flesh missing and exposed bones glistening with blood. Its eyes burned with a desperate hunger.

The Kambura was followed by other abominations, creatures that had once been part of the planet's diverse wildlife. A giant predatory bird, its feathers matted with gore, shrieked as it flapped its mangled wings. A wolf-like Dengo, its fur hanging in tattered strips, snarled and snapped at the air.

Panic erupted as the creatures lunged at the nearest people. The lobby transformed into a nightmare. Visitors and scientists alike were caught in the frenzy, their screams of terror mingling with the roars of the undead animals.

Helena grabbed Nguyen's arm. "We need to get out of here! Now!"

Trenton fired his pulse rifle, the shots echoing through the lobby as he tried to hold off the advancing creatures. "Head to the upper level! It's our best chance!"

Helena and Nguyen ducked as a grotesque bird swooped overhead, its talons narrowly missing them. They sprinted towards the central staircase, weaving through the carnage. The floor was slick with blood, and the air was thick with the stench of decay.

As they reached the staircase, Helena glanced back. A monstrous wolf had pinned a young woman to the ground, its jaws closing around her throat. Her scream was cut short, and Elena's stomach churned with horror.

"Keep moving!" Trenton shouted, covering their retreat. "We can't save them!"

They bounded up the stairs, the sounds of the massacre below spurring them on. As they reached the top step, a loud cry flew from Trenton's mouth, followed by a series of loud thuds. Helena looked back and was horrified to see his body falling to the floor below in two separate pieces. While the winged beast that had sliced him in half with its sharp talons flew down to gorge itself on the dead security officer's insides, a second one landed on the railing only inches away from them. Helena's scream only lasted a second before the beast lunged.

Amid a spray of blood and guts that flew out of his fallen comrade like a geyser, Nguyen rushed toward the door at the edge of the mezzanine, only to be horrified when he couldn't find his key-card to open it. In a last-ditch effort to escape the madness, he dove for cover under a short and narrow maintenance cart, wedging himself into a tight ball. His body shook profusely as he laid there whimpering, praying for deliverance.

CHAPTER 5

Jensen led the scientists through the bowels of the facility, each step a silent drumbeat in a march of vengeance. His blood simmered, a slow burn stoked by the embers of his rage, and a low growl of curses spilled from his lips. The specter of Aldin, framed by the inferno of her own making, was etched into his mind's eye—a vision that ignited a primal urge to extinguish her existence with his bare hands. Yet, he reined in the beast that pulsed with hatred just beneath the surface of his skin, sparing her life by a thread of restraint. Distance was his ally now; the further he got from her toxic aura, the better.

Aldin had become his nemesis, her very presence a thorn in his psyche. Her relentless probing, her audacious defiance of his authority, her stubborn chase of that damned research —despite the warnings, despite the risks—her voice, a grating symphony of dissent, threatened to fracture his sanity. The endgame was near, and with it, the promise of liberation from her annoyance. Jensen harbored no illusions; her departure was imminent, either by his hand or by the nightmare she herself had summoned. Should death claim her in a macabre twist of fate, borne from the hellish landscape she had birthed, well, Jensen would shed no tears for her demise.

They'd barely taken a few steps when the sound clawed its way into their ears, freezing them in their tracks. At first, it was a mere whisper, a sinister murmur echoing in the dimness, but then it grew into a cacophony of desperation crashing towards them like a relentless tide.

The noise seemed to be coming at them from all directions overhead. The ceiling buckled and groaned under the weight of something massive. Metal shrieked in protest, a chilling prelude to the inevitable collapse that followed. From the mouth of the chaos emerged grotesque figures, their flesh mangled, their eyes ablaze with the same insatiable hunger. Each wore the guise of death, the twisted face of an unholy animation, as they descended upon the group with ruthless savagery.

Jensen, gripped by terror, watched as his comrades were ripped apart, with two of his assistants yanked to the floor immediately amidst a flurry of fangs and claws. their screams swallowed by the frenzied onslaught. A symphony of agony filled the air, a discordant chorus of growls and dying gasps that reverberated through the narrow corridor. He watched in horror as the dying screams from those attacked rang through the corridor. Panic clawed at his throat as he rushed forward, using his companions as a shield against the ravenous horde.

Frantically, Jensen whirled and bolted away from the blood-soaked chaos. His heart thundered in his chest as he sprinted towards the nearest door, the gateway to the main temperature control station looming ominously to his left. With trembling hands, he groped for his key-card.

As he fumbled with his card, he was joined by three of the scientists, Chantel, Chastine, and Anon, a tall and silent, imposing man. Only Anon, with his stoic demeanor that bordered on madness, seemed impervious to the looming specter of death. Trailing behind them was Darin, a lab assistant, his eyes wide with terror, stumbling in their wake.

"Jensen, open the door!" Chantel's desperate voice echoed loudly through the corridor.

Initially, Jensen was irritated that they had followed him, but then he realized that having them close would provide him with a shield against the creatures if needed.

"I'm trying, Chantel!" Jensen snapped, his nerves frayed to the breaking point. "But your incessant clamoring isn't exactly helping matters!"

He finally pulled his key-card from his jacket and with a shaky breath, swiped the card through the reader, praying for salvation. Nothing happened. He tried it again, and still nothing. He looked at the card and saw that it had a large splash of blood on the front, which prevented the scanner from reading his code. Everything had moved so fast that he hadn't noticed that the front of his lab coat was covered in blood.

With a curse, he wiped the blood away and tried again. This time, a soft chime filled the air, a fleeting glimmer of hope in the encroaching darkness.

As the last person shuffled inside, Jensen's hand hovered over the button. The metal door whined and groaned as it descended, sealing them inside just as a pack of grotesque monstrosities lurched toward them. Among them, Jensen spotted one he knew all too well—Poxy, a monstrous marsupial with a twisted ear, a creature he had watched grow in the lab. But what froze him in horror was the sight of her pouch, torn open, revealing a newborn hanging by its umbilical cord. The wails of both mother and child filled the air as they collided with the closing door.

Chantel's voice quivered, breaking the tension. "That's Poxy! She was... she was just about to give birth when the explosion happened!"

Darin's eyes darted between Jensen and the unfolding nightmare on the other side of the door, where the howls and cries of the beasts continued unabated. "Doctor, what's happening?"

Jensen's lips twisted into a grimace of hatred and frustration. "How the hell should I know? But if I had to guess, I'd say that Aldin is responsible. Her inexcusable recklessness in the lab has unleashed hell incarnate—a virus gone berserk, spreading like wildfire. And if we don't put an end to it, we're all as good as dead."

"But how?" Chantel's voice trembled with fear.

Before Jensen could respond, Darin crumpled to the ground, convulsing violently. His body writhed in agony, eyes rolling back into his skull, until finally, he lay still.

Jensen darted to Darin's side, his gaze fixating on the vicious claw marks etched into his flesh. A shiver of fear rippled through him as he staggered back, his eyes wide with terror. With a sudden surge of urgency, he scoured the room, his movements frantic, desperate.

Returning moments later, Jensen brandished a long, metal rod, gripped tightly as though preparing for an imminent attack. As he poised to strike, Chastine lunged forward, seizing his arm in a frantic plea. "What are you doing?" she cried.

"He's been exposed! Look at his arm!" Jensen exclaimed.

Chastine, Chantel, and the ever-silent Anon crowded around, their expressions a mix of concern and disbelief, as blood and viscera oozed from the deep gash marking Darin's arm.

"That proves nothing," Chantel countered, her voice

wavering.

"It proves everything!" Jensen snapped desperately. "He's infected. And unless you're eager to see him transform into a raving lunatic before he tears through your flesh, we need to end this now, before it's too late."

"You're suggesting murder?" Chastine's voice quivered with disbelief.

"No, I'm talking about survival."

Chastine inserted herself between Jensen and Darin, her gaze piercing. She saw the hysteria brewing within Jensen's eyes, replacing the once-authoritative demeanor with raw, unbridled terror. It made him unpredictable, dangerous. "You can't do this," she implored. "He's just a boy."

"And I suppose you'll be the one to stop me?" Jensen challenged.

"No, I will," Anon's voice cut through the tension.

The weight of Anon's words forced Jensen to pause. He understood the gravity of Anon's silence broken, the unspoken authority it carried. Reluctantly, he lowered the rod, though his grip remained firm.

Another convulsion seized Darin, propelling Jensen forward, poised to strike. But before his weapon could find its mark, he watched with a blend of terror and scientific intrigue swirling in his mind, as a dark, viscous ooze expelled itself from the wound on Darin's arm and slithered across the floor like a sinister amoeba, a sight that both fascinated and horrified.

"Quick! Capture it before it vanishes!" Jensen's command sliced through the tension.

Chastine darted past him, clutching a nearby container in a futile attempt to ensnare the elusive substance. But she was too slow. With a deft maneuver, the organism flattened and vanished through the minuscule crevice beneath the door.

Outside, the chorus of howls and wails intensified, echoing a macabre symphony of hunger and anticipation, as if the creatures beyond were receiving instructions from the escaped entity, directing them to their prey.

As the cacophony of undead clamor swelled, Darin stirred, slowly regaining consciousness. Anon offered a steadying hand, assisting him to his feet. "How are you holding up?" he inquired.

"Just sore," Darin muttered. "And... clammy."

Jensen regarded him suspiciously, the steel rod still clutched tightly in his grasp.

The relentless pounding on the door intensified, driving the group further into the room's depths. Only a couple of temperature control units hummed with life, fueled by emergency backup power, while the rest lay dormant. The dim lights cast eerie shadows throughout the space, obscuring their surroundings, which only served to heighten the level of fear rising in the room.

But even with limited visibility, they could see well enough to know that there was only one way out of the room and that was the same way they got in. With a horde of blood-thirsty animals circling outside the door—which seemed to be growing with each passing minute—the realization hit each one hard that they were completely and hopelessly trapped!

CHAPTER 6

Aldin hugged herself tight, her trembling body collapsing to the floor, teetering on the brink of a breakdown. Everything she held dear had vanished in the blink of an eye and her rational mind didn't know how to process it, leaving her grappling at the edge of the void. Anxiety and nausea surged through her as she sank against the door, her mind racing with the catastrophic ramifications of her actions.

Then, in the stillness, a faint noise pierced the silence, the sound emanating from the corridor outside. It sniffed and snorted at the edge of the door, searching for her scent like a wild beast on the hunt, then erupted into a flurry of throaty growls and desperate scratching. A moment later, another joined in, their combined assault shaking the door so hard that Aldin's bones tingled from the force.

With each scratch, the sound grew louder, more insistent. Aldin's breath came in ragged gasps, her pulse pounding in her ears like a drumbeat of impending doom. She cast wild glances around the room, searching for any means of escape, but found none.

Suddenly, a low, guttural growl reverberated through the door, sending shivers down Aldin's spine. It was a sound of pure menace, a warning of the horrors waiting to devour her flesh. And then, without warning, the scratching ceased, replaced by an eerie silence that hung heavy in the air like a shroud.

Aldin's heart hammered in her chest as she waited, her senses on high alert for the slightest movement. But the silence stretched on, unbroken and oppressive, until she could bear it no longer. With trembling hands, she reached out to the door, fingers trembling as they brushed against the cool metal.

She traced her fingers along the door, each movement deliberate, as if coaxing a response from whatever lurked beyond. Without hesitation, the metal reverberated beneath her touch, answering with a thunderous roar that shattered the silence. It was a primal cry, raw and desperate that echoed through the darkness.

Aldin stifled a scream as she recoiled, scrambling to the room's center, her heart pounding in her chest desperately. The door strained against their relentless assault, each impact a death knell echoing her impending doom, and she knew that soon, the barrier would crumble, unleashing a nightmare from which she would never awaken.

Slowly, she made her way back across the lab toward the main door, trying to make as little noise as possible as she skirted around fallen debris and broken equipment. She pressed the button on the wall to bring up the surveillance monitor and gasped when she saw a pair of savage and hungry eyes staring back at her.

Aldin immediately recognized the face behind those deadly eyes as Bindi, one of their Dengu test subjects, except the last time she had seen him, he still had his whole face intact and didn't have a large hole in his abdomen. He paced back and forth in front of the door with a noticeable limp, leaving trails of blood on the floor as he walked. Then he growled low and desperate and hungry.

As Aldin shrank back away from the door, Bindi let out a loud cry and was joined seconds later by several others. Before long, the cries of the dead echoed throughout the building.

A thought began creeping into her brain that she would ultimately be the person who brought about the destruction of the entire planet. She was responsible for the savage apocalypse that was on course to cause the extermination of an entire species. *Unless I can stop it...?*

Her mind suddenly started working in overdrive. *If they're infected with a mutated strain of the SYHF virus, then the virus might still possess some of its vulnerabilities. And if that's the case, then I might be able to find a cure!*

But time was running out, and she knew it. This scourge was spreading faster than anyone could imagine, and curiously it was only affecting wildlife. She surmised that her DNA was providing some sort of defense against the virus, but couldn't be sure without analyzing a specimen. And to do that, she would have to venture out of the lab.

As if the monsters in the hallway heard her thoughts and weren't particularly fond of the idea of being put under a microscope, they crashed against the door with renewed fervor. The creatures outside the rear entrance answered the call with a flurry of attacks of their own. Aldin knew she only had minutes before the beasts would converge on her from both sides.

In a state of panic, she scanned the room, her gaze examining every nook and cranny, desperately hoping to find an alternative way out or a safe haven. However, her deep understanding of the lab only heightened her despair, as she realized there was no chance of getting out. Then she spotted a small hole in the far wall where a piece of the particle accelerator had crashed into it when it exploded, and ran toward it.

The opening was just big enough for her hand to fit through, but she found that the impact had weakened the surrounding section of the wall enough that she could pull a large piece of it away. A soft squeal erupted from her mouth as something sharp ripped open her stomach as she desperately squirmed herself through the opening into the room beyond just as she heard the door at the back of the lab finally give way and crash to the floor. The front door followed suit a moment later and the lab was immediately overrun by the undead.

Aldin immediately realized she was in Jensen's office when she saw the desk that she had been reprimanded at more than once. It seemed to mock her in the face of her current misstep, suggesting that she had one more admonishment coming her way. But this time, she knew she deserved it.

She heard the loud clamor coming from the lab and worked quickly to push a large cabinet over to block the hole in the wall. Each movement brought a stinging pain to her mid-section, and she could feel the blood running down her leg from the wound in her stomach. She gritted her teeth and made one final push.

A wave of dizziness surged through her—a combination of blood loss and terror—and she had to steady herself for a minute. Luckily, every room in this wing of the research facility had a first aid panel, and Jensen's office was no exception.

Aldin walked over to the corner of the room, supporting herself on the desk so she didn't pass out, and pressed a button on the wall. A panel above slid forward. She opened the cabinet door and grabbed the numbing spray, applying it generously to the wound. Within seconds the pain was gone, and she could apply an anti-bacterial steroid patch that would help heal the injury quickly...she hoped.

She turned and saw Jensen's tablet sitting on top of his desk. Against her better judgment, she turned it on. With everything else going on, if she was caught breaking into classified information it would be over for her. She was met immediately with a password screen. "Oh, well," she mumbled. "You're already in enough trouble as it is, Aldin. Let's not add data theft to the list."

A shaky voice spoke up, "Try 321SUINEG."

Aldin looked around the desk and was surprised to see Gloria—the young, good-looking lab assistant whom she had frequently seen flirting with Jensen—lying half-naked in a pool of blood on the floor. Protruding from her stomach was a long metal rod which had shot through the wall during the explosion.

Aldin rushed around the desk and slid down beside the dying girl. "Oh, my god! Gloria! What are you doing in here?"

Gloria gave out a soft chuckle that quickly turned to a bloody cough. "Do I need to answer that?" she managed after a few moments of pained breathed.

"What can I do?" Aldin asked desperately, knowing there wasn't anything. The girl was going to die. Soon.

Gloria replied hoarsely, "He set you up." Then she pointed at the tablet, "Everything you need is in there."

"Jensen set me up? Why?"

"He's jealous... always has been."

Gloria started coughing again, this time a stream of blood poured from her mouth. She clutched at Aldin's hand. "He just left me here... he didn't care... promise me you'll make him pay?"

Aldin was at a loss for words. As the last whispers of life escaped the girl's lips, she nodded her head, agreeing to a promise she knew she couldn't keep.

Tears streamed down Aldin's face as Gloria's grip went slack and she died. As Aldin looked at Gloria lying in front of her, the realization hit her hard that the girl's death was all her fault.

CHAPTER 7

Jensen's eyes narrowed suspiciously as Darin slowly rose from the ground, his grip on the rod tightening like a vise. Every nerve in Jensen's body screamed danger, a primal instinct urging him to strike first if anything seemed out of place.

"Are you alright?" Chantel's voice cut through the tense air.

Darin nodded, his voice barely a whisper. "I... I think so. What happened?"

"You were infected, that's what!" Jensen snapped, his words laced with venom. "And mark my words, if I even catch a hint of you turning into one of those abominations—a twitch, a stutter—I won't hesitate to skewer you right through the heart! You'll be dead before your shadow touches the floor!"

"Enough, Jensen," Anon's calm voice intervened. "We can't afford to leap to conclusions. As a scientist and leader of this facility, you should understand that."

Chastine spoke up, her words cautious. "We all saw that black ooze oozing out of him. It was like it had a life of its own."

"And what does that signify?" Jensen demanded.

Chastine sensed a dangerous edge to Jensen, an eagerness for violence simmering beneath his surface. She chose her words carefully. "As Anon said, we shouldn't jump to conclusions. It could mean nothing, or it could indicate we're facing an aggressive organism."

"That's my point exactly," Jensen retorted. "We need to stay prepared."

"Prepared for what?" Chantel's voice quivered.

Jensen's reply was chilling. "Prepared to do whatever it takes."

Darin stared at Jensen, a mixture of shock and defiance in his eyes. This man was toying with his life, and he wouldn't stand for it. Despite Jensen's authority, Darin silently vowed to protect himself at all costs. "I'm fine," he asserted. "No need for talk of madness. Understand?"

But his words faded into the background as a cacophony of crashes from the corridor outside echoed through the room, a stark reminder that their true adversaries lurked just beyond the door, hungry for their deaths.

Chastine's heart pounded in her chest, her breath catching at the sudden noise that echoed through the desolate corridors. "We need to find a way out of here, and fast!"

"First, we need to restore full power to the facility," Jensen replied. "And to do that, we need to reach the main control room and reboot the system."

Unspoken motives lingered in Jensen's words. If they didn't reach the control room soon, his twisted plan to eradicate Aldin would crumble. Though success might still be within his grasp, the manner of Aldin's demise hung in the balance. The mutated beasts prowling the facility added an unexpected layer of complexity, a sinister twist to his carefully constructed scheme. Yet, if he could confine the threat to this forsaken corner of the facility, he could unleash the building's defenses and dispatch them with ruthless efficiency. Collateral damage was a mere afterthought, a casualty of war in his relentless pursuit of power.

With the air ducts compromised and the halls teeming with the undead, Jensen knew that their only passage to the control room lay hidden beneath the cold steel grating at the room's far corner. An array of meters on the wall cast ominous shadows on the floor and ceiling. With a flick of a switch, hydraulic solenoids groaned in protest as the grate swung open, revealing a passage veiled in a soft, eerie glow. It beckoned ominously to them; a gateway to the infernal depths below. The passage led a short distance away from the room and ended abruptly at a ladder leading down to the maintenance tunnels.

Jensen entered immediately and started climbing down the ladder without saying a word to anyone. The twins just rolled their eyes and shook their heads before they followed.

"What's his deal?" Darin asked Anon.

Anon looked inside the passage just as the top of Jensen's head disappeared from sight. He had never seen the man fearful of anything before in his entire career at the lab. But this was not the same Jensen anymore.

"He's scared" Anon said.

"Well, so is everyone else. That doesn't mean we're going to kill everyone we see."

"Let's hope the world doesn't come to that," Anon replied as he helped Darin into the passage and followed after.

The ladder descended to a narrow passage that splintered off in different directions under the facility. The cramped confines of the maintenance passage stretched out before them, a dark maze seemingly leading into an endless abyss. As they descended into the murky depths, each step echoed like a funeral dirge.

As Jensen led the group through a series of twists and turns, a tiny whisper of a noise, like a faint clicking, barely audible, but there nonetheless, seemed to follow them.

As they rounded another corner, they stopped suddenly, a gasp escaping each of their lips when they stumbled onto a maintenance worker laying sprawled face down on the floor, his body motionless.

The worker's arm suddenly began twitching with unnatural spasms. Anon kneeled beside the fallen man, his hands trembling as he reached his arm toward him. With a cautious nudge, he rolled the body over. Almost immediately, from every crevice and cavity, a writhing mass of grotesque insects poured forth, their twisted forms illuminated by the sickly glow of emergency lights. Like harbingers of doom, spider-like creatures crawled from vacant eye sockets, while winged monstrosities erupted from the man's nostrils and ears in a grotesque display of death and decay.

Chantel reacted with instinctive revulsion as one of the abominations lunged toward her. With a primal scream, she brought her foot down with savage force, crushing the creature beneath her heel. A chorus of mournful wails instantly rose from the writhing mass, an anguished lament for their fallen comrade.

In the chaos that followed, Jensen, his eyes cold and calculating, seized the opportunity for escape. With a callous disregard for his companions, he turned and fled down the corridor, his footsteps echoing like a sinister whisper in the darkness.

While Jensen ran away from the attack, the others found themselves quickly overrun. Screams and cries erupted from each one as they felt fangs and stingers pierce their flesh.

They flailed their arms and stomped their feet frantically to escape the onslaught.

"This way!" Anon yelled desperately as he ushered them down a nearby corridor. The passage sloped upward, and instead of ending in a ladder to the main floor, it led to a narrow door.

At first, the door wouldn't budge. As the buzzing grew louder around them, Anon strained with all of his might. With a final, frantic effort, he wrenched the door open. Once they were inside, he let it slide shut, sealing them inside just as the onslaught of horrors descended upon them with unrestrained fury.

As Anon slumped to the floor, he was dimly aware of the others laying near him, their bodies shaking amid a series of seizures. Then the seizures overtook him as well, before everything went dark.

CHAPTER 8

As Ridley sprinted down the hall toward the main lobby, Mishka matching her stride for stride, an ominous fear gnawed at her gut. Something terrible was about to unfold—she could feel it in her bones. The air was thick and oppressive, every step echoing with the silent drumbeat of impending doom. Despite Aldin not being alone, fear for her safety clawed at Ridley's heart. Jensen's impulsiveness in moments of crisis was legendary, capable of escalating any situation exponentially. They had to circle back and regain control before chaos reigned supreme.

Suddenly, the emergency lights flickered, and for a brief, horrifying moment, everything plunged into pitch-black darkness. Heartbeats stretched into what felt like an eternity, each second heavy with suffocating tension. When the lights grudgingly blinked back to life, the brief blackout had left a chilling fog of dread hanging in the air, thicker and more oppressive than before.

The sound of violent crashes erupted from the other side of the complex, the noise reverberating through the halls like the roar of an angry beast. It was coming from the maintenance corridor near the back of the lab—the very escape route the others would have taken. The realization hit Ridley like a punch to the gut: they were heading straight into the heart of danger.

Ridley's pace quickened, adrenaline flooding her system. She could see vivid images of Aldin being torn apart, the horrifying scenes playing out in her mind's eye over and over. Regret stabbed at her, sharp and relentless. The recent tensions between them, the growing distance—they had been drifting apart, caught in the undertow of unspoken grievances and unresolved issues. But their love wasn't dead. It was battered, bruised, but not beyond repair. They just needed time to figure things out. Now, she prayed for one last chance to make things right, before the nightmare swallowed them all.

Ridley's thoughts were a whirlwind of fear and hope. She prayed for Aldin's safety, for one more chance to mend their fractured bond. The image of Aldin's face, the warmth of her smile, the touch of her hand—these memories drove Ridley forward with a renewed sense of purpose.

"I'm sure your woman is fine," Mishka said with a snarl. "Although I couldn't care less if something happened to her."

"Why do you hate her so much?" Ridley asked.

"Besides the fact that she took you away from me?"

Ridley stopped running and stood there looking at Mishka in disbelief. "That is not true, and you know it! We were over long before Aldin came into the picture."

Mishka walked toward Ridley with fire in her eyes. "You don't have to put it that way!" she snapped. "You act like our relationship was the worst thing that ever happened to you."

Ridley's shoulders dropped as she sighed. She knew as soon as the words had left her mouth that she had misspoken. Mishka might put on a tough front, but Ridley knew that she kept a certain level of insecurity hidden inside that made her vulnerable, especially with their past. "I didn't mean it like that, Mishka, and you know it."

"How did you mean it, then?"

Now she was getting irritated. When Mishka caught hold of something, she wouldn't let it drop. It didn't matter that the world was falling apart around them. "This really isn't the best time to do this, you know."

Mishka was about to respond when they heard an explosion in the distance right before the building started to shake. The tremor only lasted a few seconds, but it was enough to remind both of them of the severity of the situation.

They both turned and ran down the hallway toward the lobby area, where they hoped they'd be able to double back along the maintenance corridor. They were a short distance from the door when they heard a chorus of screams and cries coming from the other side, accompanied by the sounds of desperate animals.

As they neared the door, the air grew heavier. The emergency lights flickered again, casting long, distorted shadows that twisted and writhed on the walls. It felt as though the building itself was alive, its very structure possessed by a sinister presence.

Ridley and Mishka exchanged a tense glance, slowing their pace to a cautious tip-toe, the oppressive silence amplifying every creak and whisper of their movements. As they approached the door, Mishka's hand trembled slightly as she reached for the handle, her gaze darting to Ridley, who gave a ready nod.

Ridley crouched low behind her, blaster at the ready. With painstaking slowness, Mishka cracked the door open, her own blaster clutched tightly in her grip. As the door inched open, a sliver of the scene beyond came into view, and

Mishka's breath caught in her throat. The madness before her was almost too much to bear, and a gasp slipped out despite her efforts to contain it.

Carnage was the only word that could describe the scene. The lobby floor was filled with blood, a gruesome river flowing from the bodies of countless visitors along with those of their fallen colleagues. Lifeless forms lay scattered, their once-familiar faces now masks of death. But it was the creatures that truly made the horror sink in—ghastly abominations that had once been animals, now twisted and deformed beyond recognition. Large patches of flesh were missing, ripped away in savage attacks, only for the corpses to be reanimated by an unholy hunger.

These monstrosities moved with an unnatural gait, some dragging themselves along on mutilated limbs, others hobbling on broken appendages. Yet all shared the same ravenous, burning hunger in their eyes, a relentless desire to consume and destroy.

As Ridley and Mishka slipped into the surrounding gallery, Ridley's heart pounded in her chest. She tried to secure the door quietly, but the lock engaged with a loud, echoing click. The sound was like an explosion in the stillness, and immediately, the creatures' heads snapped in their direction. The gallery erupted into a cacophony of cries and howls, the bloodthirsty chorus of the damned.

"Oops," Ridley whispered, her voice trembling.

Mishka shot her a scathing glare, but there was no time for blame. The beasts were upon them, their snarls echoing through the hall as they scrambled forward, a horrifying tide of death. They had to move, and fast. Standing their ground would be suicide against such overwhelming numbers. "The door!" she shouted.

They sprinted toward the door on the other side of the

mezzanine, their hearts pounding in sync with their frantic footsteps. The distance seemed to stretch endlessly, every step a desperate race against the inevitable.

Just as they neared the door, Nguyen, his clothes in tatters and covered in blood, and his face slashed with deep cuts, staggered toward them, crying out in sheer desperation. He believed they would save him; that they were his last hope. But hope was a cruel illusion. In an instant, a Kambura leaped up the stairs, its jaws snapping shut around the man's throat. The gruesome sound of tearing flesh filled the air as the creature ripped his windpipe out, a crimson spray staining its mottled fur a deep, dark red.

The man's lifeless body hit the ground with a sickening thud as the Kambura began its grotesque feast. Ridley and Mishka, driven by pure terror, covered the last few steps to the door. Mishka's hands shook violently as she fumbled with her key card. Each failed attempt sent waves of panic through her until, finally, a beep sounded, and the lock clicked open.

But it was too late. A second Kambura had joined the first, its eyes gleaming with hunger. The two monstrous felines snarled through their broken, ravaged mouths, their gazes fixed on the women.

Before Ridley could fully grasp what was happening, Mishka yanked the door open and shoved her through with a forceful push. "I love you," Mishka gasped, her voice breaking. "I never stopped loving you." With that, she slammed the door shut, sealing herself on the other side.

Ridley collapsed against the door, her mind reeling. The muffled sounds of blaster fire were quickly followed by an agonized scream that cut through her like a knife.

CHAPTER 9

Aldin stared at the tablet screen, her disbelief morphing into horror. Every muscle in her body tensed as the realization washed over her. Gloria had been right. The evidence was overwhelming, meticulously detailed, and damning. Jensen had chronicled nearly every step Aldin had taken during her tenure, even documenting the events leading up to the catastrophic explosion. And now, in her hands, she held the blueprint of the particle accelerator, complete with Jensen's chilling sabotage—loosening a critical dampening ring to trigger a pressure tank failure. But why? Out of sheer spite? Jealousy? The questions swirled chaotically in her mind, each one more unsettling than the last.

"This makes no sense!" she exclaimed, her voice trembling as she spoke to the empty room. "I can't believe he would do something like that!"

Her eyes continued to scan the tablet, her heart pounding in her chest. She landed on a disciplinary report, her breath catching in her throat. The document suspended her indefinitely, pending an investigation into the explosion. An explosion that hadn't even occurred yet when the report was written. Jensen had set her up from the very beginning, orchestrating every detail of her downfall, just as Gloria had warned!

She exhaled shakily, a complex mix of emotions swirling within her. There was a small sense of relief, knowing the disaster wasn't entirely her fault. Yet the weight of guilt gnawed at her relentlessly. It was her obsession with her research that had led her to neglect basic safety protocols. She had fallen asleep at her post, just as Jensen had predicted, causing the explosion. But he hadn't foreseen the full scope of the consequences that followed.

The emergency lights flickered momentarily before stabilizing, casting an ominous, intermittent glow. It was a stark reminder that time was running out. She slipped the tablet into her jacket pocket, her hands trembling slightly. She gave Gloria one last sorrowful glance, before rifling through Jensen's desk. Her search yielded a large assortment of pharmaceuticals—explaining his erratic behavior—a multi-tool, and a blaster. Each item she found felt like another piece of the grotesque puzzle.

As Aldin crammed everything she could into her pockets, her fingers brushing against something odd. A strange key sat beside a red button in the bottom drawer. It was a small, yet heavy, iron rod with a triangular head, pulsing faintly with magnetic energy. She turned it over in her hand, its weight and coldness sending a shiver down her spine. She pocketed the key and pressed the button, holding her breath. For a moment, nothing happened, and she feared the worst. Then, the entire desk slid forward with a mechanical whir, revealing a staircase descending into darkness.

Tentatively, she stepped down, each footfall echoing ominously in the confined space. The edges of the stairs lit up with an eerie glow, casting elongated shadows on the walls. The lump in her throat grew, feeling as if she were walking into the belly of a beast. The building trembled, a low rumble resonating through the structure, as if that very beast was stirring from its slumber.

Her descent twisted and doubled back, spanning what felt like three floors, before she faced a solid, blank wall. Confused and increasingly anxious, she pulled out her multi-tool, shining its light over the wall. After several frustrating minutes, she noticed an outline in the corner, matching the shape of the key.

She pulled out the strange key and pressed it at the keyhole. With a sharp twist to the right, a loud 'click' echoed through the narrow passage, and the wall slid down with a heavy thud, revealing a large, hidden room beyond.

Aldin stepped inside, her heart pounding, and immediately regretted it. She had entered a madman's lair. Jensen had always seemed eccentric, unorthodox, but this—this was the work of a deranged psychopath.

Navigating the room, she shivered not at the jars and vials of animal specimens, but at the grotesque display of deformed, mutated species. Some were born with physical abnormalities, others were grotesque hybrids—a twisted attempt at playing creator. Her stomach churned as she saw containers filled with Terran body parts—hands, feet, eyes—suspended in thick gel. The horror of Jensen's experiments settled heavily on her, a chilling reminder of the darkness that lay beneath the surface of his mind. Each grotesque vessel whispered a story of pain and perversion.

Aldin backed away from the grotesque display, her heart pounding wildly. Suddenly, she felt a sharp crunch beneath her feet. Glancing down, she saw shards of broken glass littering the floor, glinting menacingly in the dim light. Her gaze followed the trail of debris upward, where she discovered the source of the destruction. A large containment chamber, big enough to imprison a person, loomed before her, its emptiness screaming silently. The outward spray of shattered glass indicated a violent impact from inside the chamber, as if something had forcefully escaped its confines.

A low, guttural growl rumbled behind her, sending an icy shiver down her spine. She turned slowly, her breath catching in her throat. Emerging from the shadows were two eyes, cold and menacing, glinting with a predatory hunger. For a brief moment, the creature remained partially hidden, then as it stepped forward, Aldin gasped in horror.

The beast that revealed itself was a nightmarish amalgamation of nature and abomination. Black fur, matted with blood and mucus, covered its large canine body. A gruesome chunk of flesh was missing from one of its hind legs, causing it to limp. The front legs, replaced by grotesque, spider-like appendages that 'clicked' ominously on the stone floor, chilled her to the core. The most horrifying aspect of the creature, though, was the head of a Terran grotesquely grafted alongside the beast's original head, both dripping black mucus. They simultaneously snapped at her hungrily, their eyes filled with a predatory gleam.

Aldin screamed as the monstrosity lunged at her. Instinct took over; she jumped backward, narrowly avoiding its massive claws as it swiped at her. Pain seared through her left arm as its nails raked her flesh. She rolled desperately, trying to escape its reach. The beast gathered itself for another attack, its dual heads snarling in unison.

Fumbling frantically, Aldin managed to extract the blaster from her pocket. With trembling hands, she fired a shot, hitting the creature squarely in the chest. But the blast barely slowed it down. A second later, the beast launched itself at her, airborne and unstoppable.

Facing imminent death, Aldin closed her eyes and

squeezed the trigger repeatedly, firing blindly in a desperate bid to fend off the beast. A second later, she heard a crash as the creature fell heavily to the floor beside her. Opening her eyes, she saw her wild shots had miraculously severed the Terran head from the body, blasted off one of its front legs, and left a gaping hole in its abdomen. Yet, the abomination still moved, its remaining head gnashing and snarling as it clawed toward her.

Aldin aimed the blaster at the creature's head and fired repeatedly. The blasts echoed throughout the room, finally killing the creature for good. As it lay inches away from her still and lifeless, she allowed herself a moment to breathe.

Her respite was short-lived. Tremors wracked her body, and she collapsed to the floor as violent spasms overtook her. The blaster slipped from her grasp, clattering uselessly to the ground. The last thing Aldin saw before darkness claimed her was the disembodied Terran head, its mouth frozen in an eternal scream. A fleeting thought crossed her mind: *Is this my ultimate punishment, my penance for the horrors I've unleashed upon the world?*

As she slipped into unconsciousness, the darkness seemed to whisper a grim answer, wrapping her in its stiff embrace.

CHAPTER 10

The control room was a cacophony of blaring alarms and flashing red lights, a far cry from its usual state of cold efficiency. Demri's heart pounded in his chest as he barked orders, his voice barely audible over the chaos. The facility had been rocked by a series of explosions, and now the system was compromised, teetering on the brink of collapse.

"Antasia, divert power from the auxiliary generators to the primary system! We need to stabilize the core!" Demri shouted, his eyes darting between the screens.

Antasia, her face pale and slick with sweat, frantically typed commands into her console. "I'm trying, but the circuits are overloaded! If we push too much power, we could cause another explosion!"

"Just do it!" Demri snapped, his fear turning into anger. "We don't have a choice!"

The door to the control room slid open with a hiss, and Lucas stumbled in, blood oozing from a gash on his forehead. He looked around, taking in the pandemonium. "What the hell is happening?"

"Explosions in sectors 3 and 4! The whole system's going haywire!" Demri replied in a raw voice. "We need to stabilize it before the core goes critical."

Lucas didn't waste a second. He rushed to a console, his fingers flying over the keys. "I'll reroute the coolant system to prevent overheating. Antasia, watch the pressure levels; we can't let them spike!"

Dak, the lab's Dengo, was huddled in a corner, his usual calm replaced by a terrified whine. "Dak, stay there, boy. It's going to be okay," Antasia whispered, though she didn't believe it herself.

Another explosion rocked the facility, this one closer. The floor shook, and dust rained down from the ceiling. Demri gripped the edge of his console, knuckles white. "We're running out of time! Antasia, status report!"

Antasia's hands trembled as she checked the readouts. "Power is rerouting, but it's unstable. We've got less than five minutes before the core overheats!"

"Dammit!" Demri swore, slamming his fist on the console. "Lucas, any luck with the coolant?"

Lucas wiped sweat from his brow, wincing as his fingers brushed the cut on his forehead. "I've got it rerouted, but the valves are stuck. We need to manually override them!"

Demri nodded grimly. "Antasia, keep an eye on the core. Lucas, with me."

The two men raced out of the control room, leaving Antasia behind. She stared at the screens, each flashing warning messages and error codes, her breath coming in short, panicked gasps. Dak whimpered again, and she spared him a glance. "It's okay, boy. Just a little longer."

Minutes felt like hours as she watched the core's temperature rise, the pressure gauges inching towards the red. "Come on, come on," she muttered, trying to will the system to stabilize.

Finally, the door burst open, and Demri and Lucas

stumbled back in, covered in grime and sweat.

"The valves are open," Demri said. "Coolant is flowing. Check the readings."

Antasia's eyes darted to the screens. The pressure levels were dropping, the core temperature stabilizing. She let out a shaky breath, tears of relief streaming down her face. "The core's been stabilized. Now, we just need to get the system back on-line."

But the relief was short-lived when Dak suddenly let out a loud yelp. Antasia turned just in time to see him run off into the corner in a state of terror.

Immediately, Demri rushed to his side, with Lucas and Antasia right beside him. "What's the matter, Boy?" he asked in a trembling voice. His heart was wrenched in two as he watched Dak lying on the floor breathing raggedly. He looked up at Demri with a sadness in his eyes as if he were saying goodbye.

Then Dak's body thrashed violently, foam bubbling from his mouth. A moment later, he went still, his life extinguished. An anguished cry flew from Demri's lips, "Dak! No!"

Demri tried to resuscitate the Dengo, but his efforts were futile. Without proper equipment and training there was no hope in bringing his lifelong companion back from the dead. Demri crumbled to the floor sobbing uncontrollably, with Antasia and Lucas beside him in a state of shock.

Caught up in grief and disbelief, they failed to notice Dak's body twitching beside them. It started out slight and nearly imperceptible, then grew in intensity until his whole body was shaking. A moment later, a loud snarl erupted from Dak's unholy mouth.

The three of them looked at Dak in terror as he rose from the floor with a deadly gleam in his eyes. His fur was matted to his skin in large patches with a black, oily mucus oozing from a number of open wounds. Without warning, he lunged at Lucas, teeth bared. Lucas fell back, scrambling to protect himself. "Demri, help me!" he cried before his voice was cut short when Dak's jaws clamped down on his face.

Demri grabbed a metal rod from the floor, hesitating for just a moment before bringing it down on Dak's head. The Dengo yelped and staggered, but didn't stop. Demri swung again, harder this time, and the rod pierced Dak's eye. The animal collapsed, twitching once before going still.

Silence fell over the room, broken only by the ragged breathing of Demri and Antasia as they stood there in disbelief.

Demri looked at the lifeless body of his pet, tears mixing with the grime on his face. "Why? What the hell happened to him?"

Instead of answering, Antasia dropped to the floor, huddling against the wall next to Lucas' still body, crying profusely.

***

When the swarm of insects attacked, Jensen felt a cold clarity settle over him. This was his moment, the slim window of opportunity he'd been waiting for. He darted away from the others, sprinting down the corridor toward the control room at the end, feeling the sharp, relentless sting of insects on his neck and hands. He swatted at them with desperate intensity, his fingers scrambling for the key-card in his jacket pocket.

As he grasped the card, a grotesque spider-thing scurried down his arm with unnerving speed, its fangs piercing his skin with a fiery sting. He shook his hand violently, the key-card slipping and falling to the floor as the creature was flung away, landing a few feet away.

Bending down to retrieve the card, Jensen saw the spider-thing lunge. Instinct took over, and he stomped down with all his might, feeling a grim satisfaction at the crunch beneath his shoe. He picked up the card and glanced at the creature, noticing its head and one of its legs still twitching in a futile, macabre dance to get at him. With a resolute finality, he crushed it again, this time leaving no doubt of its death.

Jensen swiped the card in front of the scanner, the door opening with a soft, mechanical whirr. As he stepped inside, a thought struck him, clear and chilling. He wouldn't deploy the safety measures he had meticulously planned. No, he'd let the chaos reign. In the ensuing disaster, he could lay all the blame at Aldin's feet, finally ridding himself of her once and for all.

He slipped into the control room, the door closing behind him with a reassuring click. The room was bathed in the soft glow of monitors and control panels. He felt a rush of exhilaration, a dark thrill at the thought of the havoc he was about to unleash. The world would see Aldin for the villain she was, and he would be free.

Instantly, he was surprised to find that he wasn't alone. Demri, an older man who supervised the control room operation, sat huddled in the corner next to Antasia, one of the technicians. Across from them lay the body of another technician, unrecognizable because his face was missing.

Beside the dead man was the source of the attack: a large lump of fur—that resembled what used to be a Dengo—with a long metal rod protruding from one of the eyes. Jensen looked at the normally docile canine and saw that it still had pieces of the man's flesh hanging from its mouth. Then he realized that the dead animal was Dak, Demri's pet, and the lab's mascot.

"What happened?" Jensen asked.

"I don't know?" Antasia replied. "One minute Dak was fine, then I heard him squeal like something had bitten him. He ran away and hid in the corner for a bit until Demri and Lucas came back. Then he just went crazy and attacked!"

Antasia started crying again and Demri wrapped his arms around her to calm her down. "It's okay, dear," he said. "It's over now."

"I'm not so sure about that," Jensen said.

Demri gave Jensen a critical look, suggesting that he keep his comments quiet for the moment.

"It was horrible!" Antasia finally said. "I tried to save him...but it was too late." Then she broke down again.

The skin on the back of Jensen's neck suddenly started to itch and burn. Then he remembered the insect bites he had suffered just outside the door. A moment later, a sharp pain flew down his spine, causing him to cry out as he fell to the floor. His body started shaking violently and his vision grew blurry, before he blacked out, realizing that he was under the same attack that Darin had gone through shortly before.

***

The voices were soft, muffled, like whispers carried through thick fog. Jensen's eyes fluttered open to an abyss of darkness, and panic surged through him, hot and sharp. Was he blind? The thought clawed at his mind, his life's work, his purpose, threatened by this consuming void. His breath came in ragged gasps, each one louder than the last. Then, slowly, mercifully, shapes began to form, shadows giving way to the dim light. He could make out the worried faces of Demri and Antasia hovering over him, their concern evident in the furrows of their brows and the tight lines of their mouths.

Struggling to sit up, Jensen felt a warm stream of liquid trickle from the back of his neck, sliding down his arm with an unsettling sensation. He reached back, his fingers coming away slick and dark. He watched in horrified fascination as a black puddle of oily slime oozed away from him, writhing with a sinister life of its own. It slithered towards the door, a sentient, malevolent entity seeking to rejoin its kin beyond. But this time, Jensen was ready. He grabbed a glass container from a nearby workstation, and with a swift, practiced motion, he scooped up the organism.

He watched it squirm and undulate, its movements frenzied and desperate as it tested the confines of its new prison. The glass felt cold and solid in his hands, a barrier between him and the writhing, alien thing within.

"What in the world is that stuff?" Demri's voice was a mix of awe and disgust, the words tinged with the faintest tremor as he peered over Jensen's shoulder.

"I think it's a new life-form," Jensen replied, his voice thick with a mixture of fear and excitement, each word feeling heavy on his tongue.

"Is that what caused Dak to behave the way he did?" Demri's question hung heavy in the air, the silence that followed filled with an unspoken dread.

"I believe so," Jensen said.

"Then we need to get the system back on-line quickly and implement quarantine protocols!" Demri's urgency was clear, his eyes wide with fear.

"That's why I raced in here!" Jensen stood up, the motion causing the glass container in his coat pocket to jostle. The creature within writhed more violently, as if sensing its captor's intentions. Though he did need the system rebooted, he had no intention of activating quarantine protocols. "I'm surprised you haven't done it yet."

Demri frowned, confusion marring his features. "I didn't know what was happening. I saw the explosion in the lab on the monitors and the core's temperature spiked drastically, nearly causing a melt-down until we were able to manually stabilize the cooling system. I was just about to sound the alarm when Lucas was attacked."

Jensen nodded, moving towards a door at the far corner of the room. "Are the security monitors still up?"

"They should be," Demri replied, "They're independent of the primary system, so we can still monitor the facility."

Jensen gave a curt nod and slipped into the adjacent room, the door closing behind him with a soft, ominous click. The room was dimly lit, shadows creeping along the walls like silent specters. He knew he only had a few minutes before Demri would come looking for him.

Quickly, he approached the nearest workstation and typed in a series of commands to access the security cameras, the keys clacking under his fingers. As the images flickered to life, he scanned through them, his heart sinking when he saw Gloria's lifeless body sprawled across the floor of his office. Her eyes were open, staring blankly, her face twisted in an ultimate moment of terror.

Oh, well, he thought, a cold detachment seeping into his mind. *All good things must come to an end.*

His eyes then caught sight of his desk moved aside to reveal the hidden stairway, its lights glowing softly. Jensen typed in more commands, his fingers moving with a frantic urgency to access the secret camera he had installed in his private lab. As the image loaded, he grabbed a blaster from the table beside him, the cold metal a comfort in his hands, and placed it on his lap.

The screen cleared, and Jensen's heart ached as he saw his life's work lying broken, scattered over the lab floor. Each twisted form, each failed experiment, was a testament to his tireless ambitions. "My greatest accomplishments, gone!" he muttered, his voice a strained whisper. He had poured his soul into gene-splicing, achieving a monumental breakthrough, only to see it destroyed. At least Aldin's lifeless body lay next to it—a minor consolation for the loss.

Jensen was so absorbed in the image, he didn't hear the door open or notice Demri until the man was standing over his shoulder, his breath warm against Jensen's neck.

"What are you looking at?" Demri's voice was filled with confusion, the words a harsh jolt in the quiet room. "I've never seen that lab before."

Jensen jumped at the sound, his heart pounding. His finger instinctively tightened around the blaster's trigger. "It's too bad you had to see it now," he said, his voice cold and final.

Spinning his chair around, he pointed the blaster at Demri. "I've always considered you a good friend, Demri. It's too bad it has to end this way."

"Please, Jensen," Demri pleaded, his eyes wide with fear, his hands raised in surrender. "Don't do anything rash. I promise, whatever it is, I won't tell anyone."

A look of sorrow crossed Jensen's face as he pulled the trigger, the blaster's shot echoing loudly in the enclosed space. Demri's body crumpled to the floor, his eyes wide with disbelief. "Sorry, old friend."

Seconds later, Antasia burst into the room, her scream piercing the air. "What did you do?" she cried.

Jensen's voice was eerily calm, detached. "Like I told someone else recently, I'm simply doing what I have to."

Antasia turned to flee, her footsteps frantic on the cold floor, but she made it only a few steps before Jensen pulled the trigger again, hitting her in the back so that her body slid across the floor and came to rest in a silent, lifeless heap.

Jensen stood there, the blaster still warm in his hand, the weight of his actions settling over him like a shroud. The room was silent now, save for the hum of the monitors and the distant, echoing screams from the chaos outside. He turned back to the monitor, the image of his ruined lab still glowing on the screen, and a single tear slid down his cheek. His greatest accomplishment was gone, but the darkness he had embraced was just beginning.

CHAPTER 11

As soon as Mishka closed the door on Ridley—whispering her last goodbye and letting herself feel the weight of their separation for the first time—she spun around, her heart pounding in her chest, and fired wildly at the nearest Kambura. The monstrous creature lunged at her, its fetid breath assaulting her senses with a stench of decay and blood. Her hands trembled as she squeezed the trigger, the blaster's recoil jolting her arm. One of her shots struck true, piercing the creature's grotesque, mottled skull. It collapsed with a guttural roar, its claws scraping against the floor as it fell.

No sooner had it fallen than the second Kambura surged forward, snarling, its eyes glowing with madness. Behind it, a horde of undead creatures scrambled up the stairs. The air grew thick with the acrid smell of their decaying flesh.

Mishka only had seconds to react. As the Kambura charged, its slavering jaws snapping, she squeezed the trigger of her blaster repeatedly, the shots echoing like thunder. With a desperate leap, she vaulted over the mezzanine railing, plummeting toward the lobby below. At the last moment, she reached out and grabbed a dangling light fixture. For an agonizing second, it held her weight, swaying precariously. Her fingers burned as they clung to the metal. Then, with a metallic twang, the suspension wire snapped, sending her crashing to the floor.

Pain exploded in her left arm with a sickening crack, a white-hot flash that stole her breath. She landed hard, the impact jarring every bone in her body. The sharp, metallic taste of blood filled her mouth.

Guttural growls filled the air like the roar of an approaching storm as the horde regrouped. Mishka bit back a cry, rolling onto her right side and pushing herself up, her vision swimming. She glanced toward the front entrance, but the way was already blocked.

Her only option was the corridor leading to the museum and visitor centers. The problem, though, was that it took her further from the main research labs. Her pulse raced as the beasts closed in behind her, a drumbeat of terror that drove her on. She sprinted, her legs trembling with the effort, her breaths coming in ragged gasps. Each step sent a jolt of agony through her injured arm, but she forced herself forward.

Reaching the door, she swiped her key-card over the pad, the beep of the lock disengaging a slight relief in the chaos. She pushed on the door, but something heavy on the other side was obstructing it. Panic surged through her as she threw her all of her weight against the door, forcing it open just enough to slip through.

Inside, she stumbled over the cold, lifeless body of a young man, his eyes vacant and unseeing. His flesh was pallid, as if all of the pigment were sucked from his body as his skin was stretched taut over his bones, and a faint, putrid smell clung to him. As the door closed behind her, his body slid to the floor, twitching unnaturally. Mishka watched in horror as his stomach bulged grotesquely, the skin tearing, before bursting open. A writhing mass of large, worm-like creatures spilled out, their slick bodies glistening in the dim light.

She fired into the squirming mass, her shots tearing through the writhing pile, but it did little to stop their advance. The creatures hissed and writhed, spreading out across the floor. Turning quickly, she ran, the sound of the undead beasts pounding at the door behind her reverberating through the floor.

"That won't hold them for long," she muttered through gritted teeth, panic tightening her throat, as she rounded a corner and entered a large display area filled with glass-encased artifacts.

She darted to the museum's glass door, which opened with a soft hiss, the hermetically sealed room a momentary sanctuary. Inside, the air was cooler, the smell of antiseptic mingling with the faint mustiness of relics that dated from as far back as the creation of the planet. She slipped further inside, her shoulder throbbing with every step, but she forced herself toward the back of the room. The space beyond was dimly lit, the glass cases casting long shadows that danced eerily on the walls.

Pressing her left shoulder against the cold stone wall, she bit her lip against the pain and shoved hard. With a nauseating pop, her dislocated joint snapped back into place, sending a fresh wave of agony through her. She stifled a scream, her vision blurring with tears.

She swung her arm gently, testing the injury, the movement sending sharp stabs of pain through her. Then, exhausted and overwhelmed, she sunk to the floor, tears streaming down her face. The world outside raged on, the sounds of the undead growing fainter but still present, and for a moment, she let herself feel the crushing weight of her fear and despair, her sobs echoing softly in the silent room.

For the first time since she could remember, Mishka poured out her soul. Tears streamed down her face, each one a torrent of regret that had gripped her heart and refused to let go. Seeing Ridley happy with someone else was almost more than she could bear. Each moment she watched her and Aldin together brought the painful reality crashing back: she had made a mistake. Mishka silently cursed herself for not voicing her feelings earlier, but that was her way—always keeping her emotions bottled up to avoid getting hurt. Ironically, it was that very trait that had driven them apart.

"I hope you're okay, Ridley," she mumbled, seeking some form of atonement.

But the savage apocalypse she found herself in offered no time for regret or redemption. The lights flickered again, and the building trembled briefly. Mishka pulled herself up from the floor, cradling her injured left arm against her body, her shoulder still throbbing from its recent dislocation. She made her way across the back of the main display room toward the storage area in the rear. Finding a first-aid panel, she quickly ingested a pain repressor before skirting around numerous crates and supply shelves toward the security exit.

The lights flickered once more and then went out entirely, plunging everything into darkness. Mishka reached to her side, wincing, and pulled a small multi-tool from her pocket, switching on its light. She pressed her ear to the door and thought she heard a faint, distant hum, but couldn't be sure of its source.

Slowly, she opened the door and stepped into the security corridor, swinging her light in both directions to ensure it was clear. As she made her way down the hall toward the rear of the facility, the humming grew louder behind her. Spinning around, her light caught a swirling inky mass, blacker than the surrounding darkness, speeding her way.

Panic surged through her as she turned and raced away from the mass. The humming intensified, and she realized with a jolt of terror that it was the sound of an insect swarm chasing her. And it was gaining ground fast.

She sprinted for the nearest door, a security training room, and rushed inside. Instantly, the swarm pummeled the metal barrier, sounding like rapid-fire laser blasts. Mishka jumped back as a few of the insects began crawling under the door. She fired her blaster, quickly incinerating them, but knew there wasn't enough energy in her pistol to kill them all. Desperately, she grabbed a training robe from a rod on the wall and stuffed it along the bottom of the door, praying it would keep them out long enough for her to find a way to escape.

Running toward the back of the room, Mishka stumbled over something and fell to the floor, a cry of pain escaping her lips as she landed hard on her injured shoulder. She managed to roll over and shine her light on the spot where she had tripped. A huddled mass lay there, and she instantly recognized the man as Nalon, an officer who had been at the facility since its inception, and who had also been her mentor.

She rolled his body over and gasped at the sight of a large, gaping hole in his chest. "Nalon! No!" she cried, trying to staunch the flow of blood with trembling hands.

His eyes fluttered weakly as he struggled to stay alive, blood bubbling between his lips as he whispered his last goodbye. Mishka sat in stunned silence for a moment, cradling her mentor's lifeless body, the weight of her growing grief pressing down hard on her. The world outside seemed to fade away, leaving her alone, even if only for a brief time, with her sorrow.

A deafening explosion nearby rocked the building, jolting her out of her moment of mourning. The walls shook, and dust rained down from the ceiling. Mishka forced herself to her feet, wiping the tears from her face, her resolve hardening. There was no time for grief, no time for anything but survival. She had to keep moving.

She cried out when she suddenly felt a series of sharp stings on her arm and looked down to see a large Arachnoid attacking her feverishly. The thing refused to die when she jumped up and stomped on its body, sending a spray of insect guts squirting out from under her foot. Finally, she blasted it with her gun. Immediately, a chorus of screeches sounded outside, as the swarm grew angry and pelted the door. Within seconds, a slew of insects had scurried into the room.

Mishka jumped up and ran toward the closest door—one of a number of video control rooms scattered throughout the facility—fumbling with her key-card for a moment as the buzzing grew closer. Once inside, she slammed the door.

The buzzing in the room outside grew to a tempest as she backed into the room. An obscure figure appeared in the glass a moment later, and Mishka screamed when she saw Nalon's face looking back at her. For a brief second, she feared she had left him out there still alive. Then his mouth opened, his lips moving in a wavelike motion from left to right, and an army of insects poured out. A loud screech flew from the insects, mimicking what would've been Nalon's ending cry for help, before the body slumped back to the floor. Then the insects attacked the door relentlessly.

Mishka scanned the room desperately, her eyes darting over the blank monitors lined up on the far wall. They seemed to stare back at her with a cold, mocking indifference. She pressed the button on the main control panel, her breath holding in her throat, but the system remained lifeless. Panic gripped her until she remembered that the security cameras operated on a separate power system with their own generator.

She stumbled to the panel along the back wall, her movements clumsy and pained. With her right hand, she tried to pry the cover off while clutching her throbbing left arm to her stomach, each movement sending jolts of anguish through her body. Unable to get any leverage, she fired a blaster shot at each corner of the cover, the loud blasts echoing in the small room. The metal panel fell to the floor with a clang, the sound reverberating through the space and agitating the insects outside even more. The door to the security room, thankfully sealed to prevent unauthorized access, trembled under the insect assault.

Mishka sighed, her breath shaky, as she stared at the array of switches and buttons inside the exposed panel. "I guess I should've paid better attention during training," she muttered, her voice tinged with a mixture of frustration and fear.

For a moment, she stood there, her mind racing as she tried to make sense of the circuits. Then, with a desperate resolve, she began flipping every switch and pressing every button, hoping for the best. An instant later, a tiny beep rewarded her efforts, and she spun around to see the monitors flickering to life.

She rushed to the nearest terminal, her fingers flying across the keyboard in a one-handed flurry of movement. Camera views popped up on the screens, a dizzying array of angles and locations. Her eyes darted from feed to feed, searching frantically for the maintenance hallway where she had left Ridley.

When she finally found the correct feed, she breathed a brief sigh of relief seeing it empty. But her relief was short-lived. A violent convulsion suddenly seized control of her body, sending her crashing to the floor, writhing in agony. The room seemed to spin around her, the shadows growing darker and more oppressive. She clutched her stomach, feeling as if something inside her was trying to tear its way out. The cold, mocking stare of the monitors was the last thing she saw before the darkness swallowed her whole.

CHAPTER 12

Anon was the first to stir, his eyelids fluttering as if awakening from a terrible nightmare that refused to let go. He rolled onto his side, each movement bringing a sear of pain through him; every breath was a shallow gasp. Sweat cascaded from his face, mixing with the dirt and grime that clung to his skin like a second layer. He forced himself into a sitting position against the door, peeling off his lab coat with a wince. The fabric adhered to his flesh, pulling away from pus-filled boils and blisters that had erupted over his body. The pain was excruciating, its only saving grace was that it reminded him he was still alive — even if just barely.

A low groan broke the silence, followed by the rustling of fabric as Darin began to move. His skin was a sickly sheen that glistened with fever. His arm hung awkwardly at his side, the injury turning each movement into a struggle. Gritting his teeth, he pushed himself up on one elbow, forcing his eyes open. "Where are we?" he croaked, his voice raw and strained.

Anon glanced around, his mind still in a fog as he tried to surmise their situation. "Maintenance supply room, I think," he replied, his voice barely above a whisper, as if speaking

74

louder might summon the horrors lurking just out of sight.

"What about the others?"

Darin's eyes followed Anon's gaze to the twins, who were sprawled on the floor like broken play things discarded in haste. "Are they...?"

"I don't know."

With a groan, Anon crawled towards Chastine, every movement sending sharp spikes of pain through his battered body. He reached her and carefully turned her onto her side, watching her chest rise and fall with shallow, labored breaths. She was alive. Her face was a battlefield of bite marks and swelling, one eye grotesquely swollen shut, the other fluttering open. Tears blurred her vision as she saw her sister lying next to her, unmoving. Her body shook with sobs, her grief raw and all-consuming.

"Chantel?" she whispered, the word barely escaping her trembling lips. She knew the answer before she spoke. The void inside her confirmed what her eyes feared. The preternatural bond they had shared was severed, leaving only a gaping chasm in her heart.

Darin staggered to his feet, his legs shaking beneath him, and stumbled towards the back of the room. "There should be an emergency medical kit here," he muttered, his voice tinged with desperation. He began tearing through the shelves, searching frantically.

"It's no use," Chastine said in a soft, hollow voice. "She's gone."

"But we have to try!" Darin's pleaded.

Darin's hand closed around the medical kit just as a thunderous explosion rocked the building. The tremor subsided after a few agonizing seconds, but the emergency lights flickered ominously before stabilizing. He grabbed the kit and hurried back to the others, his heart pounding with a mix of fear and determination.

Above them, the ceiling vents erupted with a cacophony of bangs and crashes. The cries and howls of the dead filled the air, growing louder, closer, more insistent with each passing moment.

"We need to get out of here!" Anon stated.

Darin fumbled through the first-aid kit, scattering supplies in his frantic search. The noises above grew deafening, pressing down on them.

Chastine placed a trembling hand on Darin's, her eyes brimming with sorrow and resignation. "Darin, it's over. There's nothing you can do."

Tears streamed down Darin's face as he nodded, his lips quivering. "I'm sorry," he whispered hoarsely.

A violent coughing fit suddenly seized Darin, wracking his body hard as he struggled to breathe. Finally, he spat out a thick wad of phlegm and mucus, his breathing easing slightly, the air coming back into his lungs begrudgingly.

"There should be antihistamine injections in the kit," Anon said as he crawled over to join them.

His hands shook uncontrollably as he rifled through the scattered contents, his fevered brain barely able to focus. He found the glass capsules and injection gun, loading it with trembling fingers. After what felt like an eternity, he managed to inject himself, feeling the fever begin to cool almost immediately, a small mercy in the midst of their nightmare.

Anon quickly repeated the process for Darin and Chastine, then found a nebulizer which he passed around. After applying antibacterial salve to Chastine's eye and wrapping Darin's arm with bandages, he slumped back, exhausted, the effort draining the last of his reserves. That's when he noticed the room's only door.

"We have a problem," he said, dread seeping into his voice.

"What now?" Darin asked, his voice weary and defeated.

"The only way out is the same way we came in."

"We have to go back out there?" Chastine's voice trembled. "Can't we just stay here until help arrives? They must be sending a task force to contain the threat."

Anon shook his head. "We don't know that," he said. "We can't stay. The beasts will find us here, eventually. We need to move, now. Plus, if something gets in here, we're all dead."

"We're dead regardless," Chastine said as her gaze traveled slowly to her sister's body.

A series of deafening bangs echoed from the other side of the door, sending shock-waves of terror through the room. The sound was like a sledgehammer striking their nerves, jolting them with a surge of icy fear. Anon's heart raced as he fumbled to bring the image up on the monitor beside the door. But the screen displayed nothing but a sea of writhing static.

He moved to open the door, his hand trembling, but Chastine seized his arm, her grip ironclad and urgent. "What are you doing? You can't open that door!" Her voice was a hiss of panic, eyes wide and wild.

"It might be one of our colleagues out there!" Anon shot back.

"Or it might be one of those monsters!" Chastine's voice quivered.

Driven by a surge of frantic energy, Darin dashed to the corner of the room. He rifled through the cluttered shelves, his movements a blur of desperate urgency. Finally, he returned, clutching a welding rod and a small tank, his eyes gleaming with a desperate plan.

"What are you going to do with that?" Chastine asked, her

voice a shaky whisper.

"Watch," Darin replied. He turned the valve on the tank slightly, then pressed the switch on the rod. A stream of fire shot out, a fierce, hissing jet of flame that narrowly missed igniting a box on a nearby shelf. The heat washed over them, almost tangible in its intensity. He quickly switched off the rod and turned the valve closed.

"It's not ideal," he said, glancing at Anon and Chastine, "but it's the best we have."

Another thunderous bang rattled the door, more insistent, more urgent, each strike reverberating through their bones. Anon exchanged a glance with Darin, his eyes filled with grim resolve. He nodded, steeling himself, and pressed the button to open the door, his heart pounding like a war drum. The door slid open with a hiss, and Darin immediately unleashed a torrent of fire into the hall beyond, the flames roaring with a savage, hungry life.

They held their breaths, the seconds stretching into a suffocating eternity, ears straining for any sound, any clue as to what lay beyond. Then, to their horror, a figure stumbled into the room, silhouetted against the flickering light of the dying flames. Ridley staggered forward, eyes wide and empty, before collapsing to the floor in a lifeless heap.

The room was instantly plunged into a heavy silence, the air thick with the acrid stench of burned flesh and the lingering echoes of their own racing hearts. The flickering emergency lights cast eerie shadows over Ridley's still form, obscuring any sign of life. Her chest, if rising and falling, did so imperceptibly.

Chastine dropped to her knees beside her, fingers trembling as she reached out, afraid to touch her. "Ridley?" she whispered, her voice barely more than a breath, straining to detect any response, any sign that she was still alive.

CHAPTER 13

The acrid stench of formaldehyde mingled with sulfur hit Aldin like a physical blow, its pungent odor slithering down her throat and making her gag. Her eyes watered as she struggled to breathe, the foul mixture choking her. Suddenly, a cold downpour drenched her. Blinking rapidly, she realized the automatic fire suppression system had been activated. Her reckless barrage of blaster fire had ignited several workstations, and the resulting sparks had set half the lab ablaze.

Aldin scrambled to her feet, her boots slipping on the slick, mucus-covered floor. The wetness mixed with the slime created a treacherous surface, making every movement a struggle. The crackling of the fire grew louder, each pop and hiss announcing the inadequacy of the sprinklers to combat the growing inferno. Panic surged through her as she cast about desperately for an escape route.

Then she heard it—a cacophony of sounds that would haunt her nightmares forever: the wet, sticky slaps of appendages on the stone floor; the skittering taps of sharp nails against metal tables; and gurgled, inhuman cries protesting her presence. Each sound layered with a grotesque symphony of terror.

Movement at the edge of her vision made her whip her head around, her heart pounding in her chest. Her blood turned to ice as she saw the source of the terrifying sounds. Numerous jars had toppled and shattered, freeing the grotesque experiments and embryonic horrors from their stasis prisons. She watched in horror as twisted, malformed creatures reanimated and began to crawl toward her with a predatory hunger.

A scream tore from her throat, raw and primal, as she kicked and stomped in a desperate bid to escape. Each squish and crunch underfoot sent waves of revulsion through her, but her fear was stronger than her disgust. She backed away, pressing herself against another door, her fingers fumbling for the latch. Just as she reached it, something banged violently on the other side, making her jump. She pictured another abomination, perhaps even more monstrous, poised to lunge at her.

Panicking, she scampered away from the door, her breath coming in short, ragged gasps. The fire had grown too large, cutting off access to the stairs that had led her into this nightmarish laboratory. The flames danced and roared, consuming everything in their path with relentless ferocity. She was trapped. Her mind raced, searching frantically for another escape.

Suddenly, the sprinkler system shut off, as if conceding defeat to the relentless blaze. Thick, black smoke filled the room, its suffocating tendrils curling around her. The air grew heavy with the noxious fumes, and Aldin coughed violently, her vision blurring as the smoke stung her eyes and filled her lungs. The heat became unbearable, the fire's hungry tongues licking closer and closer.

The sound of skittering grew louder, more frantic,

accompanied by the grotesque, gurgled cries of the reanimated experiments. Aldin's fear spiked, adrenaline surging through her veins. Her heart pounded in her ears, drowning out all other sounds. She knew she had to find a way out before either the smoke and flames, or the monsters, claimed her life. Desperation fueled her actions as she scanned the room once more, her eyes darting through the thick haze.

In the dim, flickering light, she spotted a ventilation duct near the ceiling, partially obscured by the thickening smoke. It was a slim hope, but it was her only chance. She staggered towards it, every step an agonizing effort against the slick floor and the oppressive heat. She grabbed a nearby chair, dragging it beneath the duct, her movements frantic and uncoordinated.

With a strenuous effort, she climbed onto the chair, her hands trembling as she fumbled with the vent cover. The heat and smoke made her dizzy, her vision narrowing. She pried the cover off, dropping it with a clang, and hoisted herself into the narrow duct. The metal was hot to the touch, burning her hands and knees as she crawled, but she forced herself onward, driven by the sheer will to survive.

Behind her, the lab was a cacophony of chaos: the roar of the fire, the skittering and slapping of the abominations, and the ever-present crackle of burning materials. The air in the duct was marginally clearer, but the heat was intense, and every breath felt like inhaling shards of glass.

As she crawled through the duct, the sounds of the lab began to fade, replaced by the echoing clang of her movements. She had no idea where the duct led, only that it was away from the immediate danger. Her progress was slow and painful, her body screaming in protest with every inch.

Finally, she reached a junction in the ductwork. One path led downward, promising a way out, but it was almost completely blocked by debris. The other path continued horizontally, deeper into the unknown labyrinth of the building's ventilation system.

Aldin crawled on, praying that her luck would hold and that this nightmare would soon end. The duct seemed to stretch on forever. Her body ached, and her lungs burned, but she forced herself to keep moving.

Eventually, she saw a faint light ahead, a beacon of hope in the darkness. She crawled towards it, and as she reached the end of the duct, she peered through the grate and saw a small storeroom below, mercifully free of fire and abominations.

With a last burst of energy, she kicked the grate open and lowered herself into the room. She collapsed onto the floor, gasping for air, the coolness of the storeroom a blessed relief from the inferno she had escaped.

A tremor tore through the building, shaking it to its core and signaling to Aldin that she needed to keep moving. Panic surged through her as she looked around and realized with mounting horror that this was apparently Jensen's warehouse —the heart of his mad-scientist operations. The room was lined with shelves filled with empty bottles and vials, along with boxes labeled with a dizzying array of chemicals. A small refrigeration unit sat silent in one corner, while the main body of a miniature particle accelerator lay ominously on the floor next to it.

For a moment, sheer panic gripped her as she scanned the room for an escape, her eyes darting from one shadowy corner to another. The tremors were becoming more violent, and she could feel the building's instability in her bones. Her breath caught in her throat when she couldn't immediately find a way out, but then she saw it—the vague outline of a door in the room's corner.

Staggering forward, arms outstretched, she reached the door, only to find it frustratingly solid with no apparent handle. *The key!* Her mind screamed. She fumbled frantically in her pocket until she found the outline of the key once more and jammed it into the slot. A second later, the door clicked open, and she rushed through, finding herself in a small elevator. She pressed the single button on the wall, praying fervently as it began to ascend.

Her prayers were cut short by a massive jolt. Another explosion rocked the building to its foundation, bringing the elevator to a sudden, jarring stop. The emergency lights flickered and then went out, plunging her into an oppressive blackness. Alone, trapped in the dark, Aldin huddled into the corner of the small chamber, her body shaking with fear and exhaustion. Tears streamed down her face as she muttered to herself, "I can't do this!"

Then, as if conjured by her desperation, Ridley appeared before her, crouching gently. "Yes, you can, and you will," Ridley said, her voice a soothing relief.

"But I'm not a soldier like you. I'm just a scientist," Aldin replied, her voice quivering.

Ridley placed a comforting hand on Aldin's cheek. "You're the love of my life, and that's all that matters. You've always been stronger than you give yourself credit for." As Ridley leaned in, their lips almost touching, a series of loud crashes and bangs sounded from below the elevator, jolting Aldin back to reality.

Ridley vanished, and Aldin realized she had only been a phantom of her eroding hope. Yet the words lingered, fueling a renewed resolve. She was stronger than she gave herself credit for, and she had to find a way out and fix this disaster.

Aldin pulled the tablet from her pocket, using its light to

illuminate the small area. Her eyes scanned the space, landing on a maintenance panel in the ceiling. She groaned inwardly, regretting her lack of athleticism. The walls of the elevator were sheer metal, and the only way to reach the ceiling was to jump off the wall and push herself up—a maneuver that would challenge even a skilled acrobat.

Her first two attempts ended in painful failure, her body slamming back onto the hard floor. Desperation clawed at her, but on her third attempt, her fingers brushed against the edge of the panel. Hope ignited within her. She tried again, this time with more zeal, her fingers finally grasping the edge of the panel, causing it to swing down as she fell to the floor.

The black abyss of the maintenance shaft loomed above her, its darkness both foreboding and inviting. A series of loud bangs echoed again from below, a notice that whatever monstrosity had been trapped in Jensen's lab was now free. If she didn't find a way out, she was as good as dead.

Scrambling to her feet, she made another attempt, knowing her time was running out. With a final, desperate lunge, she grabbed onto the edge of the opening. Her fingers, cut and bleeding, struggled to maintain their grip. The slick mixture of sweat and blood made her grip tenuous, and she could feel her hands slipping. Determined not to fail, she summoned every ounce of strength and pulled herself up, bracing herself with her elbows.

Her muscles burned, and her body trembled with exertion as she hauled herself into the shaft. She used the tablet's dim light to survey her surroundings, revealing a seemingly endless vertical tunnel stretching upward into the oppressive darkness. A metal handrail, slick with age and neglect, was mounted on the wall and led up one side. She could make out the faint outline of a doorway just a short distance above her, teasing her with the promise of escape.

Carefully, she skirted to the edge, her hands trembling as she grabbed hold of the lowest handrail. She took a deep breath, steeling herself for the arduous climb into the unknown. With a last glance down at the black abyss below, she began to pull herself upward.

Each rung was a battle. Her muscles screamed in protest, and her breath came in ragged gasps. She soon found herself level with the doorway she had seen earlier and realized, with a sinking heart, that it was just out of reach. There was no ledge to stand on, no way to safely jump without risking a deadly fall. She held tightly to the rung, stretching out her other hand in a futile attempt to grasp the door-frame, but it was too far away. Defeated, she continued her climb.

Sweat poured down her face, mingling with the grime and blood on her hands, making each rung increasingly slippery. Her strength dropped with each passing moment, her muscles burning with exhaustion. Then it happened. Her hand slipped from one of the rungs, and her feet followed suit a heartbeat later. She clung desperately to her last fleeting chance of survival, her heart hammering in her chest and her lungs burning for air. For a terrifying moment, she dangled in the darkness, the abyss below threatening to swallow her whole. With a tremendous effort, she swung her other hand up and snatched onto the metal bar, her fingers gripping with the desperation of the damned.

Her feet found purchase once more, and she quickly wrapped her arm through the bottom of the rung, cradling it firmly in her elbow. She held on tightly, every muscle in her body rigid with fear. The darkness seemed to close in around her, the silence punctuated only by the sound of her own labored breathing and the distant, ominous creaks of the building's failing structure.

Aldin remained still, too afraid to move, her mind racing

through a thousand scenarios, each more terrifying than the last. Finally, summoning every remaining ounce of strength and courage, she adjusted her grip and continued her climb, hoping for salvation but fearing there was none to be had.

CHAPTER 14

Darin watched in terror as Anon lunged for Ridley, dragging her limp body into the room before slamming the door shut. "Is she okay?" his voice trembled.

"I don't know?" Anon replied nervously as he kneeled beside Ridley. His hands shook as he began to examine her, his eyes darting over her still form.

A minute later, Ridley's soft moan pierced the silence, a fragile sound that brought a rush of relief to everyone. Her eyes fluttered open and she glared at Darin. "Watch where you're pointing that thing next time," she rasped, her voice barely more than a whisper.

Darin exhaled. "We didn't know what was out there," he said. "We thought it was another swarm chasing us, or something worse."

Ridley grimaced, her hand reaching up to touch the back of her neck. When she pulled it away, her eyes widened at the sight of black, oily mucus covering her fingers. "Something bit me in the corridor," she said, her voice unsteady. "I started blacking out and pounded on the door."

Their eyes followed the writhing substance as it slipped from her fingers and squirmed across the floor, sliding under the tiny crack beneath the door. "What is this stuff?" Ridley asked, clear disgust in her voice.

Chastine spoke up, her voice strained. "My best guess, given how everything happened so fast, is that it's a mutated strain of the virus Aldin was working on."

Ridley looked at her in shock. "Are you suggesting that she's responsible for all of this?" She glanced around the room, her expression then growing frantic. "Where is Aldin?"

Chastine's voice was heavy with resignation. "To answer your first question, although it was certainly an accident, yes, I think she is responsible. As for your second, Jensen left her behind. He wouldn't let her come with us."

Ridley bolted upright, horror etched on her face. "He left her by herself?"

"Yes. He was determined that she should pay for the damage she'd done."

"And you didn't stop him?" Ridley demanded, as she paced back and forth.

"You know how Jensen is, Ridley. When he gets worked up, he's capable of anything. And given the severity of the situation, there was nothing we could do."

Ridley looked at Anon and Darin, searching their faces, and saw the same grim acceptance in their eyes. They had felt as helpless as she did now.

Her gaze shifted to Chantel, who had been eerily silent. The realization hit Ridley like a punch to the gut. She had been so focused on Aldin's fate that she hadn't noticed Chantel's absence from their frantic conversations. When she saw her sister's still body, the truth dawned on her instantly. "I'm so sorry, Chastine," she said softly.

Chastine turned away, holding her feelings tight, knowing that any word she spoke would shatter her.

Darin quickly changed the subject, seeking a distraction

from the moment, "Where are the others?"

Ridley's face darkened, haunted by memories of Jasper, Kalen, and Mishka. She struggled to form the words, but her silence spoke volumes.

Darin's eyes widened in horror. "All of them?" he asked, his voice barely above a whisper.

Ridley nodded slowly, the weight of their loss settling over them like a suffocating shroud.

Darin's fear erupted. "Well, that does it then! We're all doomed!"

"No, we're not!" Ridley snapped. Aldin was still out there, somewhere, alone and scared. She had to find her. "We'll find a way out of here."

"The only way out is back through that door," Anon said grimly. "And if we go back out there, that swarm is going to eat us up in no time!"

Ridley absently reached her hand to the back of her neck and felt the boil that had formed there. She was lucky to have escaped her attack with so little damage, and she knew it. She closed her eyes for a brief second, remembering, and could almost hear the buzzing in her ears as the swarm rocketed down the hall toward her while she sat with her back against the door in silent mourning. It had all happened so fast!

Mishka! she thought sadly as a tear rolled down her cheek.

***

As the swarm got closer, Ridley jumped to her feet and turned the dial on her blaster that changed her energy beam into a wider blast. She knew it would burn through its power reserves quickly, but it was all she had. Then she started blasting frantically as she ran forward, through the middle of the swarm, yelling with all the fury she could muster.

When she finally made it through the tempest, she kept running, as fast as her legs would carry her, until she came to the fork in the corridor and saw the flesh-less body of the fallen worker. She immediately noticed the footprints leading off in different directions, stamped onto the floor in a mix of blood and ooze—a single set leading off in one direction, and a group of prints heading the other. She had little doubt who the single set of prints belonged to.

She was almost to the door where the group of prints disappeared when a seizure wracked her body. Desperately, she pounded on the door. Then the world turned upside down.

When she woke up a minute later on the hallway floor, her body stiff and sore from the recent spasms, she felt a stream of liquid ooze across the back of her neck and down her shoulder. She reached back and ran her hand along the wound. When she pulled her fingers back, she was shocked to see them covered with a thick, black, oily substance. She looked at it closely, trying to figure out what it was, then it moved.

Immediately, she shook the stuff from her hand in disgust, then watched in amazement and terror as the substance all came together to form a small puddle on the floor that slithered away down the hall.

Scared that the swarm would come back, she pounded on the door again, hoping her intuition was correct and the rest of the group was hiding inside. When the door began to open, she breathed a sigh of relief. Then, the flames shot out!

***

A series of thunderous bangs overhead snapped their heads upward. The ceiling bowed and buckled ominously under the weight of something enormous, the metal creaking and groaning like a dying beast. Darin's hands shook violently as he clutched the makeshift flamethrower, his face a mask of sheer terror. "We're never going to make it out of here alive!" he cried.

Ridley sprang to her feet. She snatched the rod and canister from Darin just as another explosion rocked the building. The ground beneath them shuddered, and the lights flickered before plunging them into darkness.

"Stay near the door!" Ridley commanded, her voice a fierce whisper in the pitch black. She braced herself, holding the equipment at the ready.

A second later, the ceiling above them gave way. A massive, grotesque form fell to the floor with a deafening crash, sending dust and debris billowing through the air. A scream tore through the darkness, a sound so unnatural and unholy it seemed to claw at their very souls.

Blind and frantic, Ridley twisted the valve on the tank and pressed the button on the rod, sending a scorching jet of fire into the darkness. The flames illuminated a nightmare vision of skull and exposed sinew, the creature's eyes bulging from their sockets. The abomination shrieked, its fur igniting in a burst of hellish light.

Immediately, the creature swung at her, forcing Ridley to scurry backward, narrowly evading the beast's massive claw. "Get that door open, Anon!" she yelled in terror.

"I'm trying, but the power's out!" Anon shouted back, his voice filled with panic.

The beast reared back, towering over Ridley. For the first time, she saw the full horror of the Kantor, a creature on the brink of extinction. Its legend spoke of unparalleled ferocity, attacking anything and everything without mercy. Its teeth, long and razor-sharp, jutted from a cavernous mouth designed for tearing flesh. It moved with unnatural speed, a demon cloaked in fur, once hunted to the brink for the safety of the entire planet. The realization that Jensen had housed one at the lab was an extremely disturbing thought, demonstrating just how far he was willing to go in the name of science.

For a fleeting moment, the lights flickered back on, and the door lifted a few inches before the power cut out again, plunging them back into darkness.

Another feral scream erupted from the Kantor as it lunged forward. Ridley fired another blast of flames, striking the beast, but it charged through the inferno undaunted, ignoring the flames that engulfed it. Ridley dodged its gnashing teeth but wasn't quick enough to avoid a massive claw that raked across her shoulder, tearing flesh and muscle. The force of the blow sent her crashing to the floor, the rod and cylinder clattering away.

As she lay there, pain radiating through her body, she watched in horror as the Kantor gathered itself for another attack. Her mind raced, memories flashing by: Aldin, Mishka, the people she had failed. A bittersweet acceptance washed over her. Maybe in the next life she would do better and live up to her potential?

Before the creature could strike, a torrent of flames engulfed its face, this time forcing it to retreat momentarily. Ridley scrambled away and saw Chastine wielding the torch, her face set in grim determination.

"Get out of here!" Chastine screamed.

Ridley hesitated, her face clouded with sadness and guilt. Yet again, another person was sacrificing themselves for her. "Now!" Chastine shouted again.

With no choice, Ridley quickly followed Darin and Anon, slipping under the barely open door. Behind them, the beast's roars were matched by Chastine's defiant shouts until they were abruptly cut off by a final, savage strike a moment later. The silence that followed was absolute, a testament to the ultimate price Chastine had paid.

CHAPTER 15

Almost immediately, Jensen felt a twinge of regret roll through him, a cold, creeping sensation that gnawed at his insides. It wasn't because he had killed them—Demri had simply been in the wrong place at the wrong time, a necessary casualty; and Antasia, well, he had hardly known her, reducing her in his mind to someone small and inconsequential. No, the regret was much more practical, more calculating. It would have been much easier to reboot the system with two pairs of hands instead of one.

He sighed. Now, he would have to do it the hard way. The first thing he needed was Demri's thumb, and for that, he required something sharp. Before he could begin his search, a grating, scratching noise from the far corner of the room froze him in place.

Gripping the handle of the blaster in his right hand, Jensen cautiously crept from his chair, each step deliberate and measured. The sound led him to a large panel set in the wall about a foot off the floor. He knew what lay behind it: a series of air ducts used by maintenance, running from the cooling room and spreading out to most of the labs. These ducts ensured that proper temperatures were maintained, preventing the equipment from overheating.

As he drew closer, the scratching morphed into a low, tortured moan that stretched out in an eerie, drawn-out wail before falling silent. Jensen's pulse quickened as he tighten his grip on the blaster. He listened closely, the silence pressing in around him, thick and suffocating.

When everything stayed quiet, he slowly reached for the handle on the side of the panel. His hand shook slightly as he turned it, and the panel swung open, pushed from behind by the weight of a dead maintenance worker. The body tumbled out, landing heavily on the floor with a sickening thud. Jensen gasped when he saw the enormous creature attached to the man's face, its serpentine body coiled tightly around his neck.

The Vispar wriggled violently, its movements jerky and erratic, as it wrenched one of the man's eyes from its socket and swallowed it whole. Jensen's stomach churned at the sight, a wave of bile rising in his throat. The creature must have sensed him, because it turned its head quickly, its hood flaring out menacingly. It reared back, ready to strike, and for a moment, Jensen saw the outline of the eyeball the creature had just ingested sliding down its undulating body.

Jensen quickly raised the blaster and fired, the blast echoing through the room as it struck the thing in the head, obliterating it. The creature's body convulsed before going limp.

The sound of the blast brought a series a series of angry, vengeful hisses streaming from the depths of the duct system. Jensen could only guess how many of their former research subjects were racing toward him on decaying forms. He quickly closed the panel and turned the latch tight.

Returning to the monitor station, Jensen rifled through the lockers on the wall behind him, searching for anything sharp.

As he did, his mind wandered to the fate of his security personnel. How many of them were still alive? Not that he cared about any of them, his curiosity was purely academic. He guessed that Mishka was probably okay, given her strength and deadly accuracy with a blaster. Ridley might survive too, despite her nauseating relationship with Aldin. The others? He doubted their chances. Some were too weak, others too new and inexperienced.

As he continued to search, Jensen's hands finally closed around an ionic knife, the blade glinting in the dim light. He turned back to Demri's lifeless body. The regret he had felt earlier was now a distant echo, replaced by a cold, relentless focus.

As he kneeled beside Demri, he pressed the button to activate the blade and sliced through Demri's hand at the base of his thumb. Although he seldom had use for such weapons, he liked the efficiency of the blade as it melted through the flesh easily, cauterizing the wound as it went to prevent a spill of blood.

Jensen took the severed appendage and walked back into the control room. His destination was the master switch panel in the back, the heart of the facility's control system. Just as he was about to place the thumb on the sensor pad to initiate the override procedure, the lights flickered, casting eerie shadows that danced briefly before plunging the room into darkness.

Above him, in the vents, came the sound of something massive shifting its weight. The scratching and scraping were unmistakable, confirming that his secret was no longer hidden. A little smile tugged at the corners of his mouth as he pictured the Kantor in action. He had analyzed the creature extensively in a controlled environment, but had never witnessed its full fury unleashed. He certainly hoped he'd get the chance before he left this accursed place. There was one person, in particular, he wanted to see ripped apart.

Jensen paused, his mind briefly wandering. His disdain for Aldin had crept in slowly, insidiously, over the past few years until it consumed him. She had always seemed weak and whiny to him, and her insubordination had been the final straw. When he had taken her off the SYHF project, she had defied him, continuing the research behind his back. That betrayal had ignited a spark of hatred, driving him to concoct a scheme that would discredit her completely, ruin her career, and shatter her life. To say his plan had succeeded beyond his wildest expectations would be an understatement.

In the oppressive darkness, Jensen could hear the ceiling above him groan under the weight of the Kantor. He longed to see the beast in action, to witness its destructive power firsthand. But putting himself in harm's way was folly; survival was paramount. He needed to ensure Aldin's downfall, and for that, he had to live.

After the creature moved on, Jensen waited a few more minutes before pressing the tip of Demri's thumb onto the scanner. He flipped the switch next to it, and the system hummed to life. He raced to the main terminal, typing feverishly. For a brief, triumphant moment, the power roared back to life, illuminating the room with a harsh, artificial light. But almost immediately, everything went dead again, plunging the room back into darkness.

Jensen pounded his fist on the counter. He needed to salvage what was left of his research, but he was trapped inside the control room. The hissing in the air ducts grew louder, more insistent. He took a deep breath, forcing himself to stay calm, and let his mind work through the problem. No acceptable solution presented itself, and he sighed in defeat, absently sliding his hand into his jacket pocket.

His fingers brushed against the glass jar, and his eyes widened with sudden realization. He had completely forgotten about it. Even in the darkness, he could feel the specimen inside, undulating back and forth, seeking an escape. The organism pulsed with a sinister life of its own. At that moment, clarity struck him. He knew what he needed to do.

CHAPTER 16

The pounding in Mishka's head as she recovered from the seizures was almost drowned out by the relentless banging of the insect horde on the other side of the glass. She sat up, the soft glow from the monitors casting eerie shadows around the room. Disgust welled up in her throat as she watched a stream of black, oily mucus pour from the wound in her arm, slithering across the floor like a living thing before escaping under the door.

Clenching her teeth against the pain, she pulled herself from the floor and began typing at the nearest terminal, her fingers trembling. She brought up the security feed for the hallway where she'd left Ridley only minutes before. Her heart skipped a beat when she saw the spot next to the door empty, and she exhaled a brief sigh of relief. But dread quickly returned as she frantically searched through other feeds, her breath catching when she saw Ridley's body lying still in front of a maintenance room door. A tear rolled down her cheek. "Ridley, no!" she sobbed, her voice breaking.

As she stood there, lost in memories of the past and the love she'd lost, she failed to notice the cracks spidering through the glass door. Then a sharp, splintering sound jolted her back to the present, a warning that the nightmare was about to descend upon her, again.

Without waiting to make sure the path was clear, she raced to the door and threw it open, rushing into the hallway beyond. Each step sent a jolt of pain through her injured shoulder, and she cried out as the edge of the door caught her arm while closing behind her.

She closed her eyes for a brief second, focusing her mind to push away the pain as her mentor had taught her. His image flashed in her mind, and she whispered a final, silent goodbye before continuing down the hall.

It wasn't long before signs of death blocked her path. The hallway was painted in blood and littered with bodies, so much so that she had to stop or risk falling prey to the same beast that had caused the devastation. Ahead, she saw it crouched low, its back to her, crunching on bones with its powerful jaws, while ripping at flesh with deadly claws.

Slowly, Mishka lifted her blaster and aimed at the beast. With its head bent low, it was hard to get a clear shot. She took a careful step to the side to get a better angle, but her foot slid on a pool of blood. The wet sucking sound broke the silence just enough to make the Kantor stiffen for a second before it turned its head toward her.

A low, throaty growl issued from the beast, blood gurgling from a hole in its throat as it stood to its full height. Mishka gasped as the creature towered over her, its charred flesh and the stench of burned fur filling the air.

She only had a split second to react, diving to her right to avoid its massive arms swinging wildly at her. She landed squarely on the remains of a scientist, unrecognizable now from the other carnage except for the white lab coat. A stream of blood ran from Mishka's neck, and she realized one of the beast's claws had found its mark.

Fortunately, the layer of blood on the floor created a slick surface that caused the Kantor to slide past her. Mishka quickly jumped up and fired several blasts at the beast, dropping it to the floor. Something told her it wouldn't stay down for long.

She forced her left arm up with her right, gritting her teeth in agony, and used her hand to staunch the flow of blood from her neck before turning and racing down the hall as fast as she dared. The corridor took a sharp turn to the left, then jogged back again for a long stretch. Mishka had just made the turn when she heard movement behind her—not the heavy pounding of the Kantor, but soft, uneven footsteps.

She spun around, holding her blaster tight, readying herself. A figure slowly emerged around the corner, stepping forward with one leg while dragging the other behind, leaving a streak of blood trailing away. The scientist reached out to Mishka, her eyes pleading desperately. "Help me, Mishka," the woman said weakly.

Mishka started to take a step toward her, but a low rumble made her stop. An instant later, the Kantor sprang into view, its mouth opened wide. It grabbed the scientist tightly with both hands and rammed its deadly teeth into the woman's skull. The razor-sharp daggers penetrated the bone easily, sending a spray of blood and brain matter spewing out like a volcanic eruption.

Once again, Mishka found herself running for her life. She sprinted down the long hallway, her heart pounding in her chest, and each step sending fresh waves of pain radiating through her broken body. The only way to escape the beast was to get out of the building completely, and the only viable exit was the service transports at the back of the building in the loading zone.

The hallway stretched endlessly before her. An eternity

later, she reached a junction and immediately turned right, her feet sliding on the blood-slick floor. Without pausing, she burst through a door and bounded up a series of stairs, her body protesting with every step. The metallic taste of blood filled her mouth as she bit down hard to keep from screaming.

At the top of the stairs, she pushed through a heavy set of double doors and stumbled into another long corridor, this one much wider than the others. The walls seemed to close in on her, the sterile white tiles smeared with gore and the acrid scent of death hanging in the air. Mishka only made it a few steps when an ear-piercing alarm sounded, followed by a mechanical voice overhead, "Emergency quarantine protocols initiated. Please exit the structure immediately."

The only thought on her mind as she raced down the corridor toward the loading zone was that she would find Ridley safe, waiting for her. It was the final hope she could cling to.

The corridor seemed to stretch on forever, each second an eternity. Her legs burned and her vision blurred as the pain and exhaustion took their toll on her body. The sounds of the insect horde and the roar of the Kantor grew distant, replaced by the incessant blare of the alarm and the mechanical repetition of the evacuation order.

Suddenly, the building trembled violently, causing the floor beneath her feet to shift. She stumbled and barely managed to keep her balance, propping herself against a door-frame for support. The walls shook, and ceiling panels crashed down around her, shattering on the floor. With each second, the tremors grew more intense, the structure groaning as if in agony.

Mishka pushed herself harder, her breath coming in ragged gasps. She could see the doors to the loading zone ahead, the promise of escape just within reach. But as she neared the exit, another violent tremor sent her sprawling to the ground, her body skidding across the cold tiles. She cried out in pain as her wounded shoulder slammed into the floor, the impact blurring her vision. The fall made her instinctively pull her hand away from the wound on her neck, which was the only thing preventing the blood from flowing.

Gritting her teeth, she forced herself up onto the slick floor, her muscles screaming in protest and her strength waning from the loss of blood. She could hear the structural supports creaking, the sound of metal bending and breaking under the strain.

With a last burst of energy, Mishka surged forward, slamming her body into the doors of the loading zone. They swung open with a deafening clang, and she stumbled blindly into the open space beyond hoping and praying for a miracle.

CHAPTER 17

The sterile, clinical scent of antiseptic hung thick in the air, mingling with the faint aroma of soap and something slightly metallic, like blood. Andrena hummed softly as she washed Janeen, her hands moving in a practiced rhythm. The warm water cascaded over Janeen's fur, and for a brief moment, it almost felt like a normal day.

Janeen, a gentle-eyed simian, relaxed under Andrena's touch, her tiny body limp from exhaustion. Andrena's humming grew softer, almost a whisper, a lullaby even. She dipped the sponge into the soapy water, squeezing out the excess with a quiet sigh.

"There we go, almost done," Andrena said soothingly. The sound of the running water was like a balm, washing away the tension of the strenuous day Janeen had undergone during her extensive testing, the results of which would hopefully be used to develop a steroid to help combat an immune deficiency commonly found among her species.

Janeen replied with a wide smile before her eyelids started to droop and sleep overtook her.

Then the explosion hit.

The floor bucked and heaved, and Andrena barely had

104

time to react. Instinct took over as she threw herself over Janeen, shielding the small animal from the shards of glass and debris that rained down from the ceiling. The overhead lights flickered madly, casting grotesque shadows that danced and swayed.

As the alarms blared, the piercing sound reverberated through the air, causing Andrena to cringe. She heard muffled screams and frantic shouts echoing down the corridors outside her lab.

"What the hell was that?" Andrena gasped. She disentangled herself from Janeen, who looked as scared and confused as she felt.

"I'll be right back," Andrena said nervously as she scooped up the wet Janeen with a blanket and quickly shoved her inside a nearby cage. "Stay here," she instructed as she turned to leave, unaware that she had forgotten to latch the door to the enclosure.

She bolted from the lab, her mind a whirlwind of fear and confusion. The corridor outside was a nightmare come to life. Smoke and dust choked the air, and the walls seemed to close in on her, the flickering lights casting long, ominous shadows.

Andrena pushed her way through the chaos, her breath coming in short, panicked gasps. The main lab on this wing of the facility was a hive of frantic activity. Researchers huddled together, their faces masks of terror and disbelief.

Dr. Harris, a tall man with a shock of white hair, met her gaze, his eyes haunted. "From what we can tell, there was an explosion in one of the virus research labs. We don't know the extent of the damage, but it appears to be extensive."

The words hit Andrena like a physical blow. Immediately, she thought about Aldin, who had become a close friend the instant they were both new recruits at the facility. The virus

Aldin had been studying—the one that had claimed the lives of countless Terrans over the years—was more just research to her. It was her life work. The implications were too horrifying to fully grasp.

A chorus of tortured animal cries rose up all around them, their anguished voices reverberating throughout the facility like a tidal wave of despair.

"I need to get back to Janeen!" Andrena exclaimed as she turned and sprinted back down the corridor.

A nightmare waited for her as she burst into the lab. Janeen lay on the floor, a dark pool of blood spreading around her small body. Andrena cried as she dropped to her knees beside the tiny creature.

"No, no, no," she whispered, her voice breaking. She reached out with trembling hands, checking for a pulse, but there was nothing. Janeen's fur was matted with blood, her eyes staring lifelessly at the ceiling.

Her mind raced, trying to make sense of the horror. But then, Janeen's body twitched. Andrena's heart leaped into her throat as she dared to hope that the animal was still alive. Then, Janeen's eyes snapped open, but they weren't Janeen's eyes anymore. They glowed with an unnatural, terrifying light, filled with hunger and rage.

Janeen—or what had once been Janeen—let out a guttural snarl, lunging at Andrena with terrifying speed. Andrena barely had time to react, scrambling backward as Janeen's teeth snapped inches from her face.

"Janeen, stop!" Andrena cried, but the creature showed no recognition, no sign of the gentle animal it had once been.

Pain exploded in Andrena's side as Janeen's claws raked across her flesh, tearing through her shirt and skin. She bit back a scream, using all her strength to push the creature away. She stumbled to her feet, clutching her side where blood now flowed freely.

With a final, desperate glance at the monster that had once been a harmless lab specimen, Andrena fled down the corridor, her heart pounding and her vision blurring.

The sound of her own ragged breathing was all she could hear as she ran, the distant growls and screams of the undead echoing through the halls like a chorus from hell. All Andrena could do was run and hope that somewhere, somehow, there was a way out of this nightmare.

CHAPTER 18

Jensen took a deep breath to prepare himself, feeling the weight of his decision press down on him. He didn't relish what he was about to do, but after wracking his brain for hours, he found no alternative. The thought of losing all his previous work—years of painstaking research, countless hours of dedication, blood, sweat, and tears—gnawed at him. But as his hand brushed against the container in his pocket, a wide grin spread across his face. The specimen inside pulsed with sinister life, reminding him of his ultimate goal.

The racket from the ventilation duct grew in intensity, a cacophony of scrabbling claws and guttural growls. Jensen walked cautiously back to the wall panel, the severed thumb cold in his hand. He placed it on the sensor again, feeling a grotesque satisfaction when he pressed the dead flesh against metal. This time, instead of rushing back to the terminal, he pressed another code on the panel and presented the appendage once more. After a brief delay, an alarm sounded, and a voice crackled overhead, "Emergency quarantine protocols initiated. Please exit the structure immediately."

A soft hiss echoed through the room as a series of hydraulics engaged, lifting the door so he could escape. He raised the blaster and stepped cautiously into the hallway. A collection of small reflectors dotted both sides of the floor, casting eerie pools of light in the otherwise dark corridor.

Jensen crept silently toward the end of the hall, where the passage joined another and stretched in opposite directions. The alarm continued to blare, and the voice overhead repeated its warning with relentless urgency, "Emergency quarantine protocols initiated. Please exit the structure immediately."

Instead of heading toward the front of the structure, Jensen turned right, holding his blaster ready. Sweat beaded on his forehead, betraying his attempted portrayal of a fierce soldier, even though he was anything but. He knew deep down that he was nothing more than a scientist—albeit, a genius one—but his pride wouldn't allow him to show weakness. This crisis, and the exciting prospects it created, only strengthened his resolve. He would prove his superiority to everyone, in every way. He would be the god of a new world.

The warning rang overhead again, more urgent this time, "Emergency quarantine protocols underway. Please exit the structure immediately. Countdown to thermal-genesis will commence shortly."

Jensen quickened his pace, pushing toward the rear of the building. All around him, howls and screams overlapped the cry of the alarm, making it difficult to determine their source. But he knew they were close. Too close.

Suddenly, a dark mass rushed toward him, accompanied by the sound of ragged breathing. Jensen fired a quick shot, the blaster's recoil jolting his arm. The shot missed by a wide margin, hitting the wall with a bright flash. A voice yelled from the darkness, "Hey! Watch where you're aiming that thing!" Seconds later, a figure came into view, shuffling gingerly and bracing against the wall for support.

"Andrena!" Jensen exclaimed, his voice a mix of surprise and indifference when he recognized who he had almost shot. "You're alive!" The statement carried no genuine emotion—her survival meant little to him—instead he offered it as if it were merely a formal greeting.

As Andrena came closer, he saw the wound in her side, the blood trailing down the hall behind her. "What happened?" he asked, forcing his voice to sound sincere.

Andrena's face contorted with pain and fear. "It all happened so fast! One second, I was bathing Janeen, and then there was an explosion. I left the room for a few minutes to make sure everything was okay, and when I came back, she was lying on the floor in a pool of blood. She had been attacked by something! I knew she was dead, lying there unmoving, but then she suddenly sprang back to life, only it wasn't Janeen anymore. She was something different. Then she attacked me! I barely got away!" Her voice cracked, and tears welled in her eyes.

"What is going on here, Jensen?" she pleaded, her voice trembling.

The warning system declared once again, "Emergency quarantine protocols underway. Please exit the structure immediately. Countdown to thermal-genesis has begun."

"Who started the emergency protocols?" Andrena asked in a panicked voice. "And what happens during thermal-genesis?"

Jensen replied calmly, "I suspect Demri was the one who set the emergency protocols in motion. He was always quick to react with extreme measures in the face of a crisis. As far as thermal-genesis goes, it's a failsafe. If a biological threat escapes containment and poses an environmental danger, the contagion must be eradicated. At all costs."

"The building is going to be destroyed?" Andrena's voice was a mix of disbelief and horror.

"That's a mild way of putting it, but yes."

"But what about all the animals? We can't just leave them to die!" she cried, desperation in her eyes.

"They're already dead... except they refuse to stay dead. This will ensure their demise once and for all. The protocols are in place to contain the incident at the source and prevent a worldwide catastrophe. Unfortunately, once the system is engaged, there's no way to override it."

Andrena lowered her head, the enormity of the situation sinking in. The chorus of howls grew louder, their guttural echoes reverberating through the narrow corridor. Jensen's grip tightened on his blaster, the metal cool and reassuring against his palm, his mind racing with a mix of dread and the grim satisfaction of impending success.

Without hesitation, Jensen started walking down the hall in the direction Andrena had just come from. His steps were measured and purposeful.

"Isn't the exit this way?" Andrena asked in a wavering voice.

"That way is blocked," Jensen answered curtly. "There are service transports at the rear loading zone that we can use to escape, provided we get there in time." He picked up his pace, not waiting for Andrena's response. A second later, he heard her shuffling behind him, her steps uneven and pained. A slight frown crossed his face for a moment. *She better not get in the way*, he thought darkly.

The sounds of the beasts in the shadows grew louder as they rounded the corridor leading away from the labs and toward the loading zone. "Final warning for evacuation," the system blared. "Lock-down will commence in five minutes. Thermogenesis will then be activated."

"Five minutes?!" Andrena cried, panic rising in her voice. "We'll never make it!"

Jensen glanced over his shoulder and saw a hulking mass approaching from behind, its silhouette a monstrous shadow. He knew immediately which beast belonged to the shadow chasing them. Without thinking twice, he pulled his blaster out and shot Andrena in the leg, crippling her.

As she fell to the floor, crying out in pain, he looked at her with cold indifference. "Oh, I'll make it in time. But I'm afraid you're not going to be so lucky." He watched, transfixed, as the Kantor pounced on her, ripping and devouring her flesh with a savage hunger. Then he turned and ran down the corridor, his heart pounding with adrenaline and a twisted sense of triumph.

The corridor opened into a wide space filled with an assortment of large machines, most of which were broken and mangled. Smoke filled the expanse, stemming from several fires scattered throughout. A series of transports lined one side of the area, all of them damaged beyond use except for one. Undead creatures roamed the area, their movements erratic as they searched hungrily for anything that moved.

Disappointment reared its ugly head as Jensen neared the transport and saw a group of people approaching from the other direction. Although he had hoped to escape the building's annihilation alone, he took solace in the fact that Aldin wasn't with the surviving group. Did he dare to hope that she had finally perished?

Another shudder shook through the building, and the warning blared again through the speakers, "Please exit the structure immediately. Lock-down will be initiated in sixty seconds."

Jensen met the group at the transport, noting the absence of the twins. He didn't need to ask what happened to them.

He could almost picture it in his head—one of them ripped apart by the creatures, the other either refusing to go on without her, sacrificing herself so they could enter the afterlife together. *What a waste!* he thought with contempt.

He was just about to reach for the handle of the transport when a low growl sounded behind him. Jensen spun around, the stench of decay assaulting his nostrils as a creature lunged for him. Its gnashing teeth were inches from ripping his throat out when a blast rang out, hitting the beast in mid-air and sending it crashing into the side of the transport.

The shot did little to stop the beast, which immediately scrambled back on all fours, preparing for another attack. The shooter fired a second shot, hitting the thing in the head and killing it for good.

Anon and Darin supported Ridley as the trio limped toward the transport. No one was more surprised than Ridley when Mishka stepped from the shadows, limping severely herself.

"Mishka!" Ridley exclaimed, her voice a mixture of relief and astonishment. "You're alive!"

Mishka replied, "Yeah. Just barely, though." Her left hand clamped tightly to the side of her neck, where a long streak of blood originated, running down her chest and abdomen to the floor beneath her feet. The rest of her body was covered in cuts and bruises.

Ridley broke free from Anon and Darin, ignoring her own pain to support Mishka. The warning blared again, "Final warning for evacuation. Lock-down will commence in thirty seconds and thermal-genesis will begin."

"I hate to break up this little reunion," Jensen said impatiently, "but we're running out of time."

The group scrambled into the transport as Anon jumped into the driver's seat and turned on the power. A moment later, a flurry of crashes against the side of the transport sent the vehicle rocking as a horde of undead creatures attacked.

Anon quickly engaged the accelerator, rocketing forward down the entrance shaft toward the exit. As they neared the exit, the warning sounded through the transport's intercom system, "Countdown to Lock-down: ten, nine, eight..."

CHAPTER 19

Once Aldin's heart calmed down and returned to normal, she gathered herself and resumed her grueling climb. The darkness made each handhold, each step, each breath a desperate grasp for safety. Her lungs burned and her muscles screamed in protest, stretched to their breaking point. Yet, she pushed herself upward, driven by Ridley's voice echoing in her head to keep going.

Just when a glimmer of salvation seemed within reach in the form of the faint outline of a door shimmering overhead, she heard it—the unmistakable sound of flapping wings, a frantic, eerie sound racing up the shaft toward her. Panic immediately surged through her.

She quickly fumbled for the tablet, holding onto the rungs tightly with one hand while using the other to light up the shaft below. The beam of light sliced through the darkness, revealing a dark, swirling mass rocketing upward like a horrifying storm of shadows.

Desperately, Aldin grabbed for the next rung to pull herself up, and as she did, the tablet slipped from her grasp and plummeted downward. As it intersected with the rising mass, the darkness momentarily broke apart, the light from the screen glinting off sharp beaks and razor talons. Crowlochs. Their collective shriek pierced the air as they surged toward her.

Aldin scrambled up the remaining rungs with every ounce of strength she had left, her fingers slick with sweat and blood. She reached the top, only to be met with a solid, unmoving slab of metal. Frantic, she put her shoulder and back into the overhead door and tried to push upward, but it refused to budge. The shrieks grew louder, closer. Her hand finally found a lever on the side of the shaft. When she yanked the tiny piece of metal with all her might, the door gave way, flying open with a loud bang!

She pulled herself out of the shaft onto the roof just as the flock surged past her into the open sky. Aldin collapsed in a heap, gasping for breath, and watched as several creatures fell to the ground. The rest of the flock flew away sporadically, as if on broken wings.

Picking herself off the ground, she walked over to the nearest Crowloch and jumped back in horror. The creature gnashed and clawed at her with half its face eaten off, a gaping hole in its chest, and only one wing still attached to its body. *The rest of the flock had been carrying it. That's not natural!* she thought in horror.

She looked around, seeing the others scattered across the rooftop like forgotten soldiers, trapped in a grotesque state between life and death. Their chilling cries echoed through the air, sending shivers down her spine. Her heart sank further when she realized her only escape option was a small airship sitting nearby.

When she stood up, her attention was drawn to the horizon. Clouds of smoke dotted the sky in every direction, signaling that the world around her was burning!

Suddenly, an alarm blared, followed by a cold, mechanical

voice. "Emergency quarantine protocols initiated. Please exit the structure immediately."

Aldin stood in stunned silence as another explosion rocked the building, shaking it to its foundation. The magnitude of the tremor sent her flailing to the rooftop, landing inches from one of the undead avians. A shriek flew from her mouth as the thing gnashed at her, prompting the rest of the fallen creatures to respond with a chorus of chilling cries.

The building continued to shudder violently. Aldin scrambled to her knees and scurried toward the edge of the rooftop. Peering over, she saw clouds of dust rising from below, a herald of the structure's imminent collapse. She had to find a way out, and quickly, or become just another casualty in Jensen's nightmarish legacy.

***

"You better step on it, Anon," Darin cried, "or we're not going to make it!"

"We'll make it!" Anon assured, even if he wasn't completely convinced himself.

Anon's grip tightened on the transport's controls, his knuckles white against the backdrop of flashing emergency lights. With a surge of adrenaline, he pushed the vehicle beyond its limits, the engine's roar drowning out the clamor of impending doom echoing through the corridors.

"... five... four... three..."

The countdown hung in the air like a death knell, each passing second a grim reminder of their dwindling mortality. Sweat poured down Anon's brow as he willed the transport to go faster, his heart hammering in his chest.

The transport's metal frame groaned in protest as it hurtled toward the exit, the barriers of time and space blurring in their frantic escape. Just as they breached the threshold, a thick steel wall crashed down behind them.

Through the crackling intercom, the voice of the warning system stated with indifferent finality, "Thermogenesis has begun."

In the eerie calm that followed, a sense of impending catastrophe hung so heavy inside the transport that it seemed to constrict their very breath.

Then, in a cataclysmic crescendo, a deafening explosion tore through the building, unleashing a maelstrom of fire and debris that split the air and shook the planet to its core.

As the ground quaked beneath them, Ridley's thoughts turned to Aldin. *I hope you made it out,* she thought sadly.

***

Aldin stood on the roof of the once bustling laboratory, her heart racing desperately as she watched a transport emerge from the rear of the building. With a surge of hope, she began to jump up and down frantically as she attempted to attract the attention of anyone who might help.

"I'm up here!" she screamed. But her cries were swallowed by the deafening roar of the building's destruction, lost amidst the cacophony of crumbling walls and falling debris. As the transport continued on its path, Aldin's hopes plummeted like a stone sinking into the depths of the blackest ocean.

Collapsing to her knees, she felt a suffocating shroud of despair settle over her. Tears welled up in her eyes as she whispered a silent plea to the heavens above, *I hope you were in there, Ridley. Please, be safe.* The words hung heavy in the air, a desperate prayer to a universe indifferent to her suffering. Almost reluctantly, as if questioning her own worthiness, she mumbled sadly, "I love you."

As the relentless rumble of destruction echoed around her, Aldin's will to live plummeted. If this was the world she had helped create, then perhaps she deserved to perish within its ruins. She tried to shift the blame onto Jensen, to convince herself that she was merely a pawn in his sinister game. But deep down, she knew the truth—she was just as complicit in the devastation that now surrounded her as he was.

In that final, agonizing moment, as the world trembled on the brink of oblivion, Aldin's thoughts drifted back to the first time she had felt a connection to Ridley. Memories flooded her mind like a torrential downpour, each recollection a bittersweet reminder of the love she had once known, now lost amidst the wreckage of their shattered world. The image of Ridley's face, etched with a mixture of determination and vulnerability, burned bright in her mind's eye, a beacon of hope amidst the encroaching darkness. As everything crumbled around her, Aldin clung to that fleeting spark of connection, a solitary glimmer of light in a world quickly being consumed by chaos.

***

Aldin sat at her cluttered workstation one evening, her eyes straining under the dim glow of a soft lamp. Papers and data sheets lay scattered around her, a testament to the relentless hours she had poured into her research. The lab was a sanctuary of silence, broken only by the occasional hum of the cooling systems and the distant echoes of machinery. Lost in the intricate details of her work, she barely noticed the soft sound of footsteps approaching.

The door to the lab swung open, and Ridley and Mishka walked in, their presence a familiar routine during their nightly security rounds. The sharp contrast between their polished uniforms and Aldin's disheveled appearance was stark.

"How's the research going?" Ridley asked, her voice cutting through the quiet.

Aldin's head jerked up, startled. It was the first time Ridley had engaged her in a conversation beyond the perfunctory 'hello'. Her heart skipped a beat, and for a moment, she was speechless.

"Um... okay, I guess," she finally stammered. "Making some progress."

Ridley offered a brief smile. "Well, keep at it. You'll figure it out."

Mishka, standing beside Ridley, grabbed her wrist, tugging gently to pull her away. But in that brief moment, Aldin caught a fleeting look on Ridley's face—a silent plea for help, a glimpse of vulnerability. Their eyes locked, and an unspoken understanding passed between them. In that instant, a small spark ignited in Aldin's heart.

Over the weeks, that spark grew, kindling into a slow-burning flame. Each brief encounter, each stolen glance, fed the fire until it blazed uncontrollably. One fateful day, the dam broke. Ridley stormed into the lab, her face a mask of determination, and before Aldin could comprehend what was happening, Ridley's lips crashed onto hers in a fervent, desperate kiss.

When Ridley finally pulled away, Aldin was left reeling, her mind a whirlwind of confusion. "But... what about Mishka?" she whispered.

"It's over between us," Ridley replied, her voice tinged with a mixture of relief and sadness. "It has been for a long time."

As the weight of Ridley's words sank in, Aldin caught a

movement in her peripheral vision. Mishka stood in the doorway, her face a canvas of pain and betrayal, before she turned away, disappearing into the shadows.

***

Now, as the world around her crumbled in flames and chaos, Aldin's heart ached for the feeling of that first kiss one more time. It was a moment of pure, unadulterated connection, a lifeline in the midst of darkness. With that memory fueling her resolve, she turned her back on the encroaching doom and made one final, desperate bid for survival.

Aldin sprinted toward the airship, her breath ragged and her legs burning. The air was thick with the stench of burning flesh and the screeches of monstrous creatures. She dodged and weaved through the snapping beaks and grasping claws like she was navigating a deadly minefield, her every step a dance with death.

With a final leap, she flung herself into the cockpit, slamming the hatch shut behind her. The interior was a confusing array of buttons and switches, a chaotic mess to her untrained eyes. Her hands shook as she frantically pressed buttons and flipped switches, her mind racing and her heart pounding. Silently, she cursed herself for never having taken the time to learn how to fly.

Miraculously, the engine sputtered and then roared to life. Aldin's eyes widened with a mix of shock and hope. She grabbed the steering handle and yanked it back with all her might. The airship lurched, its frame shuddering as it clawed its way into the air. For a heart-stopping second, it soared, clearing the edge of the rooftop. But her relief was short-lived when the ship immediately began to plummet, spiraling downward in a wild, uncontrolled descent.

The ground rushed up to meet her, a blur of smoke and debris. Aldin gritted her teeth, fighting the controls with every ounce of strength she had left. The ship bucked and veered, her desperate attempts to stabilize it barely making a difference. The roar of the engine mixed with the cacophony of destruction outside, creating a symphony of chaos that threatened to suffocate her.

In those last moments, Aldin's mind was a whirlwind of fear and determination. She thought of Ridley, of the life they might have had, and of the kiss that had ignited her soul. With a final, desperate scream, she pulled on the controls one last time, praying for a miracle as the ground loomed ever closer.

***

The transport had only traveled a short distance when Ridley cast a glance through the rear window panel. Dust and rubble billowed into the sky, obscuring the building's annihilation in a dense, swirling cloud. Through the haze, her eyes caught a fleeting image: an airship leaping from the rooftop, only to plummet swiftly toward the ground. The erratic movement suggested that someone untrained was at the controls.

Her heart pounded as she strained to see more, her mind racing with possibilities. *Is that you, Aldin?* The sight of the airship struggling for flight, teetering on the brink of disaster, kindled a spark of desperate hope within her. Ridley's breath caught in her throat, and for a moment, she forgot the surrounding chaos—the transport's rumbling, the alarms blaring, the groans of the undead just beyond the thin walls of their vehicle.

Her thoughts focused only on Aldin. Images of their

shared moments flashed through her mind: Aldin's shy smile, the warmth of their first kiss, the unspoken connection that had grown between them. Ridley's hope fought against the reality of their dire situation, clinging to the belief that Aldin might have found a way out.

As the transport sped away, the structure of the lab began to crumble in earnest, the sound of its collapse a distant roar. The airship, now a speck in the distance, continued its erratic descent. Ridley's eyes remained fixed on it, willing it to stabilize. The seconds stretched into an eternity as she watched helplessly.

Finally, the transport rounded a bend, and the collapsing building, along with the struggling airship, disappeared from view. Ridley sank back into her seat, her body trembling with a mixture of fear and hope. She wanted to believe that Aldin had made it out against all odds and had escaped the inferno.

But as the dust settled and the echoes of destruction faded, Ridley knew that hope alone wouldn't be enough. She turned her gaze forward, steeling herself for whatever came next. The battle for survival was far from over, and she needed to stay focused. Yet, in the depths of her heart, a small, fragile glimmer remained—a spark that refused to be extinguished, no matter how grim the circumstances.

CHAPTER 20

Aldin opened her eyes slowly, wincing as pain lanced through her body with even the slightest movement. The cockpit was dimly lit by the flickering control panel, casting erratic shadows across the shattered glass and twisted metal. She found herself lying sideways, her left leg twisted backward and wedged painfully beneath the airship's control wheel. Her right arm was pinned underneath her body, numb and tingling.

The sharp smell of smoke and burning electronics filled the air, stinging her nostrils and making her eyes water. She could taste the metallic tang of blood in her mouth, and every breath brought a fresh wave of agony from her bruised ribs. Gritting her teeth, she reached with her free left arm and grabbed the control wheel. Using it as leverage, she pulled herself out of her entrapment, her muscles screaming in protest.

Finally free, Aldin stretched her arms and legs gingerly, her joints protesting with each cautious extension. She braced herself for the worst, half-expecting to find broken bones or torn tendons. To her immense relief, her injuries, while severe, seemed survivable. Her body was a tapestry of bruises and cuts, blood oozing from numerous gashes, but nothing appeared life-threatening.

With a groan, she pushed herself up, swaying slightly as she stood. Her vision swam, and she clutched the control wheel for support, the cool metal grounding her in the chaos. The cockpit was a mangled mess, the instruments were a jumble of twisted metal and shattered glass. Sparks flew from exposed wires, casting brief, blinding flashes of light that illuminated the destruction. The control panel flickered weakly, the once-steady hum of the machinery now a series of sputtering gasps.

Night was approaching quickly, the encroaching darkness bringing with it a deep, primal fear to add to the terror already racing through her. She sighed heavily and slumped into the broken seat, the rough fabric scratching her skin. Her eyes, weary and bloodshot, landed on the control panel. Amidst the chaos, one small light blinked steadily—the switch for the communicator. *Could it still work?* She thought. A tiny sliver of hope surfaced, fragile but persistent. She had to try.

"Please, let there be someone there," she whispered to herself. Her fingers trembled as she flipped the switch. The signal light flickered on, casting a faint glow in the dim cockpit. Her voice, sharp and desperate, filled the small cabin. "If anyone is out there, I'm outside the Startac Labs building, and there's been an explosion. Please send help."

For agonizing seconds, there was nothing but static, a harsh, grating sound that filled the silence. Then, a burst of garbled sounds crackled through the communicator, and a voice broke through the noise. "Hello? *...static...* Is someone there?"

"Yes! I'm here!" Aldin pleaded. "Please send help. There's been an explosion at Startac Labs! I'm trapped outside the building."

"*Static*... Did you ... *static*... Startac Labs? ...*static*... Aldin, is that you? ...*static*... Are you okay?"

Aldin's voice broke as tears streamed down her face. "Yes, it's me! Please help! I'm all alone!"

"*Static*... losing connection ...*static*... breaking up ...*static*... are you there?"

"I'm here! Help me! Anybody!" she screamed.

"*Static*..."

Then the communicator went dead, the light extinguishing in an instant. The silence was deafening, a void that swallowed Aldin's cries. She slumped back in the seat, her tears falling harder. "How am I supposed to make it out there by myself?" she mumbled feebly, her words coming out in stuttered sobs. "I'm not trained for this."

A loud thud sounded on the roof of the airship, cutting through her despair like a knife. She froze, her breath catching in her throat. Seconds later, a gigantic mass of tangled fur jumped down onto the front of the craft, the creature's eyes glowing eerily in the dim light. It scampered away, its movements jerky and unnatural. The creature was enormous, grotesque, and most likely already dead.

Aldin's heart thudded in her chest as she slowly slid from her seat, moving to the small compartment below the instrument cluster. She worked to make as little noise as possible, her breaths shallow and controlled. Huddling close to herself, she tried to hide from whatever horrors might come next. It was all she could do.

As she cried herself softly to sleep, the weight of her isolation settled heavily over her. She was truly alone, with no hope for rescue, and no hope of seeing Ridley again. That stark reality brought her nightmares of a broken world—a world she had helped create.

***

A slight movement of the airship woke Aldin sometime later. It was very subtle, a slight shaking that lasted briefly and then was gone, but enough to jolt her from a restless sleep. She cautiously scooted from her hiding place, her muscles stiff and sore, and slowly stood up to peek through the window. She wasn't sure how long she had slept, but a soft light was filtering through the glass, marking the beginning of a new day.

Dawn was breaking over the devastated landscape, casting a pale, eerie glow that illuminated the ravaged world outside. Under normal circumstances, this gentle light might have brought a sense of renewal and hope, but today it only highlighted the stark devastation that had engulfed everything. The aftermath of the catastrophe was laid bare in the cold, indifferent light of dawn. Buildings lay in ruins, twisted metal and concrete sprawled like the bones of some colossal beast slain by an unstoppable force. Fires still smoldered in the distance, their columns of smoke curling into the sky and blending with the morning mist.

Aldin had to turn away from the destruction before the tears started again. Her eyes were already red and swollen, feeling as though shards of glass were sandwiched inside her eyelids. She reached for a hydration cylinder and practically inhaled its contents, hoping it would offer some relief from the parched agony of her throat. The cool liquid soothed her dry mouth, but it did little to ease the deeper pain gnawing at her soul.

She searched the rest of the ship for anything of use—tools, weapons, nourishment—but came up empty. She found her blaster in her jacket, though, its energy meter showing that its power was halfway depleted, and held it close.

The ground started shaking again, a low, menacing rumble that seemed to come from directly beneath her. Aldin braced herself against the side of the ship, her heart pounding. This time, the rumbling didn't stop. The vibrations grew stronger, more violent, and she felt the ship sliding backward. Panic surged through her as she peered through the broken window and saw the ground in front of her rising. The airship was sinking!

Quickly, she clamored out of the ship, climbing onto the nose and balancing precariously as it continued to slide further into the gaping chasm that had opened beneath it. The ground was splitting apart, the sinkhole growing wider with each passing second, threatening to swallow her whole. With a desperate push, she ran forward and leaped from the airship.

She hit the ground hard, the impact jarring her bones. She rolled like a pebble down a hill, dirt and debris scraping her skin until she finally came to a stop at the foot of a large tree. Gasping for breath, she propped herself up on her elbow and watched in horror as the last edges of the airship disappeared from her sight, swallowed whole by the savage apocalypse that had been unleashed upon the world.

After the dust settled, Aldin saw for the first time just how total the destruction of the lab had been. Absolutely nothing remained of the place where she had spent most of her life. It had practically been her home, a sanctuary for her research and aspirations. Now it was gone, reduced to rubble and ash. Her heart sank as the weight of her actions bore down on her. *My research... I did this!* she thought. *The world is dying because of me!*

She looked around and saw towers of smoke and burning embers rising toward the sky in all directions, casting the world in a fiery glow. The smell of decay was overwhelming, a horrible stench that clung to everything. In her mind, grisly scenes unfolded: widespread attacks by dead beasts feasting on the insides of fellow Terrans. A deep shudder passed through her, and she quickly forced the images from her mind even as she realized the grim truth they represented.

A soft rustling nearby jolted her from her thoughts. She jumped nervously, afraid of what might be lurking in the shadows, waiting to attack. Moments later, a Derian, untouched by the madness, sauntered from the nearby brush. Its eyes were wide and cautious as it regarded Aldin, trying to gauge whether she posed a threat.

The tall and lean herbivore slowly inched its way toward her outstretched hand, its breath warm and moist against her skin. For the first time since the nightmare began, she felt a flicker of hope, a sense that the world might make it back from the edge of the precipice. Then she heard the distant cries of the beasts that had succumbed to the madness. They were a chilling reminder that the nightmare was far from over.

The Derian sensed it too. A high shrill issued from its mouth as it spun around in panic and rushed back into the trees. Facing the imminent prospect of being eaten alive once again, Aldin followed the creature's example and set off at an urgent pace. She had to find shelter soon or she would be lost.

She rounded a grove of trees and stopped suddenly. Transport tracks entered the forested area from the opposite direction, zig-zagging erratically before disappearing around another bend. Her heart beat like a tempest as she considered the possibility of the transport's occupants.

Her worst fears surfaced as she raced to follow the tracks and saw the transport overturned. She approached the vehicle cautiously, her breath coming in short, sharp gasps. A sharp cry escaped her lips when she saw the ravaged bodies strewn across the ground.

"Please, no!" she exclaimed as she neared the crash, then saw, with morbid relief, the body of a youngling among the deceased. Ridley wasn't among the dead. *At least, not these dead,* she thought.

The cries grew louder around her, signaling that the beasts were closer than she had thought. Immediately, she jumped and ran as fast as she could away from the wreckage, hoping to find refuge from the nightmare.

At the edge of the trees, the body of the Derian lay unmoving, a ravaged mess of torn flesh. Aldin wept for the creature, saying a silent prayer for the safe passage of its soul to the Beyond before she ran into the surrounding forest.

Then the Derian's eyes opened again. And they were the eyes of the dead. Its body twitched for a moment before it rose on mangled legs and stumbled into the brush after her.

CHAPTER 21

Mishka cried out in pain with each jarring movement as the transport sped away from the lab, bounding over rocks and debris while twisting and turning through the winding path. Her screams cut through the tense silence inside the vehicle, each one sharper and more desperate than the last.

Jensen's patience wore thin, and a deep scowl furrowed his brow. "There should be a medicine kit up front," he barked at Darin. "Pass it back here so we can shut her up before she attracts unwanted attention."

Mishka threw Jensen a deadly glare, her eyes filled with pain and fury, as Darin scrambled around, his hands shaking as he searched for the kit. After what felt like an eternity, he found the box and handed it to Ridley.

Ridley worked quickly, her hands steady despite the chaos around her, bandaging Mishka's wounds with as much care as she could manage in the bouncing transport.

Suddenly, the communicator sprang to life, crackling with static. Through the cloud of interference, they could just make out a series of desperate words. "*Static...* If anyone is *...static...* Startac *...static...* an explosion *...static...* send help."

Anon started to press the button to respond, but Jensen

interjected sharply, "What are you doing? We don't have any idea who that is. It could be a trick. I think we should just keep going."

Ignoring Jensen, Anon pressed the button to activate the microphone. "Hello? Is someone there?"

The response was filled with more static, but they could distinguish the voice a little better. "Yes! I'm here! Please, send help ...*static*... There's been an explosion at Startac Labs! ...*static*... trapped ...*static*..."

"That sounded like Aldin!" Ridley exclaimed, her eyes wide with hope and fear.

"You don't know that," Jensen said, his tone dismissive. "There was so much static it could've been anyone."

Anon shook his head at Jensen before responding to the call. "Did you say an explosion at Startac Labs? Aldin, is that you? Are you okay?"

The reply was frantic but weakening, "*Static*... Please help! ...*static*... alone."

"We're losing connection," Anon said, frustration creeping into his voice. "You're breaking up."

The static grew louder, drowning out the last desperate pleas before the communicator went dead, the abrupt silence deafening.

"We have to go back!" Ridley exclaimed desperately.

"We are doing no such thing!" Jensen snapped in an icy tone.

Ridley nearly leaped at him, her fists clenched, but somehow, she found a sliver of restraint and held herself back. Losing her temper wouldn't help Aldin.

"We can't just leave her back there! She'll die out there all by herself," Ridley pleaded.

Jensen met her gaze steadily, refusing to entertain the idea. "I'm not entirely convinced that was her on the communicator. It could've been anyone. And besides, it's too dangerous to stop now. We have to get to the Startac ancillary lab so we can figure out a way to stop this madness... madness that your girlfriend started!"

"That was her and you know it!" Ridley said, her finger pointed accusingly at Jensen's face.

Jensen spread his hands out before him in a mocking gesture of surrender. "Maybe, maybe not."

Ridley, her frustration boiling over, quickly reached over and yanked Mishka's blaster from her hand before she could object, pointing it at Jensen. "I said, turn this thing around! Now!"

Jensen didn't hesitate to pull out his own blaster, aiming it directly at Ridley. "You're not the only one with a weapon, Ridley. And unlike you, I won't hesitate to fire it."

Ridley regarded him coldly, her gaze locking onto his. His animosity toward Aldin, coupled with the uncertainty in his eyes, made her pause. She recognized that look—unstable and dangerous—a look she had seen in her own reflection a long time ago. She couldn't jeopardize the others. "Fine!" she said, lowering her weapon. "Just stop the transport and I'll go myself."

Jensen held her gaze for a moment before turning to Anon. "Stop the transport."

Anon gave Jensen a questioning look, then glanced at Ridley before he released the steering control and pressed a button on the console, bringing the transport to a halt.

Jensen turned back to Ridley. "Okay, fine. Have at it! But when you're out there being ripped apart, remember it was your choice."

Ridley scowled at Jensen before turning to Mishka. "I'll need to keep the blaster," she said softly.

Mishka grabbed Ridley's arm, her grip weak and

desperate. "Don't go."

Ridley looked at her gently, working to hold back a tear. "I have to. You, of all people, should understand that."

After a moment, Mishka withdrew her hand in resignation, her eyes filled with a pain she could no longer hide. "At least promise me you'll be careful?"

Ridley nodded, turning away quickly to hide her own turmoil. She gave Jensen one last scowl before exiting the transport. The clang of the door closing behind her sounded like a death knell, echoing in the sudden stillness.

Well, there's no turning back now, she thought as she gathered herself and started running back toward the demolished lab. A nagging thought tugged at the back of her mind—Jensen hadn't been completely honest with them. Sure, he had always been untrustworthy and a little too ambitious, but now she sensed he had become something more dangerous.

The ground trembled again as a series of explosions in the distance sent plumes of smoke and fire into the air. She couldn't see the structures that were falling, just like their lab had, but her imagination conjured nightmare scenarios that made her skin crawl.

Aldin! She had to get back to her desperately. The urgency in her heart propelled her forward, each step filled with the hope that she might still be able to save that which she thought she had lost.

CHAPTER 22

"We shouldn't have let her go!" Darin said adamantly. "It was wrong. She won't survive out there by herself."

"You can forget about your little crush," Anon retorted. "She's not your type. Besides, she'll be fine. She could take us all on at the same time if she wanted to."

"I can vouch firsthand," Mishka added, her mouth turned up with a hint of amusement, "she's definitely not your type."

Darin's cheeks flushed as he glanced around, his embarrassment obvious. "I don't have a crush on her!" he protested.

Anon cast a sidelong glance at him and smirked.

Mishka chuckled softly, the sound a brief relief from the tension, while Darin sulked lower into his seat as Anon steered the transport along the perilous road through the heart of the Wildlands. The vehicle jolted and swayed, the landscape a chaotic blur of twisted metal and scorched earth.

"It still wasn't right," Darin grumbled under his breath.

"I know someone who may be able to help," Anon said as he adjusted the frequency on the communicator. His fingers moved deftly over the controls. "Outpost Three? This is

Command One. Do you copy?"

Darin's brow furrowed. "Command One? Outpost Three?"

Anon chuckled. "It's a long story."

After a tense minute, a voice crackled through the static, clear yet cautious. "I read you, Command One."

"Is that you, Silas?" Anon asked urgently.

"Yes, it's me. Who is this?" Silas replied

"It's me, Anon. I need your help."

"Sorry, Anon. I didn't recognize your voice. What do you need from me?"

"We need your help locating two of our own—a security officer and a scientist from the lab."

Silas was silent for a moment, then answered sadly, "I heard the report that the structure was eradicated. Are you sure they escaped?"

"Yeah, we're sure," Anon said.

"I'll do what I can. Anything else I should know?" Silas asked, his tone cautious.

Anon hesitated, the enormity of the situation weighing heavily on him. Finally, he said, "The scientist you're looking for may or may not have had a hand in starting this nightmare. If you find her, she may be able to stop it."

Jensen's expression darkened at the exchange, irritation flashing in his eyes, but he kept silent. The transport jolted again as Anon swerved to avoid a group of rotted beasts, their decayed forms barely visible in the dim light.

The scent of decay and burned foliage filled the air, a constant reminder of the world's devastation. Yet, despite the obstacles, they moved at a steady pace.

"With any luck, we should arrive well before the sun begins to set," Anon said, glancing at the darkening sky. But he knew that luck, like a fleeting breeze, could slip through their fingers in an instant.

The eerie cries of unseen creatures echoed through the desolate landscape. Every shadow seemed to harbor a threat as Anon's hands tightened on the controls. He couldn't shake the feeling that time was running out, that every second wasted brought them closer to the edge of oblivion.

***

When the first series of quakes rumbled through the area, Silas jolted from his chair. He sprinted to the terminal on the far side of the room, the tall, dark man moving urgently. Bending low, his eyes studied the array of screens, the images causing his heart to jump. Each one depicted a horrible scene of death and destruction: buildings crumbling, earth splitting open, and fires blazing with unholy fierceness. The yellow gem embedded in his forehead pulsed ominously, casting a sickly glow over his face.

"This doesn't look good, Tandy," he muttered.

Tandy barked softly, her eyes reflecting a deep understanding. She trotted to his side, her own gem flickering in sync with Silas's, their psychic link humming with the shared anxiety that passed between them. Silas's fingers flew over the keyboard, pulling up a network schematic of the various Watch-keeper outposts. He was relieved to find that they were still on-line, but he was afraid it wouldn't be for long.

The proximity alarm shattered the moment, a shrill wail that brought up a video feed. A young boy, eyes wide with terror, was sprinting for his life with a ravenous pack of beasts racing after him. Silas quickly grabbed his black cloak and blaster rifle as he dashed to the rear hatch of the outpost. His personal transport roared to life a second later, and he sped off into the chaos with Tandy by his side.

As they hurtled through the devastated landscape, Silas checked his wrist display, cursing under his breath when he saw how far away the boy was. He pushed the transport to its limits, the vehicle bouncing violently over the fractured ground. Towers of smoke clawed at the sky and the ground convulsed beneath them, nearly flipping the transport. Tandy whined, a high-pitched sound that mirrored Silas's own fear.

"I don't like this either, girl," Silas said, his voice barely audible over the din of destruction. "Something feels wrong."

Then he saw it—a Dengo, eerily similar to Tandy but with half its face eaten away, its eyes glowing with hunger. It charged the transport, throwing itself against the vehicle in a frenzy until it fell beneath the wheels. Silas watched in horror as the creature struggled to rise again, a guttural cry escaping its mangled throat.

Silas's heart pounded as he checked the locator. Then the boy suddenly burst from the woods into a clearing, desperation etched into every line of his face as he sprinted from the snapping jaws behind him.

Silas swerved the transport, stopping just long enough to jump out and fire a burst of shots, dropping several of the creatures. He sprinted to the boy, scooping him up with his left hand while continuing to fire with his right. As he ran back toward the transport, Silas failed to see the Dengo lunging from the other side. Tandy barreled into it, knocking it to the ground in a spray of black mucus.

But the beast was relentless. It sprang at Tandy, raking its claws across her back. She yelped in pain as it sunk its teeth deep into her leg. "Tandy! No!" Silas shouted, dropping the boy and taking a steady aim. His blaster fired true, killing the beast.

He rushed to Tandy, cradling her as he turned to see an insect swarm closing in. The boy's scream was piercing, a sound of pure terror. Silas's blood ran cold as he watched the swarm lift the boy, tearing him apart mid-air, his body bursting as it hit the ground. The undead beasts nearby howled in approval, before charging Silas. He fired wildly, slowing them just enough to scramble back into the transport with Tandy in his arms.

Inside, Tandy's breathing was shallow, her eyes pleading. "It's okay, girl. We're almost home. We'll fix you up," Silas choked out, though he knew it was a lie.

The darkness inside the hangar beckoned, and as the transport stopped, Silas's heart shattered seeing Tandy's lifeless eyes.

He placed her body in a metal cage, memories flooding back to when she was a cub, scared and alone, and how their bond had grown through love and training. He felt every moment of her agony through their psychic link, the strength she had shown, and her ultimate surrender to death.

But death was not the end. A moment later, Tandy's body convulsed, her eyes snapping open, filled with a dark, insatiable hunger. Silas slammed the cage shut as she rammed against it, black blood dripping from her snarling mouth. He stumbled back, tears streaming from his eyes as his loyal companion succumbed to the madness, leaving him alone in the heart of the storm.

CHAPTER 23

Ridley pushed forward as fast as she could, ignoring the searing pain surging through her battered and broken body. As she ran, each step reverberated through her body like a hammer strike. Her heart pounded in her chest, a relentless drumbeat driving her onward, the urgency to get back to Aldin and rescue her from this nightmare obliterating all thoughts of rest.

Her left shoulder felt like it was on fire, the result of the narrow escape from the Kantor. She rolled it in a small circle, wincing as the bones ground against each other. The pain was unlike anything she had ever experienced before, a deep, gnawing agony that threatened to overwhelm her. But there was no time to rest. The only thing that mattered was Aldin. She had to save her.

The surrounding forest blurred into a chaotic swirl of green and brown, the trees whipping by as she charged through. Her legs felt like lead weights, each step a monumental effort. Her breath came in ragged gasps, her lungs burning with the effort. Every step was a battle, as if she were wading through quicksand, and the urge to collapse and give up was overwhelming. But she couldn't. She wouldn't. She had to keep going. Tears threatened to spill down her cheeks, but she bit them back, swallowing her pain and fear. She had to be strong. She had to be brave.

Smoke thickened in the air, acrid and choking, blocking out the sun and casting the world into premature darkness. The cries of tortured animals grew louder, a cacophony of agony that spurred her on. Ridley lowered her head and charged forward, a grim determination burning in her eyes. If she was going to die, she would die with Aldin in her arms.

Finally, Ridley reached the precipice surrounding the fallen lab. She looked down in horror at the tangled wreckage of the airship lying at the bottom of the sinkhole. Metal twisted and bent, fires still burning in places, casting an eerie glow in the encroaching darkness.

She fell to her knees, her strength finally giving out, sobbing uncontrollably. "Oh, Aldin. I'm so sorry I wasn't there for you." Her cries echoed off the walls of the chasm, a haunting lament that mingled with the distant sounds of the dead.

She sat there for what felt like an eternity, consumed by grief. Her life felt suddenly empty, a hollow shell of what it had been. *What am I going to do now? I don't think I can go on without you.* The cries in the distance reminded her that she most likely wouldn't have to. The beasts would come for her, and she would go willingly, knowing she had failed her true love.

The world around her seemed to grow smaller, the weight of her failure pressing down on her, suffocating her. The smell of smoke and burning flesh filled her nostrils, the acrid stench of death. The forest seemed to grow darker, the shadows deepening, closing in on her.

A faint mark on the ground then caught Ridley's eye. She kneeled down, studying the dirt, and saw a series of imprints leading down a small hill. Instantly, hope ignited within her, and she sprang to her feet, racing down the slope to follow the tracks. The ground soon became increasingly overgrown with thick foliage, and the tracks vanished, swallowed by the underbrush. Desperation gripped her as she turned in frantic circles, trying to judge the best direction. How she wished she were a natural tracker. Mishka could have found her in a heartbeat.

For a fleeting moment, the thought of Mishka made Ridley question her decision to leave the rest of the group, especially considering Jensen's recent behavior. But the doubt was quickly squashed by the certainty that Aldin couldn't survive alone. There had been no other choice.

Then Ridley heard it—barely audible over the distant groans of the undead—a faint cry for help. She froze, straining to hear above the chaos surrounding her. The sound came again, more of an urgent screech than any recognizable words.

Her heart pounded as she rounded a corner and stumbled upon an overturned transport. Panic surged through her as she frantically searched through the remains, her eyes darting everywhere to ensure Aldin wasn't among them. She paused a little longer at the sight of a youngling, the brutal realization hitting her like a physical blow—this evil killed without prejudice, an evil that Aldin had unwittingly helped create.

A series of low, throaty growls from behind caused her to jump. She spun around and was immediately set upon by a pack of beasts. Black blood and ichor dripped from their mouths, flowing freely through the gaps in their torn flesh as they snarled at her. She fired two quick shots, dropping one creature with a head shot and grazing another.

With no time to waste, she bolted toward the overturned

transport and leaped onto it just as she felt a sharp sting in her lower leg. She recalled the sting on the back of her neck earlier and braced herself for the inevitable wave of seizures. But as she pulled herself away from the savage attack, she saw it was merely a cut from a twisted piece of metal protruding from the wreckage.

Her blood trailed down the transport's side, a stark red against the white panels. Her breathing was ragged as she brought her blaster around and took aim at the remaining creatures. Three of them remained, and the Kambura she had grazed earlier launched itself onto the transport. She quickly fired another shot, hitting it between the eyes and sending it crashing to the ground. Immediately, the two Dengo's that had been hunting with it pounced on the fallen animal, their hunger driving them to tear it apart without hesitation. She seized the opportunity and dropped them both with precise shots.

Ridley tore a segment of cloth from her uniform and wrapped it tightly around her calf, staunching the flow of blood. Exhausted, she lay back on the transport, staring up at the hazy sun struggling to penetrate the thick smoke and ash choking the sky. A strong wind carried the stench of death and decay, the bitter, rancid taste filling her mouth. It stung her nose and made her eyes water.

A scream rose above the din of the pandemonium that had overrun the world. A voice she recognized. *Aldin!*

Ridley scrambled down the transport, careful not to land on her injured leg, and set off into the surrounding woods. The snap of a tree limb and the crunch of dry grass beneath her feet echoed like a thousand twigs breaking at once. The smell of rotting corpses, of blood and death, hung heavy in the air.

After a frantic search, she saw Aldin in the distance,

cowering as a mangled Derian closed in. A discarded blaster lay just out of reach. Ridley charged and blasted the undead creature in the head before it could strike, sending it slumping to the ground at Aldin's feet.

Aldin slowly opened her eyes, gasping at the sight of the beast with a hole in its head and black blood pooling around her feet. She looked up and saw Ridley standing there, blaster in hand and a crooked smile on her face. Her hair was singed, her face smeared with soot and grime, and her once pristine uniform torn and filthy, while she stood there noticeably favoring one leg and holding her arm tight against her body in an obvious attempt to block out a surge of pain. To Aldin, she had never looked more beautiful.

"You came back for me?" Aldin exclaimed through trembling lips, her voice on the verge of cracking.

Ridley looked at her for a second. "I almost didn't."

Aldin turned away. "Then why did you?"

Ridley was silent for a moment, then said, "I couldn't just leave you out here to die."

"Why not? Everyone else did."

"What did you expect, Aldin? Look around you! All of this is your fault!"

Tears started spilling from Aldin's eyes, a single drop rolling over her cheek, followed by another, until a steady stream flowed down her face. Her chest throbbed with a mournful ache that twisted her heart with each beat. She felt like she couldn't breathe. Instead of soft sobs, thick gasps came out as she cried loudly. The weight of it all had become a burden too heavy for her to carry anymore. She looked at Ridley with the pain of a shackled spirit in her eyes and said, "I'm sorry."

Ridley sighed and put her arms around Aldin, holding her tight. "I know you are."

Tears fell hard and freely from Aldin as she buried herself in Ridley's shoulder, seeking a sliver of comfort in a world spiraling out of control. As Ridley comforted her, she felt the tears welling up in her own eyes. *How could I have even considered not coming to help her?* The thought humbled her.

The surrounding woods came alive as the roar of the beasts reverberated through the trees with a frightening, deep beat. Ridley pulled away. "We need to go. Now!"

As they started running, Aldin stopped her. "But you're hurt! We need to find someplace to hide until you're better."

"We don't have time! We need to get out of here!"

Then they heard it, a cacophony of buzzing. The deafening sound of death speeding their way, the roar of one, the buzz of thousands. Ridley gritted her teeth, ignoring the pain to push herself forward. The two women charged forward, branches slicing at them as if the trees themselves were trying to keep them from escaping.

"Where are we going?" Aldin yelled as they ran.

Ridley replied, "Startac's ancillary lab."

"We'll never make it that far!"

"Yes, we will! We have to!"

The buzzing grew louder as the swarm drew closer. Soon, they would be overrun. Faster and faster, they ran, the trees whipping by in a blur, a green and brown streak of confusion, pushing their bodies past the brink until the sound of their blood rushing through their ears drowned out the swarm.

Suddenly, they broke through the trees into a small clearing with a single structure in the middle—a Watchkeeper outpost used to monitor wildlife and alert the population of weather anomalies.

With hope glimmering again, the two women gave a final push forward, only to find their path barred by a trio of

Dengo's emerging from the structure's side. One of the damaged beasts approached with its ribs visible under a strip of exposed skin. A bubbling sound came from its throat, so low and deep it made Aldin's stomach curl. One creature was missing half of its front left leg, and had a gaping hole in its side. The third one spewed black mucus onto the ground from a long slit down the front of its chest. And all of them carried the hunger in their eyes.

As the swarm closed in behind them, a putrid stench of rotten carrion filled the air, making their eyes water and their stomachs churn. Aldin and Ridley charged forward, shouting defiantly, their voices barely audible over the deafening buzz.

The forest was alive with chaos as they fired their blasters at the three beasts. Ridley's shots were precise, the crack of her blaster echoing through the trees as two creatures fell instantly. Aldin, however, struggled, her hands trembling, managing only a glancing blow on the third.

The last beast gathered itself and lunged toward them. Time seemed to slow as its snarling mouth drew closer. Just as it was about to strike, the door to the outpost flew open, and a shot rang out, piercing the air with a sharp crack. The beast collapsed, lifeless, inches from them.

Silas stood in the doorway, a shadowy figure in his long black robe. His skin, nearly as dark as his clothing, contrasted sharply with the deadly glint in his eyes beneath his hood. For a split second, he regarded them intensely, then shouted, "Get in here, quick!"

The buzzing swarm grew louder, a tempest of death bearing down on them. They raced for the door, the sound of their footsteps drowned out by the approaching horde. As soon as they were inside, Silas dropped his rifle and pulled a metal cylinder from his side. With a squeeze of the trigger, he unleashed a torrent of blue fire that arced through the air, illuminating the night. The acrid smell of charred wings and burning insect flesh filled the air, accompanied by a symphony of popping and crackling. A singular loud shriek rose from the swarm before it veered away, retreating into the darkened forest.

"We're clear for now, but they'll be back," Silas said calmly, his voice a stark contrast to the chaos outside. He turned and walked back into the structure with an unsettling serenity. The door closed behind them with a loud clang, followed by the metallic click of automatic locks engaging.

Ridley and Aldin watched nervously as Silas approached a terminal, his fingers flying over the keys with practiced ease. The soft hum of machinery filled the room as he turned a knob on a communication panel. After a moment of static, the channel cleared, and he spoke into the receiver, "Command One, this is Outpost Three. Can you read me?"

Seconds later, a voice crackled back, "This is Command One. We read you, Outpost Three. What is your status?"

Silas replied, "I have the ones you're looking for."

Ridley and Aldin exchanged nervous glances, their hearts pounding in their chests. The oppressive silence was suddenly broken by a low, guttural growl from the back corner of the room. They turned, their blood running cold, to see a mangled Dengo locked in a cage. Its eyes glowed with evil as it gnashed its teeth and snarled through decaying flesh, the sound grating and terrifying. The beast's rotting flesh hung in strips, and the sickly-sweet stench of decay filled the room. The sight of the caged monster, desperate and feral, made their skin crawl as they wondered who this madman was that had just saved them from the beasts outside, and what horror waited for them next?

CHAPTER 24

"You probably have a few questions?" Silas said as he turned away from the communication station.

Neither woman responded, their eyes fixed on him with a mixture of fear and curiosity.

Silas threw back his hood and Ridley gasped, her breath catching in her throat. His head was long and bulbous, devoid of hair, with a yellow gem embedded in his forehead that seemed to pulse with an eerie light. His left eye was normal, but his right one was a milky white orb, and his pointy chin ended in a braided beard that swayed with each movement.

"I know you!" Ridley exclaimed. "Or at least, I know of you. You're Silas!"

Silas regarded her with an unsettling calm. "It seems I'm at a disadvantage. You know me, but I don't know you."

"You served in the Third Battalion with my father, De'Andre. He told me stories about the Faction Wars and how you saved him during the Battle at Mondig Pass."

Silas bowed his head slightly, a shadow of pain flickering across his face. "I knew your father well. He was a great man. I would've gladly given more than just my eye to see him safe. I was sorry to hear of his passing."

Ridley grew quiet, her mind swirling with memories. The image of her father, strong and alive, was stark against the haunting memory of his lifeless body. Her hand twitched, fingers curling into a tight fist. Even though he had died a while ago, his memory still haunted her, and the mention of him still tore at her heart.

Desperate to shift the focus, she asked, "Did I hear you tell the person on the other end of the communication that you found the ones they were looking for?"

Silas pointed at Aldin, his expression inscrutable. "She's the one we need."

Shock washed over Aldin's face. "Me? What do you want with me?"

"My source tells me that you're the one responsible for this nightmare."

The accusation struck Aldin like a physical blow, leaving her gasping for breath. Each reminder of her transgression was a blade twisting in her gut, threatening to choke out any last remnant of her will to live. She broke down, sobbing uncontrollably. "I didn't mean to," she cried, her voice cracking. Tears streamed down her face, her eyes red and puffy as if infected. "It was an accident, I swear. Even if it wasn't entirely my fault."

Ridley stepped closer, her face filled with concern. "What do you mean?"

Aldin took a deep breath, struggling to regain her composure. "Jensen set me up," she said slowly. She wasn't trying to absolve herself completely—she was still the one who fell asleep next to a machine spitting out radioactive particles—but someone had to know Jensen's involvement.

Ridley's skepticism was obvious in her eyes.

"I'm telling you the truth, Ridley," Aldin said. "He

loosened the support bolts on the particle accelerator to sabotage my work."

"That's a strong accusation," Silas said, his voice laced with doubt. "I've known Jensen for a long time. And while he's as untrustworthy as they come, I can't believe he'd deliberately try to hurt someone."

"You don't know him very well, then," Aldin replied, her voice steely with conviction.

Silas grew quiet, leaning against the control station with a thoughtful expression.

"Do you have proof?" Ridley asked. "It'll be impossible to convince anyone else without proof."

Aldin's shoulders sagged. "I did," she replied, her voice barely a whisper. She lowered her head, recalling the spiraling light of the lost tablet as it plummeted toward the bottom of the lift amid the flock of twisted Crowlochs. The memory of their eyes, glinting with madness, sent a shiver down her spine.

"I found a tablet in his office as I was trying to get away from the lab," she continued. "He had detailed plans of the accelerator, as well as several other pieces of equipment, with notes on how to compromise them without detection. All to discredit me. He even had disciplinary documents prepared in advance that described the explosion. I don't understand any of this? Why does he want to hurt me so much?"

Silas's voice was soft but firm. "I might be able to answer that."

Aldin looked at him, her eyes wide with shock. "What do you know?"

"It involves your mother. Jensen had fallen deeply in love with her, only to have those feelings unrequited. When she fell for another man and bore a child with him, Jensen's feelings became twisted until it focused on you. As you grew older, his hate continued to fester until it consumed him. Apparently, he finally took action."

"That explains why he hates me so much!" Aldin's voice was filled with a mix of relief and despair.

Ridley asked, "Where is the tablet now?"

"Gone," Aldin replied somberly. "I dropped it while I was climbing onto the roof. It's destroyed now."

"So, it's just your word against his?"

Aldin nodded, her despair deepening.

"That doesn't matter right now," Silas said, his voice cutting through the gloom. "What does matter is stopping this plague before it's too late."

"It's already too late," Aldin said, her voice a hollow echo. "There's no way we can contain this. It's spiraled out of control too fast!"

"Then I suggest that time is of the essence!" Silas's voice was a whip-crack in the silence.

Aldin looked at him, her mind reeling. *How in the world does he think I can stop this?*

Ridley stepped closer, her eyes locking onto Aldin's. "If anybody can figure this out, it's you, Aldin. I have faith in you."

They had all but forgotten about the creature in the cage until it reminded them of its presence with a loud, guttural growl.

"Why are you keeping that thing in a cage like a personal mascot?" Ridley asked, pointing at the creature and eyeing it warily.

Silas looked over at the cage, a haunted look in his eyes. "Her name is Tandy, and she's been with me since she was a youngling. We had a situation earlier when we tried to rescue a young boy running from a pack of diseased animals. One of those monsters attacked her while she was protecting me. It didn't take long for Death to overtake her."

Aldin looked at Silas, then at Tandy. Another tear threatened at the corner of her eye. *Another death because of me,* she thought bitterly.

"What about the boy?" Aldin asked, her voice barely above a whisper.

Silas shook his head solemnly.

"You know what you need to do, right?" Ridley asked, her voice gentle but firm.

A look of shock flew into Aldin's eyes. "Ridley! This isn't the time for that. Can't you see he's hurting?"

"No, she's right," Silas said, his voice tinged with a quiet resolve. "I was about ready to help her pass on when I received a communication from Anon concerning Aldin's situation."

"How do you know Anon?" Ridley asked.

Silas replied, "We trained together at the Watch-keeper Academy until he realized that his heart resided inside the lab instead of outside in nature."

"So, now what?" Aldin asked, her voice tinged with desperation.

"Anon asked me to bring you to the Ancillary Lab, along with Tandy to use as a test subject, so you can hopefully come up with a way to stop this."

Aldin's jaw dropped. "What happened in the lab was an accident. How am I supposed to reverse that?"

Ridley grabbed Aldin's hands, her grip firm and reassured. "You have to try. If anyone can fix this, it's you."

Tandy gave a snarled growl from the corner, a reminder of the looming threat.

"Do we really have to take that thing with us?" Aldin asked fearfully.

Silas nodded, his expression grave. "She might be the key

to finding a solution. We have to try everything we can."

The atmosphere in the room suddenly grew even heavier as the weight of their situation loomed over them, almost tangible in its presence. Outside, the night was filled with the haunting sounds of the undead, a constant reminder of the terrifying reality they were trapped in.

CHAPTER 25

Anon glanced over at Jensen in the rear passenger seat and felt a shiver of unease creep up his spine. Jensen's wide-eyed stare into the glass container was unnervingly childlike, reminiscent of a youngling mesmerized by their first lightning beetle, watching in fascination as it flashed before darting away. But this wasn't a beetle. Inside the glass, a black substance undulated and writhed, searching for an escape, its movements unsettlingly alive.

Silas' voice suddenly crackled over the communicator, snapping Anon back to the present. "Command One, this is Outpost Three. Can you read me?"

Anon replied, his voice steady despite the tension. "This is Command One. We read you, Outpost Three. What is your status?"

"I have the ones you're looking for."

"Copy that. Proceed to Startac's Ancillary lab. We'll meet you there."

"Copy," Silas replied.

A soft clank against the front glass of the transport startled Anon. When he looked up, he realized the sky had grown dark prematurely. Then another object hit the glass, larger than the first. He glimpsed long, spindly appendages before it vanished. Suddenly, a barrage of objects bombarded the transport, battering it like a sandstorm. Anon yanked the steering console, bringing the transport to an abrupt halt.

The sudden stop jolted Jensen, causing him to drop the glass jar. As he kneeled to retrieve it, he saw the substance inside had grown more agitated, almost frenzied, as if it sensed its kin nearby. "Fascinating!" he whispered, excitement creeping into his voice.

"Get us out of here!" Darin cried, but it was already too late. The swarm was enormous, a black mass that filled the horizon, writhing and twisting in a grotesque dance. The transport rocked violently as the swarm enveloped it, the impact like a thousand tiny blaster strikes from all directions. The vehicle was actually lifted a tiny distance into the air, then dropped back down with a bone-rattling thud.

The sheer number of insects, a nightmarish assembly of various species, was so dense it blocked out the sun, plunging the cabin into a suffocating darkness.

Anon quickly flipped on the interior light, and immediately regretted it. The clacking of thousands of insects converging on them, combined with desperate shrieks and cries, created a cacophony of terror. The swarm scurried over the transport, their bodies pressing against the windows, obscuring any view outside.

Darin's eyes were wide with fear, his mouth open in a silent scream. He clutched the sides of his head and jumped from his seat, retreating from the glass. "Do something, Anon, or they're going to get in here!"

"The cabin is hermetically sealed," Jensen said matter-of-factly. "There's no way they can get inside."

As if to contradict him, a large, pointed beak, surrounded by a circular, suctioned mouth, slammed against the glass with enough force to send spider-web cracks branching away from the point of impact. The creature began sucking at the glass, and the fissures grew larger, spreading out like a deadly virus.

"You were saying?" Darin exclaimed, terror rising in his voice.

Anon turned to Jensen, desperation in his eyes. "Any suggestions?"

For a moment, panic flashed across Jensen's face—a sight Anon had never seen before.

"If we reverse the polarity on the main thermocouple," Mishka interjected, "it'll cause a static discharge encompassing the whole transport. That should be strong enough to fry those things."

Jensen's demeanor shifted from panic to irritation, resenting that someone else had come up with a solution before him. "That'll leave us completely powerless," he stated smugly.

"We don't have any other choice," Mishka insisted.

"Just do it!" Darin cried.

Anon powered off the transport, quickly opening a small control panel on the console. He pulled out a tray with a series of glass cylinders, flipped the first one over, and slid the tray back in. Then he flipped the switch to power the vehicle back on.

The lights inside the cabin flickered sporadically as the surge of electricity coursed through the vehicle. Each flicker plunged the cabin into darkness for a heartbeat, but it felt like an eternity. The surge rippled across the metal-skinned vehicle, creating a tangible hum.

Suddenly, a high-pitched wail echoed from the back of the transport. Darin spun around, eyes wide in terror. "What was that?"

Anon glanced over his shoulder, heart pounding. In the dim light, he saw the container in Jensen's hand rattling violently. The black substance inside was throbbing, pulsating with a frenzied energy. "Jensen, secure that thing! Now!"

Before Jensen could respond, the glass cracked, a thin line snaking its way down the side. "It's breaking through!" Jensen shouted, scrambling to reinforce the container.

A loud thud resonated from the roof of the transport, followed by another and another. The swarm was attacking from above, relentless in their assault. The metal roof buckled under the weight, creaking ominously.

"It's not working, Anon!" Darin cried desperately.

"I need more time!" Anon yelled as the lights continued to flicker, while his fingers flew over the controls.

While Anon fought with the controls to reverse the polarity, Mishka quickly grabbed a toolkit from under her seat. She yanked out a portable welder and threw it to Jensen. "Use this to seal the cracks!"

Jensen caught the welder and immediately ignited the flame. He carefully traced the crack in the container so that the blue fire fused the glass back together. Then he watched in astonishment as the substance inside grew even more agitated, slamming against the newly formed barrier with increased ferocity.

Another beak-like appendage struck the windshield, sending shards of glass flying into the cabin. Darin screamed as a piece sliced across his cheek, blood mixing with sweat on his pale skin. "We're not going to make it!"

Anon's hands trembled as he pulled the panel out again and switched the last cylinder quickly, completing the process to reverse the polarity. The vehicle hummed louder as it built up the necessary charge. "Hold on!" he shouted, his voice barely audible over the cacophony of insectile screeches and his comrades cries.

A loud chorus of shrieks followed as a fiery rush of blue flames engulfed the swarm. The insects' bodies crackled and popped, turning to ash before floating to the ground. Silence fell as the creatures disintegrating into nothingness. The stench was overwhelming, a putrid blend of decay and rot that filled the air, making it hard to breathe.

"That was too close!" Darin said, wiping sweat from his forehead as he slunk into his seat trembling. "How long until we can get this thing moving again?"

Anon replied, "It takes a couple of hours for the solar panels to recharge enough to travel."

"The problem," Jensen said, his voice dripping with disdain, "is that the sun will set before then, effectively rendering us incapacitated until morning."

The cabin fell silent as the reality of their circumstance sinking in. They were surrounded by death, with only a brief respite standing between them and the nightmares that lurked outside.

CHAPTER 26

Aldin stood nervously behind Ridley, who had her hand on her blaster, as Silas carefully hooked the end of a long, rusted chain onto the bottom rung of the cage containing 'dead' Tandy. A flurry of savage cries erupted from her as she rammed repeatedly into the cage, her eyes wild with a ferocity that chilled Aldin to the bone.

Silas grunted as he secured the chain, his face etched with sadness and concentration. Sweat glistened on his brow, and his hands trembled slightly. He carried the other end of the chain toward a door panel on the opposite wall and pressed a button. The door slid sideways with a heavy grind to reveal a small hangar containing a personal all-terrain transport. Silas secured the other end of the chain to a winch inside the back of the vehicle, which pulled the cage inside with a mechanical whine.

"Time to go," Silas said, his voice rough as gravel, Tandy's condition weighing heavy on his soul, as he closed the back and rounded the side of the transport.

Aldin looked at Ridley, her voice trembling. "I don't know about this..."

"We don't have a choice," Ridley replied.

159

"I'm not crazy about riding with that thing in there with us."

"It's locked up tight. It'll be okay," Ridley said, but the look in her eyes betrayed her fears. Her knuckles were white around the grip of the blaster, and a bead of sweat trickled down her temple.

The transport was smaller than the service transport from the lab, forcing them to ride in closer proximity to the cage than they would've liked. The creature's rancid breath and the low, guttural growls emanating from her cage were a constant reminder that death lurked nearby, waiting for an opportunity to strike. The fact that night was approaching made their situation even more precarious.

Silas climbed into the driver's seat and turned on the communicator. "Command One, this is Outpost Three. Come in."

The communicator remained silent.

"Command One. Do you read me?" he tried again, a hint of worry creeping into his voice.

Still nothing.

Silas frowned. His jaw clenched as he tried again, his voice more urgent. "Command One, please respond."

"Maybe they're just out of range?" Aldin suggested, seeing the worry etched on his face. "Or their communicator is malfunctioning?"

Silas merely grunted, his eyes fixed on the horizon as he pulled the transport out of the hangar and accelerated forward. The road ahead was littered with the twisted remnants of vehicles and their occupants that had fallen prey to the chaos.

It didn't take long for the dead to give chase, converging on them from all angles, but the advanced state of decay had ravaged the bodies of the pursuers—making some of them unrecognizable from the creatures they once were—allowing the transport to keep at a safe enough distance. Still, their persistence was terrifying.

As Silas drove, he tried unsuccessfully to reach Anon again. Each attempt was met with static and silence. When he tried to triangulate the transport's location using the electronic signature from their last communication, his screen came up blank. They had vanished without a trace.

"Is there another way we can find them?" Ridley asked, her voice tight with anxiety.

Silas tried bringing up a satellite image of the area, but was met with a 'connection error' on the screen. "It looks like we're starting to experience network outages."

He turned to Aldin, his face grave. "We may be running shorter on time than we thought."

As if to emphasize his point, the ground began to shake violently. The earth and stone buckled and shifted beneath them, the tremor sending shock-waves through the transport. Silas gripped the transport's wheel tight, struggling to keep the vehicle steady and avoid tipping over.

The tremor continued to surge through the area, forcing the three of them to hold on to anything they could inside the cabin to ride out the quake. The air smelled electric, metallic, and charged with an unsettling energy. Instead of slowly subsiding, the force of the shake continued at a steady and deadly pace. It was relentless, a constant quake that wouldn't cease.

Ridley's grip on the handrail next to her seat slipped, and she slammed into the side of the cage. Tandy immediately pounced forward, ramming her head into the thick bars as her claws sprang through the opening, barely missing Ridley's face. The beast's growls grew louder, filled with a primal rage that echoed through the cabin.

Finally, the ground settled, and the rumble died away. In its place was an eerie silence, heavy and oppressive. The deafening silence lasted only a few moments before a shrill sound filled the air.

"What is that?" Aldin asked, her hands clamped over her ears to drown out the electronic screech. After a minute, the screeching stopped and was replaced with a steady, intermittent horn, like the pulse of the planet itself warning of an oncoming heart attack.

"That's the global emergency alert siren!" Silas replied, his eyes widening.

Terror overwhelmed Aldin's face, and her eyes widened in fear. "Global emergency?"

"My guess is that an explosion somewhere, or more likely a chain of explosions, caused some sort of seismic reaction with the planet's nuclear core. That's what caused the quake."

"Is there a way to stabilize it?" Ridley asked, her voice shaky.

"I doubt it. But I'm not the scientist here." Silas looked at Aldin pointedly. "She is."

"My field is molecular biology," Aldin replied, shaking her head. "Not environmental sciences or meteorology. I wouldn't know where to begin to analyze the situation."

"Then I suggest we find someone who can, and fast," Silas said before pressing the transport forward once more.

The Wildlands, normally a vibrant and growing place, were only visible through gaps between the walking carcasses of the dead, which attacked once more as the transport moved forward. Silas maneuvered the vehicle through the chaos, the undead clawing at the windows, their decayed faces pressed against the glass.

When Silas started steering them along a different path,

Ridley's voice was filled with urgency. "What about the others? We have to find them!"

"We have to get to the lab as quickly as possible," Silas replied, his voice firm. "I trust Anon. I'm sure they'll make it there just fine. In fact, I'd be surprised if they're not already there waiting for us."

As the transport hurtled through the broken landscape, every bump and jolt escalating the fear pounding through Aldin's chest, she couldn't shake the feeling that their time was running out.

CHAPTER 27

The group sat quietly in the transport, a nervous energy coursing through them, casting occasional glances at each other. "What now?" Darin finally asked weakly.

Jensen simply leaned back and calmly replied, "We sit here and wait for morning."

"We're easy targets in here," Mishka countered.

"We're even easier targets out there," Jensen shot back.

Mishka turned toward the front. "What are your thoughts, Anon?"

Anon, deep in thought, finally spoke, "We're in trouble either way, but given how compromised the transport is now, I think we're better off trying to get to the lab as quickly as possible."

"Are you sure that's a good idea?" Darin asked nervously.

"I don't see much choice," Anon replied, his tone resigned.

Darin shifted uncomfortably in his seat and looked back at Mishka. "Are you okay to walk?"

Mishka nodded weakly, her eyes betraying her doubts.

Jensen looked at each of them and chuckled darkly. "Suit yourself, but I'm staying in the transport until morning. Feel free to carry on your suicide mission without me."

Anon looked at Jensen for a moment, hoping to persuade him, but saw it was no use. Once Jensen made up his mind, there was no changing it.

"Grab anything you see that can be used as a weapon," Anon instructed Darin.

As Darin jostled from his seat and moved towards the rear, Jensen slid his blaster further into his coat, concealing it from prying eyes. Darin rummaged through the sparse supplies, finding a large hub-wrench and a bearing extractor tucked under the rear seat. They were big and clumsy, far from ideal for defense, but they would have to do.

Anon took the hub-wrench from Darin and paused at the transport's door. "Last chance to come with us," he said to Jensen.

"No thanks," Jensen replied curtly. "Have fun dying, though."

Stepping out of the transport, Anon was hit by a wave of ash-filled wind. The air was bitter, the scent of burned death overwhelming, compounded immeasurably by the taste of fear.

Darin felt his hair, matted with sweat and filth, sticking to his skin. The gut-wrenching stench turned his stomach. "My god!" Darin coughed. "That smells disgusting!"

"Get yourself together," Mishka said, hiking the top of her shirt over her nose. "We have a long way to go."

"She's right," Anon added. "We need to get going while we still have a sliver of light left."

They had only taken a few steps when a deep rumble rippled beneath their feet. The shaking quickly escalated, throwing all three of them to the ground. They watched in horror as a large fissure split the land open only a short distance away, snaking towards the defenseless transport like a missile. Moments later, the vehicle teetered on the edge of an abyss, its weight shifting back and forth until it came to a precarious stop.

The trembling ceased, leaving the three of them looking at each other in terror. That fear only intensified when they heard the siren.

"Is that what I think it is?" Mishka asked, her voice barely a whisper.

Anon nodded grimly. "I believe so. Although I've never heard it myself."

"That's because it hasn't been used before," Mishka replied.

Darin's face was blank with confusion. "Am I missing something? What does that siren mean?"

"That's the Global Warning Alert," Anon explained. "Simply put, it means that something very bad is going on."

The ground shook and rumbled again, as if a great beast was stirring under their feet. The alarm changed to a steady, rhythmic beat. The low, deep boom shook the transport, knocking it incrementally forward until it was at the edge of the precipice.

"We have to save him, don't we?" Darin asked, his voice filled with reluctant determination.

"Yes, Darin, we have to save him," Anon answered matter-of-factly.

"You realize he'd let us fall to our deaths if the situation were reversed."

"But we're better than that. We're not him."

Despite his reluctance, Darin knew that Anon was right. He sighed, his shoulders slumping with the thought that he was rushing to save someone that would turn his back on everyone if the situation were reversed and not think twice about it.

The three of them jumped up and raced towards the

transport. "You two grab onto the back," Mishka yelled, "while I go in and get Jensen."

Darin and Anon ran to the rear of the transport, grabbing the support bumper and leaning back, putting their full weight into bringing the rear of the vehicle back down to the ground.

As soon as the rear wheels touched down, Mishka carefully climbed inside. A gasp escaped her lips when she saw Jensen lying face-down on the floor of the cab, a stream of blood flowing from a large cut on the back of his head.

Careful not to jostle him too much, she rolled him onto his back, relieved to see he was still breathing. She caught a quick glimpse of the blaster poking from his jacket and gently slid it away, tucking it behind her back just as he began to regain consciousness.

"What happened?" Jensen groaned as he tried to sit up.

The movement caused the transport to rock once more, tipping the nose forward and throwing both of them into the front console.

"We have to get out of here!" Mishka cried urgently.

Not waiting for Jensen to answer, she grabbed his arm, yanking him towards the door as she dragged herself forward. The transport slipped further, a loud creak echoing through the cabin in protest to the strain.

Mishka staggered to her knees and shoved Jensen out of the door just as the transport lost its grip and plunged over the edge into the waiting abyss.

As the vehicle slid to its death, Anon and Darin were both thrown to the ground, narrowly escaping being dragged down with it.

Anon recovered quickly and rushed to where Jensen lay, while Darin struggled to his feet. "Where's Mishka?" Anon asked, looking around frantically.

Jensen's only reply was a glance toward the open chasm.

"What happened?" Anon shouted. "Couldn't you save her?"

"I'm a little injured here, if you hadn't noticed," Jensen replied tersely. "Besides, she's the one who pushed me out before the transport fell."

Darin joined them a moment later, limping forward. After echoing the same questions and receiving the same answers, he cried out and stumbled toward the edge of the chasm, desperately praying that Mishka hadn't been swallowed up. "No! Not you too, Mishka!"

He dropped to his knees at the edge of the dark abyss, tears streaming down his face. "All this death! I can't take it anymore!"

He didn't see her hand rise over the edge, but he heard her voice, "Shut up with your whining already, Darin, and help me up!"

Darin's eyes widened as he peered over the edge and saw Mishka dangling precariously by one hand. "Mishka!" he cried out as he grabbed hold and began pulling her up.

A cry of pain escaped Mishka's lips as she stretched her injured arm forward, trying to gain better leverage. Anon immediately joined him, and a moment later she was lying exhausted on firm ground, wounded and ragged, but safe.

It wasn't long, though, before the cries of the dead rose around them once more.

CHAPTER 28

The small, quiet farming colony of Duandan lay nestled between two rugged mountain ridges, an isolated haven carved out from the untamed wilderness of the planet. The colony itself was a combination of rustic charm and futuristic design, developed as a sanctuary for those who had tired of the politics that had overtaken the scientific community, or for those who merely wanted a simpler life and commune with nature. As its inhabitants wound down from a day of toiling and working their crops, they were oblivious to the nightmare that sped their way.

At the heart of the community stood the central Watchtower, a sleek, metallic structure that rose above the cluster of buildings like a vigilant sentinel. From its top, a panoramic view of the surrounding landscape unfolded: rolling fields of exotic crops bordered by dense, ancient forests teeming with life. The mountains, their peaks dusted with iridescent snow, loomed protectively on either side, their sheer cliffs and winding paths a natural barrier against the wilderness beyond.

The colony's residential area was comprised of modest yet sturdy dwellings sloped roofs and solar-panels, that lined neatly arranged streets, each house fronted by small gardens where families grew vegetables and native herbs. The air often carried the scent of these gardens, mingling with the earthy aroma of freshly tilled soil and the subtle, metallic tang of machinery.

To the west of the residential quarters lay the communal hub: a series of interconnected domes that served as the colony's social and cultural center. Here, colonists gathered to share meals, hold meetings, and celebrate their hard-earned successes. The largest of these domes housed the mess hall, a spacious area filled with long tables and surrounded by kitchens where culinary delights were prepared.

Beyond the communal hub, the agricultural fields stretched out in a patchwork of vibrant greens and purples, the crops swaying gently in the breeze. These fields were meticulously maintained, with irrigation systems and automated harvesters working tirelessly to ensure a bountiful yield. Among these fields, the colonists toiled daily, their labor a harmonious blend of traditional farming techniques and cutting-edge technology.

On the outskirts of the colony, near the base of the eastern ridge, the industrial sector buzzed with activity. This area housed the colony's power generators, water treatment facilities, and various workshops where engineers and technicians crafted and repaired the tools and machines essential for survival.

Surrounding the entire settlement was a high, reinforced wall, a necessary defense against the planet's native predators. The gates, thick and imposing, were the only points of entry and exit, guarded by a small contingent of soldiers ready to protect the colony from any threats.

Despite its rustic appearance, Duandan was a place of hope and progress, a beacon of determination in a harsh world. The colonists lived in harmony with their surroundings, forging a life of relative peace and prosperity.

***

In a quiet room illuminated only by the soft glow of a lamp, Marina tucked her daughter, Lily, into bed. The familiar scent of lavender from the night oil filled the air, a comfort against the backdrop of an increasingly unpredictable world. Lily clutched her stuffed toy, her eyes wide with lingering fear.

"Mommy, tell me a story," Lily whispered, her voice trembling.

Marina smiled gently, brushing a strand of hair from her daughter's forehead. "Of course, sweetie. How about the one with the brave princess and the magical forest?"

Lily nodded eagerly, her grip on the toy tightening. Marina began the tale, her voice soothing and melodic, weaving a world of enchantment and bravery to ease her daughter's fears. As the princess embarked on her quest, the room seemed to become a haven, separate from the turmoil outside.

Suddenly, a faint rumble interrupted the serene moment. Marina paused, her eyes flickering toward the window. The tremor grew, causing the glass to rattle in its frame. Lily's eyes widened as a cry of fear flew from her mouth.

"It's just a little earthquake, darling. Nothing to worry about," Marina reassured her, though her own heart pounded unsteadily.

The tremors intensified, shaking the entire house. Marina pulled Lily close, wrapping her arms around her. The lights flickered, casting eerie shadows on the walls. Outside, a low, ominous growl echoed through the valley, mingling with the sound of shifting earth.

"Mommy, what's happening?" Lily cried, burying her face in her mother's shoulder.

Marina swallowed hard, trying to keep her voice steady. "We're safe here, Lily. I promise."

As if in response, a deafening roar split the night, followed by a series of crashes and the unmistakable sound of creatures clawing at the walls. Marina's blood ran cold.

"Lily, we need to go. Now!" Marina scooped her daughter up, her mind racing. She hurried to the door, pausing only to grab a small bag of essentials she had prepared for emergencies.

The normally quiet, small farming colony was suddenly caught up in a flurry of chaos, as the inhabitants rushed to barricade doors and windows in the hope of keeping the approaching monsters at bay. While the cries of the dead echoed darkly through the valley, children clung to their parents, seeking salvation from the evil that flew on broken wings and walked on four legs through the valley.

Commander Elise Marten stood atop the colony's central Watchtower, her keen eyes scanning the horizon. The tower, usually a symbol of security, now felt like a last stand. Elise's heart pounded as she saw the black shapes moving erratically toward them, a storm of death and decay. She could hear the distant screams, the unholy roars of the undead, growing louder with each passing second.

"Commander, we have to seal the gates!" shouted Jax, her second-in-command.

"Do it!" Elise barked, her voice firm despite the dread knotting her stomach. "And get the women and children to the underground tunnels."

Jax nodded, rushing off to relay her order. Elise watched him go, her mind racing. They had always known the risks of living on the frontier, but nothing had prepared them for this.

They were a peaceful and hard-working group who toiled the land and were one with nature. Although there was a small battalion of soldiers who resided among the colonists to keep away the threat of ravagers, they were hardly enough to defeat the horde that quickly advanced toward them.

Below her, the gates groaned shut, the sound reverberating through the air like a tortured spirit. The colonists worked frantically, piling crates, barrels, and anything they could find against the gates. The makeshift barricade seemed pitifully inadequate against the coming storm.

"Commander, they're coming!" A lookout pointed, his voice cracking.

Elise turned her gaze to the ridge, where the first of the undead creatures appeared. They were hideous, their bodies twisted and decayed, eyes glowing with an unnatural hunger. They moved with a disturbing speed, an unstoppable tide of death.

"Hold your positions!" Elise shouted, her voice carrying through the colony. She raised her blaster, aiming at the nearest creature.

The colonists took up positions behind their barricades, fear and terror plastered on their collective faces. The first wave of creatures hit the gate with a force that shook the ground, their claws raking against the metal, their roars filling the air.

Blaster fire erupted from the colony's defenders, beams of energy searing through the night like a lightning storm. Some of the creatures fell, their heads exploding in bursts of putrid flesh. But for every one that fell, a dozen took its place, their bodies piling up against the gate.

Elise fired again and again, her blaster glowing hot in her hands. She spared a glance to her left and saw Jax, his face grim as he fought alongside her. "We can't hold them!" he shouted over the din.

"We have to!" Elise replied, her voice a raw command. "We have to buy time for the women and children to escape!"

The gate shuddered, the wood and metal groaning under the relentless assault. Then, with a deafening crack, it buckled. The undead poured through the breach, a tide of death sweeping into the colony. The defenders retreated, fighting with all their might to stop the advance.

Elise fired at a hulking creature that leaped over the barricade, its jaws snapping inches from her face. The creature's head exploded, and it collapsed, its momentum carrying it forward to land at her feet. She stepped back, her heart pounding.

"Fall back to the inner ring!" she shouted.

The colonists retreated, forming a desperate last line of defense around the entrance to the underground tunnels. The undead creatures were everywhere now, their claws and teeth tearing through flesh and bone. The air was thick with the stench of death and the screams of the dying.

Elise and Jax stood side by side, their blasters firing in unison. "We can't hold them here!" Jax shouted.

"We have to try," Elise replied.

A massive creature, its body a grotesque mass of rotting flesh and bone, charged at them. Elise fired, but the shots barely slowed it down. It swung a clawed hand, sending her sprawling to the ground.

"Elise!" Jax screamed, firing at the creature's head. The shots found their mark, and the beast fell with a guttural roar. Jax rushed to Elise's side, helping her to her feet.

"We need to get to the tunnels," Elise said weakly.

They fought their way to the entrance of the tunnels, even as a large number of colonists were filing inside. Elise and Jax were the last to enter, slamming the door shut behind them.

They could hear the creatures outside, their roars muffled but still terrifying.

In the dim light, the survivors huddled together, their bodies trembling with fear. With a heavy heart, Elise surveyed the faces of her people, their fear reflecting her own. "We're safe for now," she said.

A young woman with cuts and scrapes across her face, who sat cradling a child in her arms, asked quietly, "What's next?"

Jax replied, "There's an old tunnel system, separate from the main system, that leads out of the colony. It's dangerous, but it might be our only chance."

Elise took a deep breath, her mind racing. "We'll need to move quickly and quietly. Gather what supplies you can. We leave as soon as we're ready."

As the colonists moved through the small entrance chamber to gather supplies, Elise turned to Jax. "We need to find help."

Jax nodded. "I'll go with you."

"No," Elise said, her voice firm. "I need you here to protect the colonists."

Jax hesitated, then nodded. "We'll meet at the maintenance shed. Be careful."

Elise gave him a grim smile. "I will. And Jax? Keep them safe."

With that, she turned and made her way to a hidden exit at the back of the chamber. As she slipped into the darkness, the sounds of the undead creatures echoed in her ears.

***

The underground tunnels twisted and turned, a labyrinth of stone and darkness. Jax led the group cautiously, every step echoing through the passageways. The air was damp and filled with the stench of decay, and every shadow seemed to promise unseen horrors.

"Stay close," Jax whispered, his voice barely audible. "We need to find a safe place to regroup."

The remaining colonists, a small group of frightened civilians barely numbering thirty, followed in a tight cluster. Their fear was palpable, every creak and groan of the tunnels amplifying their terror. Jax glanced back, his blaster ready, and saw the wide-eyed children clutching their parents, their faces pale and haunted.

They had been moving for what felt like hours when a low, rumbling growl reverberated through the tunnel. Jax stopped abruptly, raising his hand for silence. The group halted, their breaths coming in shallow, anxious gasps.

"What was that?" a woman whispered, her voice shaking.

Jax strained his ears, the growl growing louder and more menacing. It seemed to come from the depths of the tunnel, a sound filled with hunger and malice. "Stay quiet," he murmured, his eyes scanning the darkness. "And stay close."

They continued cautiously, the tunnel narrowing around them. The growls grew louder, and soon other sounds joined them—the skittering of claws on stone, the hiss of breath through rotten teeth. Jax's heart pounded in his chest as he led the group around a bend.

Ahead, the tunnel widened into a larger cavern, its ceiling lost in shadow. As they stepped into the open space, the growls intensified, echoing off the walls. Jax's blood ran cold as a massive, grotesque beast emerged from the darkness.

It was unlike any creature they had encountered before. Its body was a twisted amalgamation of decayed flesh and bone, with multiple limbs ending in sharp, clawed appendages. Glowing eyes dotted its malformed head, and a mouth filled with jagged teeth dripped with ichor.

"Run!" Jax shouted, raising his blaster and firing at the beast. The shots struck its hide, but it barely flinched, roaring in fury.

The colonists broke into a panicked run, the sounds of their footsteps and screams filling the cavern. Jax fired again and again, trying to slow the creature, but it was relentless, its many limbs propelling it forward with terrifying speed.

"To the tunnel!" Jax yelled, pointing to a narrow passage on the far side of the cavern. The colonists surged forward, their fear driving them faster. Jax backed away, firing as he went, the beast closing in.

A clawed limb swiped at him, and he barely dodged in time, feeling the rush of air as it passed. He swung his blaster like a club, smashing it into the creature's face, but it only enraged it further.

They reached the tunnel entrance and poured through, with the beast hot on their heels. Jax was the last to enter, the creature's roar reverberating through the passage. "Don't stop!" he yelled at the group. "Keep going!"

The tunnel grew narrower and more twisted, the walls closing in. The air was thick with moisture, and the ground became slick with moss.

Suddenly, they came upon a small chamber, barely large enough to hold them all. Jax ushered everyone inside, his eyes scanning for any other exits. But there were none—the chamber was a dead end.

"We're trapped," someone whispered, their voice trembling.

Jax turned to face the tunnel entrance, his blaster ready. The beast's growls grew louder, and soon it appeared, its grotesque form filling the passage. It stopped at the entrance, its glowing eyes scanning the chamber.

"Get back!" Jax shouted, firing at the creature, but it seemed unfazed. The beast roared, trying to squeeze through the narrow entrance, but its bulk was too great.

The creature's roars filled the chamber, its claws reaching through the entrance, swiping at anything within reach. Jax swung his blaster, knocking a claw away, but the beast was relentless.

"Stay away from the entrance!" Jax yelled,

The colonists retreated, forming a tight circle in the center of the chamber. The beast roared in frustration, its claws scrabbling at the stone.

As the undead creature thrashed at the entrance, Jax's thoughts turned to Elise. He could only hope she would return with help. Until then, they had to survive. They had to hold on.

For the sake of the colony, for the children, for hope itself, they had to hold on.

CHAPTER 29

The hours dragged on, turning into an endless stretch of horror and exhaustion. The chamber grew colder, the air damp and heavy with the stench of decay. Mason, one of the founding members of the colony, had experienced his share of hardship and fear in his long life, but nothing compared to the terror racing through his blood right now. The old man, with his long beard and withered skin, sat huddled together with the rest of the surviving colonists, their makeshift barricade at the entrance barely holding back the beast's relentless assaults. Every so often, the creature would retreat into the tunnels, its growls echoing ominously, only to return with renewed fury.

Time became a blur, marked only by the cycles of the beast's attacks. They had no way of knowing how long they had been trapped—hours, days? Fear and fatigue weighed heavily on them all.

Mason sat against the wall, cradling his arm, which had been injured in the chaos of their escape. The makeshift bandage was soaked with blood, but he refused to let it slow him down. Elise's face kept appearing in his mind, urging him to hold on.

Jax paced restlessly, his anxiety palpable. He kept glancing at the tunnel entrance, where the beast's growls could be heard in the distance. Finally, he couldn't take it any longer.

"We can't just sit here and wait to die," Jax muttered, his voice low and tense.

Mason looked up, exhaustion etched into his features. "We need to hold on. Elise will come back with help."

"How do we know that?" Jax snapped. "It's been too long. What if she didn't make it? What if the colony is overrun, and no one is coming?"

Mason had no answer. The same fears gnawed at him, but he couldn't give voice to them. "We have to believe," he said finally. "It's all we have left."

Jax shook his head, determination hardening his features. "I can't just wait here. I have to do something."

"What are you thinking?" Mason asked, already knowing the answer.

"I'm taking a few men. We're going to slip out when the beast is gone and try to find help ourselves."

"That's suicide," Mason warned. "The tunnels are crawling with those things. You'll never make it."

Jax squared his shoulders, a resolute look in his eyes. "We have to try. We can't just wait here to die."

Mason sighed, knowing he couldn't stop him. "All right. Take whoever is willing to go. But be careful."

Jax nodded, then turned to the others. "Whoever wants to come with me, get ready. We move when the beast is gone."

A few men stepped forward, their makeshift weapons gripped tightly in their hands and a grim determination etched on their faces. Hours later, the beast's growls faded into the distance once more. Jax took his chance. "Now!" he hissed.

The small group slipped through the entrance, moving as

quietly as possible. As Mason watched them go, a sinking feeling grew in the pit of his stomach. He prayed they would make it and find help. Their survival depended on it, yet something told him he'd never see them again.

The tunnel seemed even more oppressive in the absence of the creature's immediate threat. Jax led the way, his senses on high alert. Every shadow, every sound was a potential threat, waiting to rip them apart. They moved as swiftly as they could, knowing the beast could return at any moment.

"Keep close," Jax whispered. "We stick together, no matter what."

Time passed in a blur of darkness and apprehension. They navigated the labyrinthine tunnels carefully, praying with each step that the distant growls of the undead would stay distant.

Suddenly, a faint light appeared ahead. Jax signaled for silence, and they approached cautiously. The light grew brighter, revealing an opening to a larger cavern. Jax peered inside nervously.

The cavern was massive, its walls lined with old mining equipment and the remnants of a once-thriving operation. The light came from a series of flickering lamps, casting eerie shadows on the walls. In the center of the cavern, a group of undead creatures milled about hungrily.

Jax's heart sank. They had found another nest. He motioned for the men to retreat, but it was too late. One of the creatures looked up, its eyes locking onto them. It let out a guttural roar, alerting the others.

"Run!" Jax shouted, turning and sprinting in the opposite direction.

The men followed, panic driving them forward. The sounds of the undead echoed behind them, growing closer with each passing moment. Jax pushed himself harder, knowing their only chance was to find another way out of the tunnels.

They turned a corner and found themselves in another passageway, this one narrower and more treacherous. Jax led them through, his mind racing for a plan. They couldn't go back to the chamber; it would only lead the undead straight to the others.

"Up ahead!" one of the men shouted, pointing to a smaller tunnel branching off to the side.

Jax nodded, leading them into the side tunnel. The walls were rough and uneven, the ceiling low enough that they had to crouch as they moved. The cries of the dead grew fainter, but Jax knew they couldn't stop.

"Keep moving," he urged. "We have to find a way out."

Finally, they emerged into another chamber, smaller than the first but devoid of any immediate threats. Jax glanced around, taking stock of their situation.

"We need to rest for a moment," he said, his voice barely above a whisper. "But we can't stay here long. The beasts will keep searching."

The men nodded, their breaths coming in ragged gasps. They sank to the ground, their bodies trembling with exhaustion and fear. Jax leaned against the wall, his mind racing. They needed to find a way to signal Mason and the others, to let them know they were still alive.

"We'll find a way out," Jax said, more to himself than to the others. "We'll get help and come back for the rest."

But as the minutes stretched on, hope began to wane. The sounds of death echoed faintly in the distance, a constant reminder of the danger lurking just beyond the walls. Jax's resolve hardened. They had to keep moving, had to find a way to survive.

"Let's go," he said finally, pushing himself to his feet. "We can't stay here. We need to find another way out."

As they delved deeper into the maze of passages, Jax's mind never strayed far from the chamber where the others were trapped, or from Elise and the distant hope that she would bring salvation. He vowed silently to return with help, no matter what it took. Their lives depended on it.

CHAPTER 30

A cloud of dust and ash swirled over the land as a strong wind began to gain life. Overhead, a flurry of airships soared in desperate patterns, the pilots trying to escape the spreading madness on the ground, flying like frenzied insects trying to escape a spreading wildfire, unaware that the darkness flew on deadly wings as well. Moments later, two of the airships collided into a spectacular ball of raging fire.

The group watched in stunned silence as chunks of metal plummeted to the ground. Even from their distance, the loud crashes caused them to flinch. Then they saw the black shapes flying erratically toward them.

"We need to get out of here!" Darin exclaimed.

No sooner had those words escaped his lips when they heard movement coming from a group of trees nearby. Not waiting to see what the cause of the commotion was, they all jumped to their feet and started running.

"Where are we going?" Mishka asked through gritted teeth as she struggled to keep her wounded arm close to her body.

"There's a small colony a short distance from here over the next ridge," Anon replied. "Hopefully, we can get some help there."

"If there's anyone still alive, that is," Jensen stated, his tone a bitter edge cutting through the air.

"Forever the optimist, aren't you, Jensen?" Mishka said.

"Just being a realist. We've seen firsthand how quickly this madness can spread. I'd guess that in just a short time the entire planet will be exposed."

"Let's just hope Silas makes it to the lab with Aldin so she can figure out a way to stop this," Darin replied.

"I wouldn't count on her to fix anything!" Jensen snapped back. "Her ineptitude is what caused this damned apocalypse in the first place."

Darin opened his mouth to speak, then closed it again. He knew Aldin to be one of the smartest minds he had ever seen. To hear Jensen speak about her that way seemed wrong, like he had some kind of personal vendetta against her.

After a short trek, the colony loomed up ahead, a beacon of hope amidst the chaos of the desolate terrain. As they approached the edge of the territory, the group saw that the gates had been broken apart and the watchtower was vacant, which was odd and unnerving.

As they got closer, they could see that the colony had been overrun. Bodies littered the ground, and the buildings were ablaze. "See, I told you they'd all be dead," Jensen said smugly.

Suddenly, a low growl erupted behind them. The group turned as one to face the source of the noise, their weapons at the ready.

Out of the darkness stepped a large, black beast. Its fur was matted and ragged, and its eyes glowed with an all too familiar undead hunger. The Vulgan bared its teeth menacingly, revealing blood and bits of flesh caught in between.

As the creature lunged forward, its jaws snapping

furiously, the group scattered, dodging the initial attack. Mishka fired her blaster desperately in an attempt to take it down, but the quickness of the beast, coupled with the increasing darkness, made it difficult to get a clear shot.

The Vulgan immediately turned its attention toward Mishka, charging violently with rage and fury radiating from it. As she backed away quickly, her foot caught on the body of a fallen colonist and she went crashing to the ground. For a brief second, as she recovered from her fall, she regarded the face of the dead colonist, whose eyes, even in the dim light, conveyed the absolute terror they had felt as they died. Mishka was determined not to experience the same fate. When the creature sprang forward, she unleashed a torrent of shots from her prone position, finally hitting it with a shot that penetrated the base of its snapping jaws and continued up to exit the top of its skull.

Mishka rolled to the side to avoid the weight of the dead beast as it fell, only to cry out in pain anyway from the movement of her injured shoulder crunching against the hard ground. Anon rushed over to quickly help her up as the cries of the dead answered her in earnest.

"This way!" Darin exclaimed as he ushered them toward the entrance to the tower, with Jensen following close behind.

As they approached the building, they could hear faint growls and snarls coming from inside. When they entered through the door cautiously, the smell of death and decay was so overwhelming that it nearly dropped everyone to their knees.

They had only gone a few steps when a figure suddenly lunged at them from the shadows. Darin immediately swung his hub wrench around in a wide arch, hitting the figure squarely in the chest, sending it crashing to the floor.

A soft and raspy groan issued from the mound twitching

on the floor, and as they drew closer, they realized that their attacker was actually a woman and not one of the undead. She was covered in blood and scratches, and she clutched a knife in her hand.

The group approached her cautiously, their weapons still raised. The woman looked up at them with wild eyes, and they could see that she was on the verge of breaking down.

"Please," she whispered, her voice barely more than a croak, "help me. They're everywhere."

Anon stepped forward, offering a hand. "Are you okay?" he asked as he shot a glance toward Darin.

The woman nodded as she rose to her feet.

"Can you tell us what happened?" Mishka asked.

"They came out of nowhere," the woman stammered, tears streaming down her face. "We tried to fight them off, but there were too many. They tore through us like we were nothing."

"Are there more of you left?" Anon asked.

The woman nodded, her eyes tearing up, "There's a few of us trapped in the Mining Outpost. I barely made it alive out and came back here to try to find help."

"How far is the Mining Outpost?"

Jensen interrupted, "We don't have time for this! We need to get to the Ancillary Lab as quickly as possible."

"Please, we need your help," the woman pleaded. "The Mining Outpost isn't far from here, and then it's only a short distance to the Traveler's Outpost, where you can get a transport to take you to your destination."

Anon looked at Mishka and Darin, who both nodded. Only Jensen's eyes held a look of contempt. "It's settled then," Anon said. "Lead the way to the Mining Outpost and we'll help you in any way we can."

"This is a mistake," Jensen grumbled as the woman turned

and led them out of the building.

They hurriedly pressed forward, the woman guiding them through the bleakness of the colony. The air was heavy with the stench of decay, as lifeless bodies laid strewn across the landscape. The once lively community now resembled a desolate wasteland, echoing with the eerie silence of death and the haunting remnants of destruction.

As they neared the door to the tunnels, they heard a deep, guttural growl. The group turned to see a monstrous figure blocking their escape. The creature roared, its massive, clawed hand raised and ready to strike.

"What in the world is that?" Darin cried.

"I don't know," Mishka replied. "But whatever it is, it's ugly and needs to die."

"I agree," Anon said with a sneer.

A handful of blasters lay scattered amongst the dead, and the group quickly dispersed, each one scrambling for a weapon as the unholy beast attacked.

Anon, with a fierce determination in his eyes, lunged forward and snatched one from the ground just as the creature swung his claw around. He quickly brought the blaster up, firing rapidly. The shots seemed to do little more than annoy the monster, which bellowed in rage. Mishka and Darin followed suit, their weapons blazing as they tried to create an opening.

"Go for the head!" Mishka shouted.

Jensen, despite his earlier cynicism, fought alongside them with equal ferocity. He managed to land a shot that blew off part of the creature's jaw, but it only seemed to anger the beast more. The creature swung its massive arm, knocking Jensen to the ground. Mishka, cradling her injured arm, tried to drag him back to safety.

"Keep going!" Anon yelled, as he continued to fire at the

creature's head. He finally landed a shot directly between its glowing eyes. The creature staggered, giving them the precious seconds they needed.

"Now! Go!" Anon urged, pulling Mishka and Jensen to their feet as they darted past the stumbling behemoth and into a narrow alleyway.

Within seconds, the sounds of snarling and clawing echoed behind them, as a horde of undead beasts joined the hunt. With each passing moment, their cries grew louder and more desperate.

"How much further?" Darin panted, glancing over his shoulder.

"Not far," the woman replied, her voice shaking. "There's a hidden exit that leads to the underground tunnels."

A minute later, they reached the heavy metal door, which the woman pushed open with a struggle. They found themselves in a dimly lit tunnel, the air thick with damp and decay.

It didn't take long for the sounds of the infected to gather on the other side. With each passing minute, the banging and clamor against it grew more frantic.

"Come on, we have to keep moving," the woman urged, leading the way deeper into the tunnel.

The group pressed on, the tunnel's twists and turns disorienting them. The air was cold and dank, each breath feeling like it was coated in mildew.

"Where do these tunnels lead?" Jensen asked, his voice barely above a whisper.

"To the old mining facility," the woman replied.

"Is that where your people are?" Anon asked.

The woman didn't say anything, just nodded as she continued forward. As they turned another corner, they were met with a fork in the path. The woman hesitated, trying to recall the way. "Left," she decided, her voice wavering with uncertainty.

"I don't trust her," Mishka whispered to Anon.

Anon looked at the woman up ahead, who seemed to be leading them further and deeper than he thought was possible. "Who knows? We might be able to find supplies and a more secure place to regroup?"

"Just keep your eyes open."

They took the left path, the tunnel narrowing even further. The sound of running water echoed around them, and the ground grew slippery beneath their feet. Suddenly, the tunnel opened into a large chamber, the ceiling high above them.

In the center of the chamber was a deep pit, from which a foul stench emanated. The walls were lined with old machinery and mining equipment, long abandoned and covered in rust and grime.

"We can rest here for a moment," Anon said, his eyes scanning the chamber for any immediate threats.

The group slumped against the walls, trying to catch their breath. "How much further to the mining facility?" Darin asked, his voice weary.

"Not far," the woman replied.

"Just through that tunnel on the other side of the chamber."

Suddenly, a loud crash echoed through the chamber, followed by the sound of crumbling rock. The ground beneath their feet trembled, and they looked around in panic.

"Get back!" Anon shouted, pushing them away from the pit as the ground began to give way.

A section of the floor collapsed, sending debris and dust flying into the air. Anon grabbed the woman, pulling her back just in time. The pit widened, revealing a dark chasm beneath them. From the depths of the chasm, a series of low, guttural growl resonated, sending chills down their spines.

"What now?" Darin asked, his voice trembling.

Before anyone could answer, a pair of glowing eyes appeared from the darkness, followed by another, and another. The growls grew louder, echoing through the chamber.

"We need to move, now!" Anon shouted as he urged the group toward the far end of the chamber where another tunnel entrance was visible.

As they sprinted toward the tunnel, the creatures from the chasm began to emerge, their grotesque forms illuminated by the faint light of burning embers that emanated from deep within the abyss. The group could only glimpse twisted limbs and gnashing teeth as they ran for their lives.

Just as they reached the entrance, a massive hand shot out from behind them, grabbing Darin by the ankle and pulling him to the ground.

"Darin!" Mishka screamed.

Anon quickly grabbed Darin's arms and pulled with all his might as the creature's grip tightened. The ground again shook violently, and the tunnel entrance began to collapse around them.

With one final heave, they freed Darin from the creature's grasp and stumbled into the collapsing tunnel. The entrance caved in behind them, cutting off their pursuers but trapping them in darkness.

CHAPTER 31

The beasts came closer, their disease tainting the air like smoky acid. Jackson peered through the reinforced window of the Traveler's Outpost Tower, eyes wide with fear. His hands trembled on the intercom microphone. "They're almost here!" he shouted.

Down below, fires burned unchecked, sending plumes of smoke into the sky. The larger buildings were turning to ash, their roofs caving in. The wind carried the smoke in waves, changing directions like a slow-moving river.

In the main courtyard, Claire, a woman with steely resolve, tended to a wounded guard. Beside her, Tom, a burly mechanic, fortified a barricade with anything he could find. "We can't hold them off much longer," Tom said, sweat dripping down his face. "We need a miracle."

A growl echoed through the courtyard, followed by the shuffling and scraping of claws on stone. Undead Singa with glowing, sinister eyes emerged from the smoke, their fur matted with blood and ichor.

"Here they come!" Jackson's voice crackled over the intercom. Tom grabbed his energy rifle and took aim, while Claire drew a small plasma pistol. Around them, the few

192

remaining defenders readied their weapons, faces set with determination and fear.

The beasts charged with unnatural speed. Tom fired, the energy blast echoing through the courtyard. One of the beasts yelped and fell, but more surged forward. "Keep firing!" Tom shouted, squeezing off shots. "We can't let them get inside!"

But the undead were relentless. They swarmed over the barricades, tearing at the makeshift defenses with claws and teeth. The remaining defenders fell quickly under the gruesome attack, until only Tom and Claire remained.

"Fall back!" Tom yelled, retreating toward the main building. Once they were inside, Claire slammed the door shut.

"We can't stay here," Claire said, breathing heavily. "They'll find a way in."

Tom pointed to a narrow hallway on the other side of the room. "Through there! It leads to the basement. We might be able to hold them off down there."

Jackson, having joined them after abandoning the tower, nodded. "It's our best chance. We can't stay here and wait to die."

They hurried down the hallway, the sounds of the undead pounding against the door growing louder. In the basement, they found an old storeroom filled with dusty crates and rusted equipment. "Block the entrance," Tom ordered, pushing a heavy crate against the door. "It won't hold them forever, but it'll give us some time."

They worked quickly, piling up whatever they could find. The air was thick with dust and fear, every creak and groan of the building making their hearts race. "Is there any way out of here?" Claire asked, looking around desperately.

"There's a maintenance tunnel," Jackson said, pointing to a hatch in the floor. "It leads to the other side of the outpost.

We can make a run for it."

They pried open the hatch and descended into the tunnel, the darkness swallowing them. The sounds of the undead grew fainter, but the sense of danger never left. "Stay quiet," Tom whispered, leading the way. "We don't know what's down here."

The tunnel was cramped and musty, the air thick with the smell of mold and decay. Their beam lights flickered, casting eerie shadows on the damp walls. After what felt like an eternity, they emerged into the open air on the far side of the outpost. The sight that greeted them was one of utter devastation. Three of the four structures were engulfed in flames, the remaining one standing as a dying hope amidst the chaos.

"We need to get to the rendezvous point," Jackson said, his voice steady despite the fear in his eyes. They moved quickly, sticking to the shadows and avoiding the roaming packs of undead. The wind carried the sounds of distant screams and growls.

They hurried through the ruins, the air thick with smoke and the distant, mournful moans of the undead. Their hearts pounded in their chests, a frantic rhythm of desperation. "Stay close and keep moving," Tom growled, his voice strained and low. "We're almost there."

They rounded a corner and found themselves facing an old storage shed, its doors hanging off their hinges like broken promises. The rendezvous point, a small, fortified structure, stood just beyond. Each one clung to a flicker of hope to reunite with their comrades and escape the devastating apocalypse that surrounded them.

Suddenly, a low growl echoed from behind the shed. The group froze, their breaths caught in their throats. Out of the shadows emerged a pack of undead Singa, sleek, metallic fur and eyes glowing with hellish red light.

"Run!" Jackson shouted, but it was too late. The Singa lunged with a speed and precision that seemed almost choreographed. One leaped at Jackson, knocking him to the ground. His screams were quickly drowned out by snarls and the wet, ripping sound of flesh being torn apart.

Claire turned to flee, but another of the beasts caught her by the leg, dragging her down. She kicked and screamed, but the creature's grip was as relentless as death itself. Tom tried to pull her free, but more of the undead closed in.

"Claire!" Tom yelled, but his voice was swallowed by the chaos. He swung a metal pipe in a futile attempt to fend off the creatures, but their numbers were overwhelming. One latched onto his arm, its teeth sinking deep. Tom howled in pain, dropping the pipe, his face a mask of agony.

The beasts tore into their prey, the sounds of ripping flesh and gnashing teeth filling the air. The group's final cries echoed through the burning ruins of the outpost, their last remnants of hope extinguished by the relentless fury of the undead. In the eerie silence that followed, the undead feasted, their grotesque forms illuminated by the flickering flames.

CHAPTER 32

"Is everyone okay?" Anon asked, his voice echoing in the pitch-black tunnel.

"I'm okay," Darin panted, his voice shaky.

"Everyone else?" Anon called out.

"We're here," Mishka replied.

The group huddled together in the darkness, the sound of their heavy breathing the only thing breaking the silence. The tunnel ahead was completely black.

"We have to keep moving," Anon said. "We can't stay here."

The group hurried through the darkened tunnels, led by the woman whose name they had not yet learned. Her ragged breath and frantic pace seemed genuine, but there was something about her shifty glances that kept Anon on edge. The damp, musty air clung to their skin as they moved deeper into the labyrinth, each step echoing ominously.

"This way," the woman said, her voice wavering slightly. "We're almost to the maintenance shed. We'll be safe there."

Anon exchanged a wary glance with Mishka, but they had little choice. After what felt like an eternity, they emerged into a dimly lit chamber. Old mining equipment lay scattered around, and the faint sound of dripping water filled the silence.

"We should rest here for a moment," the woman said, leaning against a wall. "Catch our breath before we make the final push."

Anon nodded, though he kept his blaster at the ready. "Fine, but we can't stay long."

As they settled in, the woman moved to a corner of the chamber, her movements tense and deliberate. She glanced back at the group, her eyes flickering with an emotion Anon couldn't quite place.

Suddenly, the chamber's dim light flickered and went out, plunging them into darkness.

"What's happening?" Darin asked, his voice tinged with panic.

A series of clicks and whirrs echoed through the chamber. Lights flared on, revealing a group of shadowy figures emerging from hidden doorways and tunnels. Each one was armed and wore a face hardened by desperation.

"It's a trap!" Mishka shouted, raising her weapon.

Anon cursed under his breath, realizing they had been led into an ambush. "Everyone, stay together!"

As the group surrounded them, Jax stepping forward. "Drop your weapons," he ordered, his voice cold and commanding.

The woman joined him a second later, a somber look on her face. "I'm sorry, but I had no choice."

Anon slowly lowered his blaster, but kept his eyes on the leader. "What do you want?"

Jax's expression softened slightly, though his grip on his weapon did not. "We need your help. There's something in the mines—something dangerous. We've lost too many trying to deal with it ourselves. A number of our colony were trapped trying to escape the monsters up above. Now we fear that time is running out."

"And you think we'll just agree to help you?" Jensen snarled.

"You don't have a choice," Jax replied. "We need you to help us clear out whatever's in there, or none of us will survive."

Anon looked at the woman who had led them into this trap. "And you? You were just bait?"

She shook her head. "My name is Elise. I'm the governor of this colony and I'm trying to do everything possible to save those that are left. I'm sorry. We didn't have any other way."

"How do we know this isn't another trick?" Jensen demanded.

"You don't," Jax admitted. "But with the tunnel collapsed behind you, it's the only way out to get to the Travelers Outpost safely."

Mishka stepped forward with the rage of a woman scorned brewing inside. "If you double-cross us again, there won't be a next time."

Jax nodded, a grim expression on his face. "Fair enough. Follow me."

The tunnel itself groaned, the air thick and stagnant, as if the planet itself were running low on oxygen. They reached a blast door, a monstrosity of warped metal guarding the forgotten depths. Jax produced a data chip, its surface marred by countless scrapes. With a hiss and a groan, the door yielded, revealing a passage that gaped in the flickering light of their small, hand held beams.

The door slammed shut behind them with a finality that sent a shiver down their spines. The air there was like a tomb, thick with the stench of decay and something else entirely—a musky, ancient death that gnawed at their insides.

As they ventured deeper, the walls pulsed with an eerie luminescence. The ground trembled beneath their feet, and a low, guttural growl resonated from the inky depths.

Within the darkened chamber, a grotesque creature began to awaken. Its form, a desiccated husk animated by undead, diseased energy, was a grotesque parody of life, sending shivers down their spines. Glowing pustules dotted its flesh, and the sound of its claws scraping against the uneven floor echoed through the room.

The creature unleashed a sound that was more shriek than roar, the very chamber groaning in protest. The group unleashed a torrent of blaster fire, causing the creature to stagger back with a sizzling hiss. It lunged, a whirlwind of rage and decay.

"Now!" Jax roared. "Unleash everything you've got!"

In a final, defiant act, they unleashed a concentrated barrage of fire, focusing on its head. The creature shrieked, an unholy sound born from the depths of the abyss, before it expired into a lifeless heap on the cavern floor.

An unnatural silence followed, broken only by the ragged gasps of those that had just faced certain death and triumphed.

A moment later, a small group of people shuffled from an alcove hidden on the far side of the chamber where they had been trapped, hiding from the beast. Their bodies were covered in dirt and grime, while their eyes still held a look of terror in them, not sure if the demon had truly been vanquished.

A woman and child rushed to Jax and embraced him fervently, tears pouring down each face. After a minute, Jax slumped against the wall. "Thank you. You've given us a fighting chance."

"What now?" Darin asked, wiping sweat from his brow.

"We keep moving," Anon replied. "The Travelers Outpost is still our best chance."

Elise said, "If you follow the left tunnel all the way to its end, you'll come to an old mining facility that's out of commission. There are stairs there that lead out of the tunnels near the outpost."

"You're not coming with us?" Anon asked.

"We're too old and slow," Elise replied. "We'd only slow you down. We'll meet up with you at a later time."

Anon looked at Elise and nodded, knowing that he would never see them again.

They pushed forward, navigating the winding tunnels with renewed urgency. The air grew colder, and the sounds of distant snarls echoed through the darkness.

The tunnel stretched on, an unending black void that seemed to swallow the group whole. The walls were damp, the air thick with the smell of mold and rot. As they trudged forward, the air grew colder, and the sound of dripping water echoed around them.

After an eternity, they finally reached the decommissioned mining facility. Their footsteps echoed in the large, empty space as they passed old conveyor belts, rusted carts, and abandoned piles of ore. A thick layer of dust covered everything.

"Over here," Darin called out, pointing to a narrow spiral staircase leading upward. "This might lead to the surface."

Jensen immediately pushed Darin aside, nearly knocking him to the ground, and began climbing without waiting for the others. "You'd think that a few brushes with death would've changed him, at least a little," Darin said as Anon helped steady him.

"Some people refuse to change, no matter the darkness they face," Mishka said.

They climbed the stairs, their breath coming in short, labored gasps. The stairs creaked under their weight, the metal screaming in protest after years of neglect, and each step felt like it might be their last. At the top, they found another door, which led them into a narrow corridor.

They had only gone a few steps when a loud crash suddenly echoed through the corridor, and the ground beneath them shook. The walls began to crack, and dust rained down from the ceiling.

"Move, now!" Anon shouted.

They sprinted down the corridor, the sound of crumbling stone growing louder behind them. The corridor led to a large chamber with several exits. As they entered, the ceiling began to collapse, and they were forced to dive for cover.

Anon spotted an old maintenance hatch on the far side of the chamber. "This way!" he yelled, waving the group over.

They scrambled to the hatch, prying it open and slipping through just as the chamber caved in behind them. The hatch led to another tunnel, this one smaller and more claustrophobic.

"Keep going," Anon urged, his voice steady despite the chaos.

The tunnel twisted and turned, and they had to crawl through narrow passages and wade through knee-deep water. The air was stifling, and the darkness seemed to press in on them from all sides.

Finally, they emerged into a small, open space. Ahead, they could see a faint light that outlined a door.

They hurried toward the light, emerging into the open air. The Travelers Outpost loomed ahead in the distance, a beacon of safety in the desolate landscape.

As they approached the tower that stood on the outskirts of the outpost, however, the group noticed was vacant, which was odd, as there was always someone there, keeping watch. They cautiously made their way towards the entrance.

As they got closer, they saw that the entire area had been overrun. Bodies littered the ground in all directions. The group exchanged worried glances. "This isn't good," Mishka said.

A horde of undead animals surrounded the primary structure, their eyes glowing with an unnatural light.

"We have to get inside," Anon said, his voice urgent. "Stay close."

With each step toward the tower, the growls of the undead animals grew louder, their focus shifting towards the approaching group.

The group fought their way through the horde, their weapons blazing. The air instantly grew thick with the stench of decay and burning flesh, and the ground became slick with black ichor.

As soon as they reached the door to the tower, Anon threw it open and ushered the group inside. The door closed with a heavy thud, and they could hear the animals scratching and snarling outside.

"Is everyone okay?" Anon asked.

Darin nodded, while Jensen merely offered an irritated grunt.

"We're fine," Mishka replied, panting heavily. "But we can't stay here for long. They'll find a way in."

A crash behind them made the group whirl around, weapons ready. The door they had just entered through was now blocked by a mass of bodies, all clawing and snarling to get inside. The group exchanged a look of sheer terror. There was no way out.

"Is there another exit?" Darin asked urgently.

Mishka pointed to a narrow hallway at the back of the

room. "Through there!"

As they started towards the hallway, the infected broke through the door, pouring into the room in a wave of death and decay. The group fired wildly, trying to hold them back as they retreated.

Just as they reached the hallway, a massive figure loomed in the doorway, blocking their escape.

The group fired their weapons in a desperate attempt to hold back the tide of infected. It was clear they were running out of time. The hallway was their only chance, but the figure blocking it was unlike anything they had faced before.

With no other options, they charged forward, terror and determination intertwined in their eyes. The monstrous figure blocking their escape was an abomination of rotting flesh and twisted limbs. It let out a bone-chilling roar, reverberating through the tower and shaking the very foundation.

"Go for the legs!" Anon shouted, his voice cutting through the chaos like a knife through flesh. "We need to bring it down!"

Mishka and Darin focused their fire on the creature's lower limbs, while Jensen and Anon tried to target the beast's head. The creature stumbled, its corrupted flesh giving way under the relentless onslaught.

With a final, unified effort, they unleashed a concentrated barrage of fire. The creature let out a deafening scream, collapsing to the ground with a sickening, wet thud.

"Move, now!" Anon commanded.

They sprinted down the narrow corridor, the sounds of the undead behind them growing louder, closer. The hallway twisted and turned, the flickering lights casting shadows that seemed to reach out and grab at them, whispering promises of doom.

"We need to find a way to seal this off," Darin panted, glancing over his shoulder with wild, fearful eyes.

"There!" Anon pointed to a heavy, rusted door at the end of the hallway. "That might buy us some time."

They reached the door, and with a combined effort, managed to slam it shut. The sound of the undead pounding against the metal was deafening, but the door held—for now.

The group hurried through the winding passages of the tower, their breaths ragged and hearts pounding like war drums, until they finally emerged into a larger chamber. In the center stood a massive mechanism, its gears and cogs encrusted with decades of dust and grime.

"This must be the control room," Mishka said, wiping sweat and grime from her brow. "If we can activate this, we might be able to seal the entire tower."

Jensen looked at the mechanism warily, "It doesn't look like this thing has been operated for quite some time. We'll be lucky if we can move it even slightly."

"There hasn't been a reason to seal the tower for a long time. But I'm sure the Watch-keepers have maintained it sufficiently to keep it operational."

Jensen just grunted in reply.

"We have to try," Anon pushed.

Reluctantly, Jensen joined them and each member of the group took a position around the mechanism. With a concerted effort, they began turning the gears and pulling the levers. The machinery groaned to life, the sound echoing through the chamber like the moan of a dying god.

"Hurry," Darin urged. "We don't have much time!"

As the last lever was pulled, a deep rumbling filled the air. The walls of the tower began to shift and slide, sealing off the corridors and trapping the undead within their tomb of stone and metal.

They found another exit at the far end of the chamber, leading them out into the open air. The sight of the Travelers Outpost ahead filled them with both a renewed sense of hope, and a disconcerting feeling of dread.

CHAPTER 33

Silas raced through the Wildlands as if he had every inch of the land committed to memory. The transport became an extension of him as he glided it effortlessly over the rocky terrain. Off in the distance, small habitats dotted the horizon sporadically, the only visible signs of normal life amidst the wilderness.

These were the dwellings of the Kellion's, a race that had turned their backs on technology eons ago, refusing to allow its influence into their lives in any form. Some said their ancestors were members of the Architects who had disagreed with the methods used in the creation of Terran Five and were thus exiled to live as outcasts on the very world they had despised. Silas said a silent prayer for those inhabitants as he drove by, knowing they wouldn't survive this nightmare once it reached their doorsteps.

Watching Silas, Ridley sensed that being in nature was more of a spiritual act than a scientific one for him. A little pang flittered in her brain. She wished she could let herself go in such a way and just be one with the moment. But her training made that impossible. She was a fighter, plain and simple. Always on edge. Always ready. She couldn't change even if she wanted to. Plus, it had kept her alive so far.

A small lump began to form in her throat as they neared the Junction that would take them towards the Seascape, where Startac's Ancillary Lab was located. She could already hear the pounding of the surf echoing in her mind, the icy waters closing in around her, chilling her bones and making it difficult to breathe.

Silas suddenly brought the transport to a halt. Tandy's continued growls and snarls, the tires screeching against the rock, the echoes of the snarls, and the howls of the wind, combined into an ear-shattering symphony.

"Why are we stopping?" Ridley asked.

"Look," Silas replied.

Ridley climbed forward to see through the front glass and immediately wished she hadn't. Straight ahead, like a battalion of soldiers preparing for battle, a wall of savage creatures advanced toward them, each one pushing forward on decaying limbs, urged on by the hunger in their eyes.

"What are you going to do?" Aldin asked worriedly.

"The only thing we can do," Silas replied. "We have to go through them."

"Can we go around them?" Aldin asked, his voice tinged with desperation.

"That would take us to the Sandscapes, and the transport isn't equipped for that kind of terrain."

"Will it hold against those things?" Ridley asked.

"It has to," Silas said, his resolve hardening.

Silas pushed the transport forward as fast as it would go. The vehicle bucked and lurched as he steered it towards the beasts, the wheels kicking dirt and rocks out behind them.

As they drew closer, Tandy became a raging monster, ramming her head into the cage over and over, sending a spray of black ichor sailing forward. Her growls turned to roars and the cage shook, like a gigantic hammer was slamming into the metal.

"I don't know if this cage will hold, though," Ridley stated as she watched one of the welds break loose.

Tandy reared back and charged harder, snapping a second weld off. The bars bent forward just enough for her snapping jaws to jut from the front of the cage, trying desperately to snatch onto Ridley.

A second later, the sound of a blaster rang out before Tandy went silent.

"What did you do?!" Silas cried.

Ridley replied, "Something you should've done a long time ago."

Silas gripped the steering console tightly, suppressing his rising emotions. Deep down, he had known this was how it would end with Tandy, but he hadn't been able to bring himself to finish it. In a sense, Ridley had done him a favor, something he hadn't been strong enough to do. But even though it had been necessary, it still hurt.

"Are you okay?" Aldin asked, sensing his pain.

Silas didn't answer.

The beasts came closer, their disease tainting the air like smoky acid. Silas aimed forward, his wide and desperate face a shaky mask. He pushed the transport forward as fast as he could and slammed into the wall of creatures with enough force to send a slew of them flying in all directions. The vehicle bounced and swayed as it charged over others that fell beneath its weight. Black blood and ichor sprayed upward, showering them with an unholy rain as they were crushed under the transport's wheels.

Finally, they pushed through the horde and fled toward the Junction, putting a good amount of distance between themselves and what was left of the undead horde.

As they neared the Travelers Outpost, they were disheartened to see that three of the four structures were engulfed in fire and smoke. As flames engulfed the larger of the buildings, the once majestic round roof crumbled into ruins. The fires sent up thick columns of smoke, darkening the sky with shades of gray and black. The heavy wind carried the smoke in undulating waves, shifting directions like a raging river.

Silas slowed the transport and approached the fourth structure carefully. He stopped the vehicle when he saw a pack of animals round the corner. A torrent of growls accompanied the pack. Their clicking claws and growls were low and deep. More of them soon joined, until their numbers were so immense, the sound was like a storm. At the moment, they didn't seem to notice the transport, but Silas knew that could change in an instant.

Suddenly, the pack stopped and immediately rushed as one toward the untouched building and the group of figures rushing toward its entrance.

CHAPTER 34

"That's Anon!" Silas cried, his voice a knife cutting through the chaotic symphony of growls and gunfire.

Aldin and Ridley strained forward, eyes wide and unblinking, as they watched their friends fend off the initial animal attack. The creatures were relentless. Mishka fired her blaster with savage fury, dropping several of the creatures, their bodies hitting the ground with dull, sickening thuds. Anon and Darin fought side by side, their faces masks of grim determination, while Jensen stood in the background, frozen like a statue, his eyes vacant and wide.

Silas pulled out his blaster rifle, its weight a cold comfort in his hands. Ridley mirrored his movements, her own weapon ready. They exchanged a determined glance, then turned to Aldin and, in eerie synchronization, said, "Stay here."

Aldin's face crumpled, a mixture of shame and frustration. She knew they were right. She wasn't a fighter; she'd just be a liability and probably get herself and the others killed. Instead, she was left with the pressure of finding the cure to this madness. "No pressure," she muttered to herself bitterly.

* * *

***

Mishka didn't see the Kambura until it was too late. The beast, a blur of muscle and claws, barreled into her from behind, knocking her to the ground. She wrestled with the creature, desperately trying to keep its snapping jaws away from her face. Its breath was hot and fetid, and its strength was overwhelming. Her arms trembled, her breath coming in ragged gasps as she felt her grip weakening.

Just as Mishka's strength was about to give out, the creature suddenly collapsed beside her, lifeless. Gasping for breath, she looked up to see Ridley standing over her, blaster still aimed at the fallen beast. "I suppose you think this makes us even?" Mishka panted, managing a weak grin.

Ridley smiled, her eyes hard and determined. "Yeah, I guess it does."

Meanwhile, Silas surged forward, his focus razor-sharp as he advanced toward the thickest part of the battle. He moved with lethal precision, dropping a number of creatures with well-placed shots. But even with all his training, he couldn't be everywhere at once. A beast broke through and leaped toward Darin with terrifying speed.

Without hesitation, Anon threw himself between Darin and the creature, taking the full force of the attack. The beast's teeth sank deep into Anon's stomach, and he let out a choked cry.

"No!" Silas shouted. He fired another shot, killing the beast instantly, then rushed to Anon's side.

As Anon lay in Silas' arms, blood bubbling from his mouth, he said weakly, "Do you think Father will finally be proud of me, Brother?" he whispered, each word a struggle.

Tears streamed down Silas's face as he cradled Anon's head. "Aye, I'm sure Father is very proud right now."

Anon's lips curled into a weak smile. "And it only took my death to win his approval." He coughed, blood spraying from his lips.

"Father was always proud of you, Anon. He just didn't know how to show it."

Anon's laughter was cut short by another fit of coughing. "I guess I'll find out soon enough. Goodbye, Brother." With those last words, Anon's body went limp.

A deafening roar filled the air, cutting Silas' moment of mourning short. He turned to see the Kantor charging toward them. Its hide writhed, a grotesque mass of insects that moved as one.

"We need to get inside!" Ridley yelled, pulling Mishka to her feet. Together, they rushed to the entrance doors just as Darin shoved a long, metal rod into the gap, leveraging it to widen the opening just enough for them to squeeze through.

"Come on, Silas!" Ridley shouted.

"I can't just leave my brother here like this!" Silas protested, his voice breaking.

"There's no time! Now get in here! It's what Anon would want."

Reluctantly, Silas slipped through the narrow gap, leaving Anon's lifeless body behind. Jensen, though, remained rooted to his spot, eyes wide with fascination as the Kantor approached. The creature, an awe-inspiring terror, leaped into the air, its body splitting apart to reveal a swarm of insects within.

"Incredible!" Jensen exclaimed, his voice filled with wonder as the upper half of the Kantor fell upon him. The creature's jaws clamped around his throat, and his last thoughts were not of fear, but of admiration for the magnificent beast. He died with a sense of fulfillment, his blood soaking the ground in an eager spray.

The others, momentarily stunned by the horrific scene, snapped back to reality as the swarm of insects surged toward them. They pulled the rod free and the doors slammed shut, barely keeping the swarm at bay. They collapsed against the door, breathing heavily, their faces pale with shock.

Minutes later, Darin's voice broke the silence. "Where's Aldin?"

Ridley's eyes widened with fear as she looked at Silas. "She's still in the transport!"

CHAPTER 35

Aldin watched in horror as the scene unfolded before her eyes. Time seemed to stretch, elongating the moment of Anon's death into a slow-motion nightmare. She could almost feel every second pulse through her veins, each heartbeat an agonizing reminder of her helplessness. Anon's sacrifice played out in excruciating detail, every drop of blood a testament to his bravery and desperation. In stark contrast, Jensen's death was a brutal flash—quick, savage, and utterly merciless.

Inside the transport, Aldin felt a suffocating sense of worthlessness. The rest of the group had escaped into the structure, leaving her behind. Panic clawed at her throat. *I have to do something!* She thought frantically, her eyes darting around the cabin for any potential solution.

Her skin crawled as her gaze fell on Tandy's body, lying grotesquely in its cage. The creature's remains were a half-decomposed horror, the stench of decay mingling with the metallic tang of fear in the air. She noticed black tendrils of slime weaving through the creature's skull and into its brain, a nightmarish picture of rapid, invasive rot. "I've never seen decay on a molecular level like this happen so fast," she whispered, her voice barely audible over the chaos surrounding her.

The alarm's tempo increased, a sinister blast counting down to oblivion. The encroaching night cast long, sinister shadows, making their situation even more desperate.

Her eyes drifted to Jensen's lifeless body, where a swarm of insects circled a glass jar lying next to him. From her vantage point, it was difficult to make out, but it seemed to contain some sort of organism. The swarm grew tighter around the object, encapsulating it completely before lifting it into the air. High above, the insects dispersed momentarily, letting the glass fall and shatter on the ground. Aldin watched in stunned amazement as the swarm regrouped, allowing the escaped organism to join them.

"They're intelligent!" she exclaimed, the realization hitting her like a thunderbolt. "These things are alive! They're not just a mutated virus. They behave as if in a hive mind. That means there's one controlling them all!"

But which one? It had to originate from the original test specimen at the lab. If the organism was intelligent, it would have the ability to move from one host to another. *The Kantor!* The beast had been part of the swarm that rode on its back to this place. But why was it following them?

A horrifying thought struck her, chilling her to the bone, *It knows I was responsible for the accident!*

As if to confirm her worst fears, the swarm began pounding feverishly on the transport. It wanted her. Aldin's mind raced as panic surged through. She had to get to the others, fast!

She scrambled into the driver's seat and started up the transport. It was larger and bulkier than the personal vehicles she was used to. The transport lurched and swerved as she wrestled with the controls, finally straightening out and heading towards the structure. She skidded to a halt, turning in a wide arc to face the opposite direction. Her fingers flew over the controls, flipping the button to send the vehicle into reverse.

The transport hurtled backward, slamming into the metal door with a bone-jarring crash. Aldin's breath came in ragged gasps as she fought to keep her focus while the swarm's relentless pounding echoed through the cabin.

***

The structure shook violently, a deafening crash reverberating from outside. Dust and debris rained down from the ceiling, the very walls seeming to tremble with fear.

"What was that?" Darin asked, his voice trembling. He braced himself against the wall, eyes wide with panic.

A voice, muffled but urgent, called from the other side of the door. "Guys? Are you there? We need to get out of here, now!"

"Aldin?" Ridley's voice was sharp with concern. "Are you okay?"

"Yeah, just scared. Can you pry the door open again?"

Darin, his hands slick with sweat, wedged his rod into the door's edge. Muscles straining, he pried it open just enough for Silas to grab the lip. Silas's jaw clenched under the effort, veins bulging in his neck as he pulled with all his strength. Finally, the gap widened enough for Ridley to squeeze through.

Relief washed over Ridley's face as she saw Aldin sitting there, the rear door of the transport cycling upward. "Hurry up," Silas grunted, his voice tight with strain. "I can't hold this open much longer!"

Ridley climbed into the transport and quickly unlatched

Tandy's cage. Together, she and Aldin pushed the cage out of the transport, wedging it into the opening. Mishka and Darin scrambled over the cage and climbed into the back of the transport. Silas, his face a mask of grief and heartache, took a moment to close his eyes. "Goodbye, Brother," he whispered, before climbing into the driver's seat.

Aldin's voice was sharp. "We need to get out of here, fast! I think the swarm is after me personally."

Mishka scoffed in disbelief. "That's ridiculous. There's no way these things can think like that."

"You didn't see the way the swarm acted when it knew I was in here," Aldin insisted. "I think it knows I was in the lab when it mutated."

Mishka's face twisted in a mix of disbelief and horror. "So, it thinks you're its mother?"

"I don't know! What I do know is that we need to get out of here!"

Silas immediately slammed the transport into gear, sending the vehicle lurching forward. After a short distance, he stopped suddenly, reversing until the transport was beside the fallen Kantor. The beast, despite missing half its body, tried desperately to crawl forward, its eyes burning with mindless rage. It gnashed its teeth, clawing at the air.

Silas flung open his door and fired a shot into the Kantor's brain. The creature convulsed, then fell still, its death throes echoing in the silence. A shrill cry rose from the nearby swarm. The insects, now a seething mass of anger, rocketed toward them with renewed ferocity.

The transport's engine roared as Silas pushed the vehicle as fast as it cold go, the vehicle surging forward. The swarm closed in, a living wave of darkness and death. Aldin's heart pounded in her chest, each beat a desperate prayer for survival. The air was thick with the sound of wings and the buzz of a thousand tiny bodies, each one driven by a singular, terrifying purpose.

As the transport hurtled through the night, Aldin's mind raced. She had to find a way to stop the swarm, to end this nightmare. She was sure that the organism that had taken over the Kantor was the one controlling the rest, but now she wasn't so sure. *Maybe my theory is all wrong and we'll never stop this?* She thought, afraid to voice her fears to the rest.

At the moment, all she could do was hope that somewhere ahead, there was safety.

CHAPTER 36

The sun rose over the small, isolated community nestled in a lush valley on the edge of the Wildlands, casting a warm glow over the neat rows of homes and the surrounding verdant landscape. Birds with iridescent feathers sang, and the air was fresh with the scent of flowers in full bloom. For a brief moment, it seemed as though nothing could disrupt their peaceful existence.

Outside one of the homes, Raul was busy fixing a broken fence, his hands working methodically. He paused to wipe the sweat from his brow and glanced around at the tranquil scene. Life had settled into a comfortable routine in their quiet, little community, a peaceful sanctuary surrounded by all the splendor nature had to offer. *This is what perfection looks like,* he thought with a smile.

They never had a chance.

Inside the house, Kim and Jonas slept soundly, cocooned in the warmth of their beds. The early morning was wrapped in an eerie stillness, the kind that blankets a place just before something terrible happens. The sun was just beginning to rise, casting long, skeletal shadows through the windows.

Linora was sprawled on the couch in the living room, a

holographic map flickering beside her. She had fallen asleep in the middle of planning their next supply run, the weight of leadership bearing down on her even in sleep. Her brow was furrowed, as if her dreams were filled with the same worries that plagued her waking hours.

The silence was abruptly shattered by the blaring of the local emergency alarm, a harsh, jarring sound that seemed to pierce the very soul of the house. Kim and Jonas jolted awake, their hearts pounding as the alarm continued its relentless scream.

"What the hell is that?" Kim gasped.

Jonas sat up, his head spinning. "I don't know, but it can't be good."

Linora's eyes snapped open, the alarm wrenching her from her restless sleep. She sat up just as Kim and Jonas hurried into the room. Linora pressed a button and the holographic screen flickered to life, displaying a stern-faced official who looked like he'd seen the gates of hell open. The image glitched in and out as he spoke. *"This is an emergency broadcast... All citizens... remain indoors... reports of... stay inside... god help us."*

The broadcast went dead.

The room fell silent, the message hanging in the air ominously. Kim clutched Jonas's arm. "I'm scared, Jonas! What's going on?"

"I have no idea, but we need to be ready for anything," Linora said.

A second later, Raul burst into the house, slamming the door behind him. His breathing was ragged and his eyes held a look of terror in them. A long swath of blood ran from his shoulder down his arm and puddled onto the floor.

"Oh, my god, Raul!" Linora said. "What happened?"

Before Raul could reply, there was a flurry of savage

clawing and pounding on the door from the other side, accompanied by a chorus of deep, throaty growls.

"Seal the structure, now!" he finally managed to sputter.

Linora rushed to a panel on the wall next to the door and punched in a code. Immediately,, the structure went into lock-down. Metal barricades dropped down to seal the windows and doors, preventing anything but a missile attack from breaching the perimeter.

While the monsters outside continued their assault on the door, Jonas helped Raul over to the couch, where he slumped down weakly, the result of significant blood loss. Linora tried to clean his wound, bringing a cry of pain from his lips when she removed his shirt, then a loud gasp from her own mouth when she saw the large hole in his shoulder where the flesh had been ripped out. She was just about to apply a healing salve when his body started trembling violently.

Raul looked at her through tortured eyes before he fell to the floor and started convulsing violently. Kim screamed as he thrashed about, while Linora and Jonas held onto him tight, desperately trying to keep him from injuring himself.

Then, as suddenly as the seizure started, it stopped. A hushed silence fell over the room as they waited for Raul's still body to show any signs of life. After a minute of agonizing tension, his chest began to slowly rise and fall. His eyes fluttered open and he struggled to sit up.

"Are you okay?" Linora asked.

Raul nodded at her weakly. "I think so."

"What attacked you?" Jonas asked.

When Raul looked his shoulder, he was shocked to see a large oily mass wriggling out of the bloody wound and writhing down his arm like a black, inky serpent. Kim let out a loud screech when it dropping to the floor and quickly slithered toward the door. A cacophony of desperate howls and cries erupted from the beasts outside as it passed under the threshold and disappeared.

Tears fell down Kim's face as she held onto Jonas tightly. "What in the world is going on here?" she cried.

Raul replied weakly, "Baboans."

Linora looked at him in shock. "Is that what attacked you?"

He nodded.

"But they've never come down this far from the mountain before. What would cause them to do so now?"

Raul took a deep breath and swallowed hard as he fought against the pain. "These were different. They were crazed. Something… in their eyes." He shuddered.

As if to emphasize the point, the attack on the door increased with savage force, as the number of primates swelled so that their collective cries grew to an overwhelming crescendo. The structure shook violently from the onslaught. Within minutes, they were everywhere, pouncing on the windows, jumping on the roof, scratching at the dirt.

Kim, her face pale and eyes wide, gripped Jonas' arm even tighter. "We're not going to make it!" she yelled over the deafening noise. "They're going to get in! We're trapped!"

Raul, wincing in pain, struggled to his feet. "We need to reinforce the barricades. Find anything heavy!"

The reinforced door groaned under the relentless pressure, metal bending as the primal force from outside continued to build. Jonas and Raul pushed a heavy cabinet against it, their muscles straining with the effort. "This won't hold forever," Jonas panted.

Linora picked up a blaster from the table, her knuckles white as she gripped it tightly. "We need a plan. If they get in, we can't just stand here and wait to die."

Suddenly, a loud crash echoed through the building. One

of the windows had cracked under the pressure, the reinforced glass giving way. Kim screamed, dropping a knife as she backed away in horror.

Jonas turned, eyes wide with terror. "Oh, no! One of the window mechanisms must have failed!"

Before anyone could react, a Baboan burst through the shattered window, its crazed eyes filled with blood-thirsty madness. One of its ears had been chewed off and a stream of blood bubble from the stump. It snarled, black saliva dripping from its fangs, before it lunged forward with a blood-curdling screech.

Linora fired her blaster repeatedly, knocking the creature backward against the wall with a heavy crash before it slumped to the floor, leaving a wide streak of blood behind.

The group shuddered as they watched the decaying creature lying on the floor spasming as if in the throes of death, before it went still. They weren't aware that death had already claimed the beast.

"What the hell?" Jonas exclaimed.

Raul replied, "It's just like the one that attacked me! Like it was possessed or something!"

"Maybe some kind of virus or disease spread through their troop that caused this behavior?" Linora suggested.

Before anyone else could respond, they watched in horror as the creature slowly rose from the floor and stood on its hind legs, exposing the gaping hole in its chest from the blaster shots. A low growl issued from its throat, an unholy proclamation of its true nature.

The Baboan's feral eyes locked onto Linora, its lips curling into a hideous grin. She raised the blaster again, her hands shaking uncontrollably. As if in support of the impending assault from the one that had penetrated the structure's perimeter defenses, the howls outside reached a fever pitch. It launched itself at her once more, its deadly claws extended as a terrible screech exploded from its mouth.

Linora stumbled backward to avoid its attack and fell to the floor. The beast was on her in an instant, scratching and clawing at her face before it sank its fangs into her skull. Linora's dying scream echoed loudly through the small structure. A desperate gurgle then sounded from the beast as it cracked the rest of her skull open and gorged itself on the brain matter within.

When Kim's ear-piercing scream flew out of her mouth after she recovered from the shock of Linora's death, the Baboan immediately turned toward her, bits of flesh and blood dripping from its mangled mouth. As it gathered for another attack, Kim turned to run, knowing her life was about to end. She only made it a couple of steps when she heard a loud thud behind her and turned to see the creature lying on the floor with a long metal rod sticking from the back of its head. Jonas was standing beside the dead creature, his eyes wide and his body trembling.

Kim rushed over and threw her arms around him, crying uncontrollably. "Linora…" she sobbed, her voice broken and shaky.

"I know," Jonas replied softly, trying his best to calm her down, when in his mind, he was just as traumatized as her.

Another wave of attacks outside, followed by more clamor from the back of the house reminded them quickly that the nightmare was closing in and would soon engulf them completely.

Raul walked past them, holding his arm against his body to try to keep its movement to a minimum, but each step still brought an unbearable amount of pain with it. "I'm going to try to close the window barricade so more of those things don't get in."

"I'll help you," Jonas said.

"You're not leaving me out here by myself!" Kim stated. "We're all going together."

Jonas thought briefly about arguing with her but thought better of it. Time was running out, and if they didn't get the window barricade fixed quickly, they'd be overrun in no time.

Raul hobbled down the hall with Jonas and Kim right behind him. The Baboan had entered through the window at the back of the house, where the defective relay switch had been discovered weeks ago. If he had kept his promise and fixed it when he was supposed to, then Linora would still be alive. a shudder passed through him, not from the pain in his arm, but from the pain in his heart.

As they entered the rear living quarters, they saw the decaying arm of another Baboan reaching desperately through the broken glass, trying to get a handhold, throaty growls issuing from the beast as splatters of black blood painted the wall from its relentless pounding.

Raul fired his blaster at the monster, the blow effective in causing it to fall backward, but not effective enough to kill it. The creature's arm was ripped off as it fell back into the darkness, and thudded to the floor, where it twitched and spasmed for a moment before it went limp.

"Hurry," Raul said. "We have to manually pull the barricade down.

As Jonas reached up on one side, with Kim helping Raul on the other, he saw a sea of red, glowing eyes outside, overwhelming the entire community. "We're not going to survive this!" he panicked. "They're everywhere!"

"Let's just get this barricade down, then we'll figure out a plan," Raul replied.

With a heavy thud, they pulled the steel panel down and

locked it into place just before a throng of undead beasts converged on the house. Raul immediately slunk to the floor, his body on the verge of shutting down. The severed limb of the beast lying next to him a grim notice that death waited anxiously for them just outside.

"I'll get the med-kit," Jonas said before he rushed out of the room.

Kim's eyes quivered and her lips trembled as she watched him leave the room. She was helpless in times of extreme emergency, and she knew it. So did everyone else. With a look of terror and disgust covering her face, she kicked the Baboan's severed limb away and sat down next to Raul.

Growing up as a scared little girl her whole life, she had hoped that the constant fear that resided inside her would disappear as she got older. But even the security of the tight-knitted community couldn't quell the shadows in her mind that forever stayed present just under the surface of her mind. She supposed it was the result of some dramatic trauma she had experience as a young child, probably when her parents had died while their village burned. Even though she had been too young to understand, the events were still a part of her, and they surfaced frequently, even though no current danger was present. Now, she was forced to be brave in the face of certain death, and she couldn't do it.

She jumped and let out a little gasp when Jonas returned a minute later with the med-pack. With fumbling fingers, she grabbed the kit and applied a liberal amount of healing salve to Raul's seeping wound, then wrapped his shoulder and arm in bandages before making a make-shift sling out of a cleaning cloth on the counter nearby. As she did that, Jonas injected a steroid healing solution into Raul's neck, hoping and praying that it wasn't too late to overcome the severe blood loss.

Jonas and Kim helped him to a nearby chair where he slumped backward and was asleep within minutes.

"Is he going to be okay?" Jonas asked.

Kim replied, "I think so. He lost a lot of blood, but the steroid injection and salve should help close the wound. He just needs some rest."

Jonas nodded as they both collapsed in exhaustion beside Raul. As the monsters outside continued their assault on the structure to get at them, they each drifted off into a fitful sleep full of hellish nightmares.

At some point throughout the night, the cries of the dead grew distant, as the Baboans moved away from the community in search of more prey. The terror of the beasts was then suddenly replaced by the ground trembling beneath them, jolting them all awake.

"What's happening?" Kim asked nervously.

Before anyone could reply, the power went out, throwing the building into a hazy shadow as dawn began to approach.

"We can't stay here," Raul said. "We need to get to the safe zone as quickly as possible."

Jonas replied, "Are you okay to travel?"

Raul nodded, "I think so. We don't have a choice. We can't wait any longer. The longer we stay, the more dangerous it becomes."

"Are you sure about this?" Kim asked, glancing at Jonas.

"We don't have a choice," Raul replied. "The safe zone is our only chance. We could be there by nightfall."

"But that means we have to go out there with those things," Kim said, her voice quivering.

Jonas approached the barricaded window and listened carefully. After a long minute, he pulled back. "It sounds like most of them are gone now."

"Then maybe we should just stay here and wait for help?"

Kim suggested.

When the ground shook again, it gave her the answer she didn't want to hear.

The three of them made their way back toward the front, pausing to step over the dead Baboan, while also taking a moment to cover Linora's body. A wave of sorrow encompassed the room as each one said their final goodbye.

Without power to raise the front barricade, they had to manually lift the heavy metal slab. Even then, they could only get it high enough to crawl underneath, praying with each nervous movement that the monsters were truly gone.

The acrid stench of death and decay assaulted their senses immediately, sending each one to the ground retching violently. A thick fog had blanketed the area, but even through the murky air they saw the bodies of their friends and neighbors strewn everywhere.

They climbed into the nearest transport, the atmosphere inside heavy with tension and unspoken dread. As Jonas started the engine and pulled forward, the fog began to clear slightly, revealing more of the road ahead. Just as they started to feel a flicker of relief, a dark shape loomed in front of them. Another transport, spinning out of control, was heading straight toward them.

"Hang on!" Jonas shouted. He tried to swerve, but it was too late. The two vehicles collided with a sickening crunch of metal and glass. Their transport spun wildly, the world outside a blur of motion.

When they finally came to a stop, everything was eerily quiet. Jonas's head was throbbing, and a trickle of blood ran down his forehead. He looked around, dazed. "Is everyone okay?"

"I think so," Kim said, though her voice was shaky. She winced, clutching her side. "Raul?"

"I'm okay," Raul replied.

"Stay in the transport," Jonas ordered. "I'm going to check on the other vehicle."

"Be careful," Kim pleaded, her voice trembling.

Jonas nodded, grabbing his blaster. He pushed open the door, stepping out into the crisp morning air. The scent of ash and decay was strong, and he realized the fog wasn't actually fog, but instead was the byproduct of numerous wildfires scattered across the land.

As he got closer to the transport, he saw movement inside the vehicle. A woman was slumped over the steering console, blood trickling down her face.

Jonas's heart raced as he opened the door. "Are you okay?"

The woman stirred, lifting her head. Her eyes were unfocused, but she managed to nod. "I... I think so."

Jonas moved to help her out when a chilling sound froze him in his tracks. The savage cries of the Baboan echoed through the air, sending a shiver down his spine. "We need to get out of here. Now."

The woman's eyes widened as she heard the cries. She tried to move, but her leg was pinned. "I can't...I'm stuck."

Jonas's mind raced. He glanced back at his own transport, then at the woman. The creature was close, too close. He couldn't leave her here. "Hold on, I'll get you out."

He braced himself, pulling with all his might. The woman cried out in pain, but he didn't stop. Finally, with a sharp crack, the dash panel gave way, and he managed to free her leg. "Can you walk?"

She nodded, wincing as she tried to stand. "I think so."

Suddenly, a dark shape lunged out of the fog, knocking Jonas to the ground. He fired his blaster wildly, trying to fend off the creature. The Baboan snarled, its white eyes gleaming in the mist.

"Run!" Jonas shouted to the woman, struggling to keep the creature at bay.

She hesitated for a moment, then turned and limped toward the transport as fast as she could. The door opened, but just as Kim was about to pull her inside, she stopped suddenly. A spray of blood flew from her mouth as her eyes grew wide before she slumped to the ground. The Baboan yanked its claws out of the woman's back and let out a loud screech in triumph before it sank its teeth into her flesh.

A scream flew out of Kim before she could stifle it, drawing the attention of the beast to her. As it prepared to attack, Raul leaned forward and fired a shot over her shoulder, hitting the creature in the forehead. It let out a final, guttural cry before collapsing.

Jonas sprinted back to the transport, diving inside just as another pack of Baboan appeared from the fog.

"Go! Now!" Kim shouted.

Jonas slammed her foot on the accelerator, the transport lurching forward. The small group of Baboan chased them for a short distance before giving up, their chilling howls echoing behind them.

CHAPTER 37

Aldin's throat burned like fire, her eyes stinging from the thick smoke and swirling ash that enveloped the overturned transport. She wiped at her eyes with the back of her hand, smearing soot across her face as she struggled to regain her blurry vision. When her sight finally cleared, she immediately wished it hadn't.

She lay on the ground, a short distance from the smoldering wreck. The transport was a twisted hulk of metal and flame, its guttural moans filling the air with a symphony of despair. Silas's body jutted grotesquely through the shattered front view-port, his head having shattered the glass, his face a ruin of blood and bone. Darin's still form was pinned under the weight of the vehicle, identifiable only by the distinctive boots he always wore. Mishka's lifeless eyes stared blankly from the passenger seat, her body stretched forward in a futile reach for help. Only Ridley remained alive, crawling desperately toward Aldin, her movements slow and agonizing.

Aldin's ears rang with the relentless pounding of a war machine, a hellish rhythm that matched the throbbing pain in her head. She tried to push herself to her knees, only to find that she couldn't feel her legs. Panic surged through her as she turned her head and looked down. Her legs were gone, severed cleanly off. Her entire lower body was missing, her torso ending in a bloody, ragged stump.

A scream rose in her throat but was cut short by a million legs crawling over her skin, biting and pinching violently. Her body was lifted into the air, suspended by a legion of tiny wings, the sensation both surreal and horrifying. She watched in a daze as her lower torso floated up to meet her, joining her together once more in a grotesque, unnatural fusion.

Her mouth opened to scream, but the sound was stifled as a large Betylle, a nightmarish insect, scurried up her neck and clamped onto her tongue. Its long tendrils burrowed into her flesh, growing rapidly, winding their way to the back of her mouth and penetrating the soft tissue there. She felt the tendrils probing deeper, searching for her brain stem, the sensation a blend of excruciating pain and sickening violation.

Her body convulsed violently as the organism took hold, her muscles spasming uncontrollably. Her eyes turned a deep, unnatural red; her flesh began to decay, peeling off in putrid chunks. A ravenous hunger overtook her, an insatiable need to consume. She saw Ridley clawing at the ground, trying to escape, and responded with a feral cry that erupted from every insect embedded in her flesh.

Aldin swooped toward her with savage fury, her movements quick and violent. She grabbed Ridley by the throat, her fingers digging in with inhuman strength. Ridley's eyes widened in terror as Aldin bent forward, her mouth opening wide, eager to taste her flesh.

***

Aldin woke with a jolt, trembling violently. The cabin of the transport was dimly lit, shadows flickering ominously on the walls. She blinked, trying to dispel the remnants of the nightmare, and saw worried eyes watching her. Ridley immediately took her in her arms, and a tidal wave of tears crashed out of Aldin.

"It's okay," Ridley whispered, her voice a soft balm. "It was just a dream. You're safe with me now."

Mishka, sitting nearby, watched the exchange with a mixture of empathy and sorrow. Tears threatened to spill over, but she held them back. *That used to be me,* she thought wistfully. *I'd give anything to have that again.* But she knew it was lost forever.

"Do you want to talk about it?" Ridley asked softly, her fingers brushing Aldin's hair.

Aldin didn't answer. She clung to Ridley tighter, as if trying to squeeze the nightmare out of existence. But the horrific images remained, vivid and relentless. Even awake, she felt the phantom legs of insects crawling over her skin, sending a chill down her spine.

Ridley squeezed her a little tighter, as if trying to ward off Aldin's fear. They were all terrified. Staring into the abyss every second, it was hard to be brave, but they had to try.

"Where are we?" Aldin asked after a while, shifting so that she lay in Ridley's lap, seeking solace in the familiar warmth.

"We're about halfway to the lab," Ridley replied, her voice steady. "We should be there before too long."

"How long was I asleep?"

"For a while."

Aldin reached over and squeezed Ridley's hand, closing her eyes again. She didn't dare sleep, though. She refused to let the demons invade her mind once more. Instead, she rested, bathing in Ridley's warmth, the only thing keeping her from a complete breakdown.

"You're so good to me," she mumbled.

Ridley brushed a stray lock of hair from Aldin's forehead and replied softly, "Only because you're the same to me."

The transport suddenly swerved, jolting them violently. "Sorry," Silas called from the front. "A couple of roamers."

***

"Slow down!" Kim cried as Jonas tried to speed away from the pack of Baboan that had emerged from the darkness unexpectedly in front of them, as if they had been waiting in ambush.

He swerved erratically to avoid a number of the lunging beasts. Then they heard a heavy thud on the roof of the transport, followed by the sight of a decaying arm reaching down frantically to smash through the front glass. Jonas tried to swerve again to throw the thing off, and when he saw the other transport closing in, it was too late.

The impact sent the transport spinning before it went airborne, toppling end-over-end numerous times before it came to a grinding halt upside down.

When Jonas opened his eyes moments later, he instantly knew the worst thing imaginable had happened. Kim's eyes were wide and lifeless as her head hung at an unnatural angle. A soft moan of anguish issued from his lips as he looked at her, a mountain of regret rising inside him for all of the things he had wanted to tell her but were left unsaid.

He looked back at Raul, whose breathing was shallow and quick. Raul exchanged a knowing glance with him, as if to say 'it's okay', before he closed his eyes and succumbed to his injuries.

Jonas heard the monsters closing in on the overturned

transport, and for a brief moment entertained the thought of letting the demons have him. He had already lost everything. What reason was there live now? Then, he heard Kim's voice in his head, urging him to go on.

His only hope for salvation lay with the other transport and the hope that it and its occupants were still intact. With a painful exhale, he pushed open the transport door and climbed out. Maybe if providence were on his side, he would live to honor Kim's memory?

***

A heavy impact then slammed into the transport, sending it spinning out of control. Silas wrestled with the steering controls. Through the spinning chaos, another transport loomed into view, teetering on the brink of disaster before it went airborne and crashed back to the ground.

"Everyone okay?" Silas asked, his voice strained, as he brought their transport to a stop.

"Yeah, I think so," Darin muttered, wincing as he recovered from being thrown against the rear door. Mishka rotated her arm, wincing in pain from being pressed hard against her door. Ridley and Aldin sat huddled tightly together on the rear seat, their faces pale.

"What happened?" Ridley asked, her voice shaky.

"Another transport hit us," Silas replied.

"Are they okay?" Aldin asked, peering into the darkness.

"I'm not sure. Their transport crashed pretty hard. I'm going to go check it out."

"Be careful," Mishka said, her eyes wide with concern.

"I will," Silas promised, grabbing his blaster rifle. He slowly opened the door, the cold night air rushing in, filled with the scent of smoke and fear.

Cautiously, he approached the crashed transport, holding his blaster tight. The moonlight cast long, deceptive shadows that made every step more precarious. Something had caused the driver to lose control, and Silas's heart pounded as he braced himself for whatever that may be.

Suddenly, a man came running at him, screaming for help. Silas started sprinting forward until he heard it—the chilling, savage cries of the Baboan. The darkness around him came alive with movement. The Baboan emerged from the blackness, their long arms dragging the ground as they ran in a loping gait, powerful legs built for climbing and jumping.

Silas's blood turned to ice as he raised his blaster, ready to face the nightmarish creatures. The night, already thick with fear, grew darker still as the Baboan closed in.

It was a pack of black-furred primates, their white eyes glaring like ghostly orbs in the darkness, that attacked the running man from behind. Silas fired a couple of shots into the throng, knocking a few of them back. But it was too dark, and there were too many. The man's screams were brief, cutting off with a sickening abruptness as the pack overwhelmed him.

Then several of the Baboans turned their attention to Silas. He tried to remain as still as possible, hoping to evade their uncanny sense of hearing, but it was futile. They had already locked onto him and were advancing rapidly. He squeezed off a few more shots before turning to run back toward the transport.

The back door of the transport suddenly rolled up, and Darin was there with his arm outstretched as the vehicle started moving forward. "Grab my hand!" Darin shouted.

Silas sprinted, trying to gain ground on the transport as it picked up speed, while also putting distance between himself and the crazed Baboans. He was almost there when he felt one of the beasts nipping at his heels. In a desperate lunge, he grabbed onto Darin's arm just as a blaster shot whizzed by his ear. He turned to see the creature drop dead from a shot that hit it between the eyes.

"You're welcome," Ridley said, helping pull him into the transport.

"It's not over yet!" Darin warned. "You better step on it, Mishka!"

Behind them, the rest of the pack had joined the chase and were gaining ground. Mishka pushed the transport into overdrive. Crazed howls rose from the beasts as the vehicle started to pull away. At the last moment, a trio of the creatures leaped onto the roof with a heavy thud that caved the cabin inward.

"Close the door!" Silas shouted as he climbed over the rear seat, scampering to the passenger's seat and pressing the button to open the side door.

"What do you think you're doing?" Mishka yelled as Silas started climbing out onto the door sill. "Get back in here!"

"Just try to hold it steady for a minute," Silas replied.

His first shot went wide as the transport hit a large rock, causing it to jolt. "What part about keeping it steady did you not understand?" Silas shouted.

Mishka grunted, focusing on the terrain ahead. "This is why I don't like men!" she mumbled under her breath.

Silas's second shot found its mark, sending the closest Baboan tumbling backward into another, knocking both from the roof. The third creature, however, launched itself at Silas, grabbing his arm in a vice-like grip before he could fire again.

He cried out as the monster's teeth sank into his arm, causing him to drop his weapon. As it clattered to the ground, he reached desperately with his other hand for the ionic blade tied to his hip, balancing precariously on the edge of the door.

His fingers brushed the hilt of the blade just as the transport jostled again. The movement caused the Baboan to slide forward, releasing its grip on Silas and scrabbling for purchase.

"Hit the brakes!" Silas shouted.

Mishka responded instantly, slamming the brakes and sending the Baboan hurtling over the front of the vehicle. Silas was whipped backward into the cab. The heavy thud of the Baboan hitting the ground was followed by the transport lurching forward, bouncing over the beast.

Within minutes, they had put enough distance between themselves and the Baboans that the pack gave up the chase.

Mishka glanced over at Silas, who was slumped forward in his seat, cradling his wounded arm. "Are you okay?" she asked, her voice trembling with worry.

Silas turned his head slowly, his face pale and his eyes glazed with pain. "I'm not feeling too hot," he muttered, before his eyes rolled back and he slumped further into his seat.

CHAPTER 38

The voice echoed faintly through the haze of pain and confusion that enveloped him. "Stay with me, Silas," it murmured, distant yet urgent, as if calling from another realm. It promised relief, a respite from the torment he endured.

When the convulsions subsided, he tentatively peeled open his eyes. A thunderstorm pounded inside his skull, each heartbeat a hammer blow. He attempted to move, to quiet the tempest within, but the mere effort sent shards of agony coursing through his body.

His gaze found Mishka, her face etched with concern. "You'll be alright," she assured him, though uncertainty lingered in her eyes. "We'll stop the bleeding and get you patched up."

Blood cascaded from the wound where the Baboan's teeth had torn away flesh, and Silas cradled his arm protectively, fearing the worst. Aldin, quickly grabbed a medical kit from the transport's rear. She applied a neurotoxin spray, and Silas winced as dark, viscous slime oozed from the injury.

Mishka watched in horrified fascination as the black ichor slithered away, vanishing into the cabin's recesses.

"That should ease the pain," Aldin said in a strained voice. She applied a green liquid that congealed into a protective film over the wound, staunching the flow of blood. After wrapping it in sterile cloth, she leaned back, "That should hold until we reach the facility."

"Thank you," Silas managed weakly before exhaustion claimed him, his eyelids fluttering shut.

Rest, big guy, Mishka thought, casting a wary glance at the surrounding darkness. *I'm sure this is far from over.*

***

Elizabeth, a petite woman with intense eyes and a perpetually furrowed brow, adjusted her stance as she monitored readings on a nearby screen, while a number of scientists hurried between workstations behind her.

"We're running out of time," she muttered.

Chang, a wiry man with a mop of unruly hair, glanced over from the adjacent workstation. "The filtration system is compromised. I'm seeing traces of the virus in the air samples."

Elizabeth's fingers flew across the keyboard, pulling up diagnostic charts and environmental scans. "How did this happen?"

Chang shook his head grimly. "I don't know. The containment protocols should have held."

As they debated the implications, Ramirez, a no-nonsense scientist with a steely demeanor, approached with a tablet in hand. "We've lost another specimen in Tank Seven."

Elizabeth's heart sank as she processed the news. Tank Seven housed their Spiraled Octopod specimen, a creature crucial to their research on bio-adaptive defenses. She hurried over to the tank urgently.

The tank lay shattered, water and shards of glass strewn across the floor. Amidst the wreckage lay the mangled remains of the Octopod, its once vibrant form now a grotesque mass of torn flesh and exposed scales. Next to it lay the body of Mills, his face frozen in an expression of horror.

Ramirez kneeled beside the fallen scientist and checked for signs of life, knowing that the venom from the Octopod was nearly one hundred percent fatal. "He must've been checking on the Octopod when it happened."

Elizabeth swallowed hard, trying to calm herself against the panic rising quickly inside her. "We need to contain this before it spreads further."

Chang gestured to the monitors displaying the frantic movements of the various species in their tanks. "The specimens are reacting. If they breach containment—"

"We'll have a full-blown disaster on our hands," Ramirez finished grimly.

Just then, alarms blared overhead, signaling a breach in the outer corridors. The floor beneath them trembled as the facility shook violently.

"We're out of time," Elizabeth declared. "Initiate emergency lock-down procedures. We have to prevent these creatures from escaping."

Chang and Ramirez darted between consoles, fingers flying over keyboards as they activated security protocols.

As they worked feverishly, the infant Rhedocin in Tank Eight suddenly thrashed violently, its massive form slamming against the reinforced glass with alarming force. Across the lab, the other specimens displayed the same behavior, their bodies pummeling against their enclosures.

"We need to move," Elizabeth urged, glancing towards the exit. "Now!"

Chang and Ramirez exchanged a tense look before

nodding in unison. With one last glance at the shattered tank and the fallen Octopod, their dead comrade laying nearby, they hurried towards the door, Elizabeth leading the way.

The lab fell into an eerie silence, broken only by the relentless pounding of the Rhedocin against its enclosure. Outside, the facility trembled under the assault of the sea creatures.

***

"Do you want me to take over driving?" Ridley's voice broke the silence, concern evident in her tone. "You look exhausted."

Mishka glanced back, seeing Aldin nestled in Ridley's lap, a pang of envy flickering within her once more. She swallowed hard, masking her emotions. "No, I m fine. We're almost there anyway," she replied tersely, pushing forward.

As dawn painted the horizon in hues of hope, Mishka finally approached the colossal barrier that marked their destination. The glass wall, a monolithic divider rising hundreds of feet high, stood as a stark testament to their world's shattered beauty.

"It's quite something, isn't it?" Silas murmured softly.

Mishka nodded silently, her thoughts elsewhere. "How are you holding up?" she asked him.

"Better, thanks."

"Are we here?" Aldin asked.

"Yes," Mishka replied.

Aldin felt Ridley tense behind her and pivoted in her lap, worry etched on her features. "What's wrong?"

Ridley withdrew into herself, a defensive gesture Mishka knew all too well. "I just... don't like this place," she finally admitted, her voice barely above a whisper.

"But this place is awesome! What's not to like?"

Ridley snapped back, "It gives me the creeps! Okay?"

She's afraid! Aldin thought. *And I was stupid enough to push the issue. Great going, Aldin!*

Aldin's heart sank. "I'm sorry," she murmured, trying to draw Ridley close again. "I didn't mean to upset you."

Ridley's embrace lacked its usual warmth. She grunted softly, arms still around Aldin, but the distance between them was palpable. Aldin cursed the clumsiness of her own tongue, regretting her momentary lapse of judgment that had made Ridley feel uneasy.

Mishka guided the transport cautiously toward the colossal glass barrier, the structure looming like a monolith against the turbulent sky. With a tense breath, she punched in the access code, the console blinking to life. The communication channel crackled to existence, a voice cutting through the uncertainty.

"This is Command One. Please state your purpose," came a terse command.

Silas replied, "Command One, this is Outpost Three. We've reached the tunnel entrance."

"Roger that, Outpost Three. Emergency protocols are in effect. Proceed with extreme caution," the voice warned.

Moments later, a section of the glass wall slid open, revealing the dark maw of the tunnel leading into the Seascape. Ridley shrank further into herself, eyes fixed on the abyss beyond. It wasn't just the proximity to the water that unsettled her; it was the suffocating grip of claustrophobia that tightened around her throat every second they ventured further into the secure passage.

A sudden boom shattered the tense silence, the ground trembling beneath them. Another blast followed, nearly tipping the transport over. Water cascaded down the glass, a relentless assault on their fragile barrier.

"What's happening?" Ridley's voice cracked.

Aldin's replied, "Could be underwater volcanic activity?"

"Will the wall hold?" Ridley's desperate question hung in the air.

Silas's responded resolutely, "This wall has stood strong for a thousand years. It was built to withstand anything."

Mishka interjected, "I doubt the Architects foresaw this savage apocalypse when they were building it."

An emergency signal blared, piercing their ears, followed by fragmented communication from Command One, drowned out by static and urgency.

Another deluge of water hammered down, accompanied by a sickening crack.

"We need to get to the tunnel exit now!" Silas barked.

Mishka floored the transport, hurtling toward the tunnel's opening just as it began to seal shut. They barreled through, the glass fracturing behind them.

Ahead, the cause of the chaos awaited. The Rhedocin, a colossal sea predator twisted by the same deadly organism, slammed repeatedly into the barrier, surrounded by a frenzied swarm of smaller creatures.

The Rhedocin's massive form turned toward them, and the smaller sea beasts followed suit, hurtling toward the tunnel entrance. The impact sent cracks spider webbing through the glass.

"Go faster!" Silas shouted over the roar of the assault.

Mishka pushed the transport to its limits, racing toward safety. Behind them, the tunnel buckled under the relentless assault of savage sea life.

"We're not gonna make it!" Darin's panicked voice echoed from the rear.

Silas's command cut through the chaos. "Press the green

button on the console!"

Mishka's fingers found the button under its clear cover. She slammed it, and the transport surged into overdrive, hurtling forward just as the tunnel entrance began to collapse.

They burst into the primary parking area, Mishka struggling to regain control. The transport skidded dangerously, spinning out of her grip. The impact threw them all against the cabin walls.

Silence engulfed the cabin, broken only by the group's heavy breathing. Slowly, Silas spoke, "Is everyone alright?"

Mishka was the first to respond, her voice shaky. "Yeah, I'm okay."

Ridley's voice trembled slightly, but she managed, "We're okay."

The silence from Darin spoke volumes. Aldin peered over the seat and cried, "No!"

The impact had sent Darin flying into the wench with such force that he had been impaled through the chest by one of the connecting rods before it broke off. Like a broken plaything, he lay stretched out in unnatural angles with the spear sticking out from his body and a fountain of blood bubbling from the end like a fountain.

CHAPTER 39

As chaos outside raged like a tempest, the emergency alarm wailed its ominous warning, and the very structure trembled under the relentless assault of sea creatures. Inside the transport, a heavy silence hung like a shroud.

Suddenly, loud banging on the transport's exterior shattered their silence. Then, a voice cut through the clamor, calling out, "Is everyone okay in there?"

Mishka cautiously cracked open the door, her gaze meeting that of a tall, lanky man in a black security uniform. "Define okay," she replied with a mixture of skepticism and relief.

Silas peered over her shoulder, "Jeron! It's good to see you!"

Jeron's expression was grave, yet urgent. "Silas, I was hoping this was your transport. You're just in time. Evacuations are underway, and there's a ship leaving soon. We have to hurry."

Aldin's eyes grew wide. "What's happening? Evacuations? Why?"

"I'm not a scientist," Jeron said, "but they're saying the planet's core is going to explode. We don't have much time."

For a moment, the gravity of his words hung in the air, as each one in the transport grappled with the unimaginable reality that their world was on the brink of cataclysm.

"We need to move," Jeron urged, breaking their stunned silence. "Now."

Mishka was the first to step out of the transport, followed by Silas and then Ridley. Aldin hesitated, lingering for a final farewell to Darin's memory.

"I'm sorry about your friend," Jeron said softly as Aldin finally emerged. "But right now, we don't have the luxury of a proper remembrance."

Aldin nodded, tears lingering in her eyes as she joined the others.

Ridley reached out to comfort Aldin. "This isn't your fault. Don't blame yourself. It was an accident."

Jeron interjected, "Where's Jensen, by the way?"

Silas's response was grim. "He didn't make it."

Jeron was silent for a second, before he said matter-of-factly, "Well, I don't think many people will be mourning his loss."

A piercing screech echoed through the structure, and the ground beneath them trembled violently. The sound was accompanied by the panicked screams of people scrambling for safety.

"That felt like the support trusses!" Silas exclaimed. "The creatures must be trying to breach the facility from below!"

They found themselves swept up in a chaotic rush toward the primary structure's entrance. In the panic, Ridley was knocked back, her head colliding with the transport she had narrowly avoided moments earlier.

"Watch it!" Silas shouted at the young man responsible, his words drowned out by the roar of the crowd surging forward.

Aldin hurried to Ridley's side. "Are you okay?"

Ridley nodded in response, and they pressed on through the throng, their steps quickened by the looming shadow of the Rhedocin passing ominously beneath them.

The group reached the entrance only to have it slam shut before their eyes. On the other side stood the man who had inadvertently pushed Ridley.

"Let us in!" Silas pounded on the glass, desperately.

The man hesitated, then turned and fled down the corridor, consumed with terror.

"Follow me!" Jeron said as he led them to a secured door in a remote corner of the parking structure. He quickly swiped his security badge across a panel. The door clicked open, revealing a long hallway beyond.

"This way," Jeron urged as they hurried down the corridor, the incessant blare of alarms ringing in their ears.

The corridor's side panel offered a grim view of sea creatures charging toward them, slamming into the transparent barrier with the force of a plasma cannon.

A faint crack crept through the glass, barely audible over the din of alarms. Silas's eyes widened. "If that glass gives way with us here, we're done for!"

Jeron sprinted ahead, leading them through a sharp left turn into an open doorway. He swiftly sealed the opening behind them with a press of a button, then typed commands into a nearby terminal.

"That should buy us some time," Jeron explained breathlessly. "The interior of this facility is pressurized. If the outer corridors breach, we won't drown—at least not immediately."

"Well, that's comforting," Mishka said. "How much further to the ship?"

"Not far," Jeron replied. "The problem is that we have to

go through the center of the lab."

"What's so bad about that?" Aldin asked.

"You'll see" Jeron said.

After using his key-card again, Jeron led them through a door to their right and down a long hall, stopping short of the large entrance at the end. He turned to them and whispered, "Be very quiet and don't make any sudden moves. We'll need to move slowly."

Aldin peaked around Jeron and saw the main lab, a sprawling room divided into numerous workstations. Embedded into each wall were several glass tanks with specimens inside them, while the middle of the lab held a large open tank that contained an infant Rhedocin. All the creatures remained motionless, as if caught in suspended animation.

"How come they're not moving?" Aldin whispered.

Jeron replied, "Somehow, the test subjects were exposed to the virus, probably through the filtration system. They're dormant right now because of the lack of a food source. That changes in a hurry if they realize we're here."

Aldin looked again and saw that one of the tanks in the far corner was empty. Broken glass and puddles of water still dotted the floor. Her heart broke when she saw amidst the debris a mound of mangled animal flesh that, at one time, resembled a Spiraled Octopod. Large patches of scales were missing, and black ichor still seeped from the rotting flesh that once held them. Then she saw the body lying face down next to it and gasped.

It wasn't very loud, but it was enough. Almost immediately, the Rhedocin began thrashing about wildly, splashing water over the edge of the tank like a mini tidal wave. Within seconds, the rest of the specimens followed suit, throwing themselves at their glass enclosures in a maddening frenzy.

At that moment, the exit door on the opposite side of the lab seemed like a million miles away.

"We're going to have to make a run for it," Silas stated. "It's the only chance we have. Just be careful not to slip. If you go down, you may not get back up."

Aldin gulped, "I'm not exactly the most agile person here."

Ridley grabbed her hand, "Just stay with me. I won't let anything happen to you."

Mishka felt another little tug at her heart and looked away.

"I'll go first and draw their attention," Silas said.

He took a deep breath and readied his blaster rifle. Then he sprinted into the lab, firing at the Rhedocin as it thrashed about to get at him. The shots bounced effortlessly off its thick scales, but he succeeded in distracting the beast.

Ridley led Aldin quickly around the other side of the tank, avoiding the creature's gaze, and met him at the rear door.

Mishka attempted to follow suit, but slipped halfway there and had to grab onto the edge of one of the workstations to avoid falling. The noise was enough to draw the creature's focus, and it immediately shot one of its tentacles toward her. She barely escaped being impaled by its sharp barb as she regained her balance and rushed the rest of the way forward.

Jeron had taken advantage of Mishka's misstep and joined her by the others.

"Now what?" she asked, as she crouched down to catch her breath.

Jeron replied, "The hangar is just a little way down the hall."

"How many ships are there?" Aldin asked.

"We have a couple of shuttles, plus a handful of cargo ships. All the equipment on-board should be sufficient to help us recolonize."

Aldin still couldn't get over that thought. *Recolonize! It sounds like the last desperate act of a dying race.* It didn't just mean starting over. It meant global extinction had occurred.

CHAPTER 40

The alarm that had been blaring intermittently went silent for a moment to allow for an all too familiar warning to broadcast: 'All personnel, immediate evacuations are underway. Proceed to the nearest shuttle as quickly as possible.'

"Time to go!" Jeron said. He led them through the door, leaving the madness in the lab behind.

"Be careful," Silas said as he pointed to another empty containment unit on the opposite wall. Broken glass and water covered the floor, but its previous occupant wasn't among the debris.

As they ran down the hall, Aldin heard a slight whimpering and stopped.

"What are you doing?" Ridley asked.

"I heard something," Aldin replied.

"Whatever it was, we don't have time. We need to get out of here now!"

But Aldin was already heading back down the hall, stopping at the opening to a small room.

Ridley threw her arms in the air, "Why do I even bother?"

When she caught up to Aldin, she found her standing

silent in the doorway of a small supply closet afraid to move. Ridley started to say something but Aldin put her finger to her mouth to silence her.

The lights were flickering off and on, as if in the throes of an electrical seizure. Streaks of lightning arced back and forth between the walls and ceiling, centering on the serpentine figure of the Ramora as it feasted on the body of a young child.

This thing shouldn't be alive without water! Aldin thought. Then she saw the patches of rotting flesh staggering along its tail and up into its torso and she realized it wasn't.

The creature suddenly spun around, lifting itself so that it towered over the two women, its hood flared out as it prepared to attack.

Ridley quickly drew her laser pistol and fired a shot, but it bounced away harmlessly. She desperately fired a barrage of shots, trying to hit the thing in its head to no avail. The energy crackling in the surrounding air acted as a shield, protecting it from her attack.

The Ramora reared back and then lunged forward, its long jaws snapping wildly. Ridley and Aldin staggered backward to avoid the attack.

The door to the room suddenly crashed down, trapping the creature inside. A loud bang echoed against the steel as the creature slammed into it on the other side, followed by the eruption of a series of high-pitched squeals. Then tiny sparks of electricity began splintering out from around the doorway.

They were surprised to see Jeron standing there with his key card in his hand.

"If you ladies are done admiring the local wildlife, then I'd suggest we get out of here immediately," he said. "We can't have you two dying before we even get off this rock, can we?"

Ridley grabbed Aldin's hand and gave it a little squeeze as they followed Jeron down the hall. Aldin turned toward her with a questioning look regarding his peculiar statement.

A tremendous rumble tore through the complex a moment later as they joined the others just outside the door to the hangar. The structure began to twist and rock back and forth violently, throwing them all to the floor.

Jeron scrambled to his knees and reached up with his key-card once more to open the large double doors to the hangar. Screams echoed throughout the enormous expanse, as people rushed about frantically.

Another warning blared overhead, "All personnel, final evacuations are underway."

The structure groaned loudly to echo the urgency of the announcement. As if to further amplify the terror of the moment, water began seeping in from cracks throughout the perimeter of the hangar.

"This way!" Jeron shouted as he led them toward the closest shuttle.

An all too familiar scene replayed itself as they neared the ship, only to have the door close tight before they could reach its sanctuary, with the same man looking on in terror as it slammed shut. The moment proved ironic when a pair of gigantic tentacles suddenly shot through the floor of the hangar and wrapped tightly around the shuttle. A loud screech of twisted metal reverberated throughout as the sea creature dragged the craft to its watery grave.

A tidal wave of water immediately flooded through the hangar, giving the group seconds to react. As one, they all raced to the nearest cargo ship and climbed in, closing the door an instant before the water overtook them.

Everyone sat in stunned silence for a moment before

Mishka said to Jeron, "I don't suppose you know how to fly this thing?"

Jeron replied, "Uh, no. Sorry."

"Don't worry," Silas said. "I do."

Mishka smiled at Silas, "Why am I not surprised?"

As Silas jumped into the pilot's seat, he flipped a few switches and the engines immediately roared to life. He pressed a button on the front console to open the front viewport and was horrified to see the remaining shuttle burst into flames after it took off, crashing into the domed ceiling before it was completely open. A second later, it exploded into a giant fireball.

The flooding water quickly extinguished the flames, but the debris from the exploded craft became underwater missiles bent on destroying anything in their paths.

"Hold on!" he shouted as he maneuvered the bulky cargo ship upward, dodging from side to side to avoid pieces of the debris flying toward them.

A horde of creatures immediately rose from the depths, swimming erratically on broken fins to feast upon the bodies of those Terrans unlucky enough to escape the onslaught. In a matter of seconds, the surrounding sea turned blood red.

Silas steered the craft upward, toward the portal opening in the dome, only to realize that the second shuttle had damaged its operation when it exploded, leaving it stuck only part-way open. "This is going to be a tight squeeze!" he said as they neared the top.

At the last moment, another long tentacle snaked up from the depths toward them. A quick maneuver by Silas avoided the creature's attack, but it put the ship at a precarious angle as they sought to escape the watery madness. He held the steering controls tightly as he braced for impact, then guided the ship carefully through the small portal.

Aldin buried her head in Ridley's chest as the ship scraped the edge of the portal, cringing at the sound of metal against metal, while Mishka and Jeron braced themselves against the side of the craft.

When the ship began to rock back and forth, each one feared that they had finally run out of luck. There would be no miraculous escape for them this time.

CHAPTER 41

The emptiness of space paled in comparison to the emptiness in Aldin's heart as they fled their planet. Numerous ships splayed out before her of other Terran's who had successfully escaped their dying world brought her little comfort.

If only...?

It was a question that plagued her mind continuously. Sure, she knew that Jensen had tampered with the equipment. She knew that he had been out to get her from day one. And she knew that he was relentless in his pursuits. Still, she felt like she could've done something to avert this clandestine moment. Maybe if she had gone through her safety protocols more thoroughly during the experiment? Or if she had taken better care of herself and not worn herself out? *Then, maybe, none of this would've happened?*

"Stop it," Ridley said.

Aldin replied, "I'm not doing anything."

"Yes, you are."

"But—"

"I mean it."

Aldin opened her mouth for a brief second and then closed it again, knowing her words would fall on deaf ears. Instead, she just sat quietly, trying her best to be brave.

Jeron sat opposite them on a little bench seat, watching the entire exchange curiously.

"Can you open the rear-view panel?" Mishka asked Silas.

Before he could respond, the instrument panel started blaring an alarm.

"What's going on?" Ridley asked.

Silas scanned the instrument for a moment. "It's the radiation alarm! They're off the charts!"

"That can only mean one thing!" Aldin said.

Silas pressed the button to open the rear-view panel, allowing them a final view of their lost world. A collective gasp rose from the group as they looked at their planet, glowing a fiery orange. The end had begun.

"How long before it explodes completely?" Mishka asked.

Silas replied, "With these readings, I'd say not long at all."

"We're too close!" Aldin cried. "We'll be incinerated! Can this thing make the jump to light speed?"

"I'm running system diagnostics now," Silas said. "We took a little damage escaping the lab, but I think it'll hold."

"Let's hope so" Ridley said.

"We should be okay," Jeron said. "I've ridden in cargo ships like this a couple of times. They're built to withstand just about everything."

"Does that include an exploding planet?" Mishka asked.

Jeron raised an eyebrow, but remained silent.

"We have a problem," Silas suddenly said.

"Those aren't the words we want to hear right now," Ridley shot back.

Silas continued, "The quantum generator is off-line. We can't make the jump to light speed without it."

"The relay coupling must've gotten disconnected," Jeron said as he scampered toward the back of the ship. "I'll see if I can reroute the circuit."

Ridley eyed him suspiciously, "You seem to know a lot about this ship."

Jeron replied, "A little bit. I learned a thing or two from an uncle of mine."

"Anyone we'd know?"

Jeron didn't answer as he began to pry one of the side panels away from the side of the rear cabin.

Then they saw it happen—a silent moment stretched out in slow motion like a dream sequence. Terran had finally lost its battle to live and exploded in a fireball, fueled by the rage and fury of the undead.

A second later, the sound caught up with the blast, sending a shock wave in all directions that would surely be heard even in the farthest reaches of the universe.

"Get us out of here, Silas!" Ridley urged.

Silas immediately hit the thrusters, and the ship sped forward. "We have to be careful not to burn too much fuel," he said, "or we'll be dead out here floating in space."

Ridley replied, "If we don't get far enough away from the blast, we'll be dead, anyway."

He called back to Jeron, "How are we doing with that generator?"

"Almost there," Jeron shouted. "Just a few seconds more."

"I'm not sure we have seconds!" Silas shouted as the first shock wave almost sent the ship into a spin. His quick reaction saved them, for the moment

Then a barrage of meteors—fragments of their lost world—pummeled the ship, knocking it back and forth. The force sent Ridley and Aldin crashing into a large equipment locker, while Mishka was pinned against the side of the ship by a portable cryo-chamber.

"Jeron!?" Silas shouted.

Jeron was holding on tightly to the edge of the panel as the ship bounced around. Finally, he pressed the last wire in place to reroute the power to the quantum generator. A steady whirl sounded as the generator came to life. "We're good!" he said. "Hit it!"

Silas immediately pressed the button, sending them shooting through a swirling tunnel of light particles. A second later, they came to a stop near a planet on the other side of the universe; strangers in a foreign galaxy, homeless and alone.

After recovering from being tossed about, they all sat there in stunned silence until something heavy crashed against the side of the ship.

"What was that?" Mishka said.

Silas looked through the view-port and saw a large number of meteorites floating nearby, "It looks like a few meteor fragments were caught in the ship's wake and followed us through the light speed portal."

He quickly maneuvered the ship through the debris and put the ship on standby, allowing the impromptu meteor cluster to pass them and giving them a chance to plot their next course of action. As he turned around in his seat and glanced around the cabin, the faces of those that had escaped the apocalypse with him spoke volumes of loss and heartache. The emptiness radiating from each one was nearly suffocating. Pushing forward was not going to be easy. *But if anyone can pull through this,* Silas thought, *it's them.*

Aldin was the first to speak, her voice soft and timid, "Now what?"

Silas pressed a few buttons on the console and a moment later numerous graphs materialized on the display screen. "Atmospheric readings of that nearby planet indicate that it's nearly identical to that of Terran's."

"You mean, what Terran's used to be," Aldin said sadly.

Her statement caused Silas to pause. This was going to be difficult, indeed. But they had no other choice. He kept pouring through the readings. "A detailed scan of the planet's surface clearly shows that it's inhabited."

"Yeah, but with what?" Mishka said.

"Well, according to the data, they're advanced enough to fabricate living structures."

"That hardly makes them intelligent, though," Ridley stated.

"Fair enough" Silas replied.

While they contemplated their next move, watching as the meteors grew closer to the mystery planet and its gravitational pull, Jeron took the opportunity to seclude himself in the back corner of the cabin. He pulled a small tablet from his pocket and turned it on. The light chirp that sounded caused him to look around nervously, but no one heard him. After typing a few notes, he turned the device off and slipped it back into his pocket, where it clinked softly against a small vial containing a sample of the deadly organism. *Don't worry, Uncle,* he thought to himself, *I'll see that your work goes on.*

The end

BOOK TWO PREVIEW

Savage Apocalypse
Book Two:
The Howl Of The Dead

By Scott Dokey

CHAPTER 1

Tommy Patterson always looked forward to Friday nights. It was a chance to finally spend some quality time alone with his dad. And he relished every moment of it. Sometimes it was watching their favorite movie together with a tub of popcorn between them on the couch. Other times, they played a board game or two. But this Friday night was the one he looked forward to the most; when they took their rods and reels to the small lake at the edge of the woods and fished for catfish. To a ten-year-old kid, this was like heaven.

At half-past seven, Tommy rushed out to the garage, where his dad, William, had just finished restringing the line on one of his reels. "Is it time, yet?" he asked anxiously.

William looked up at the evening sky for a second, scrutinizing the angle of the setting sun, and then down at his far-too-eager son with a soft smile, "Almost. It's still a little too light out right now. Give it a few more minutes and then we'll be ready to go."

Tommy nearly stepped on his bottom lip as he stood there, pouting.

"Hey," William said. "Don't go getting all upset like that. The fish won't bite if you're upset."

"You're joking, right? I'm pretty sure my feelings have nothing to do with fishing."

William snickered. "Sure, they do. Remember, animals can sense emotion; even fish."

"Yeah, you've told me before. I just don't get how it works."

William ruffled Tommy's hair and chuckled, "Don't worry about it too much. What do I always tell you?"

Tommy replied, "Don't sweat the small stuff."

"And…?"

"It's all small stuff."

William smiled back at his son, suddenly realizing how much he had grown recently. "Just try to remember that," he said. "Life will be much easier. Now help me load the rest of the gear into the truck and we'll be ready to go."

Tommy grabbed his dad's tackle box and lifted it onto the open tailgate. When he turned around to get his own, smaller tackle box, he was annoyed to see his little sister, Kate, standing there holding her pink Barbie fishing pole in her hands. "What are you doing here?" he asked, his voice clearly irritated at her presence. This was supposed to be their special time alone, just him and his dad, and now his sniveling sister was trying to barge in.

Kate replied matter-of-factly, "I'm going fishing with you?"

Tommy turned around so he didn't have to look at her, knowing his temper would probably get the best of him, and then he'd do or say something that would probably get him in trouble and ruin the whole night, or worse. "Dad?" he implored.

William looked at Kate and smiled. *She's so determined to grow up,* he thought. "I'm sorry, Little Lady, but you're not quite old enough to be out so late."

Kate protested, "But I'm almost six years old!"

Tommy replied nastily, "So? I didn't get to go until I was eight."

"Well, that was you. Everybody knows girls are better than boys."

Tommy threw his tackle box into the truck and turned around, his face scrunched up as his eyes burned with anger, "I'll show you who's better than who."

William cut in between them, "Hey, that's enough of that."

Tommy argued, "But she started it?"

"And I'm finishing it," William stated firmly. He then turned to Kate, "Listen, next time we go fishing it'll be during the day so you can go too."

Kate's eyes grew misty for a second from disappointment until she finally gave in, "Promise?"

"I promise."

"Or maybe we can go sometime early in the morning when the frogs are still out?"

Tommy couldn't stop himself when the words quickly slipped off his tongue before he realized what he was doing, and said, "You look like a frog."

Kate stomped her foot and held her finger firmly jabbed in his face, "You take that back!"

When his dad looked at him sternly, he knew that an apology was the only thing that could still save their fishing trip. "Okay," he said. "I'm sorry."

William looked at Kate expectantly. After a moment, she finally said, "Fine. Pology accepted." Then, to show off to Tommy that she was dad's favorite, she went over and gave her dad a big hug in front of him, a wide smirk spread across her lips.

After a minute, William said to her, "Now go in and get ready for bed."

Kate trudged off, still carrying her fishing pole. On her way out of the garage, she looked back at Tommy and stuck her tongue out at him when William wasn't looking, before turning and running into the house.

***

Melinda was sitting on the small swing that ran along the back of the patio, slowly sipping a cup of tea, when William turned the corner. She didn't see him at first, so it gave him a minute to admire her as she sat there, her back against the soft pink glow of the setting sun.

A moment later, she turned to him and smiled, "Are you spying on me, William Patterson?"

"Of course I am—any chance I get."

"I guess that means I better be on my best behavior, then?"

"You better. I'd hate to have to punish you for acting up."

"Oh, really?"

"Yes, really." Then he nuzzled up close to her and softly nibbled on her ear.

Melinda responded with a soft moan, before nudging him away and saying, "Don't you have a fishing trip to get to?"

William smiled, "I'd rather do some other kind of fishing."

"As tempting as that sounds, I think you better get ready to go. You already have a disappointed little girl on your hands. If you blow this off, you're going to have to deal with your son as well. And we both know he doesn't handle disappointment well."

William snickered, "You got that right."

She smiled back at him seductively, "Plus, when you get home, we can always pick up where we left off." After a passionate kiss she pulled away from him, "You better get going before he starts getting antsy."

"One more," he said, and gave her a last, quick peck before he walked back into the house.

***

When William climbed into the driver's seat, he wasn't all that surprised to see King, their four-year-old Golden Retriever, sitting next to Tommy. "And what's this all about?" he asked.

Tommy said matter-of-factly, "King wanted to come too."

"Oh, he did, did he?"

"Yep, he sure did."

In reply, King let out a soft bark that made William chuckle as he scratched behind the dog's ears. "Okay, fine. You can come too. But you better not scare the fish." King barked eagerly in agreement.

William put the keys in the ignition, and a minute later they were pulling out of the driveway. Their neighbor Harvey Stratton, was sitting on his front porch drinking his evening beer. He was an older man in his sixties, who had lost his wife to cancer three years earlier. The alcohol was his attempt at erasing the pain of his suffering.

Harvey waved at them as they pulled away. Tommy gave a small wave back and then said to his dad, "He's a strange old man."

William chuckled, "He's not so bad."

"But he smells bad."

This time William laughed out loud, then said, "You should give the guy a break. He's been through a lot these last few years."

Tommy grew silent for a minute. At his age, he'd never really thought about how much Harvey had dealt with when his wife died. Instantly, he was embarrassed at the way he had acted. "I guess you're right. I'll be nicer to him from now on."

William added, "Plus, you have to admit that his jokes are pretty funny."

Tommy chuckled this time, "Yeah, he is kinda funny."

Then they were out of their neighborhood, heading toward Lake Cahuilla, and what he hoped would one of their best fishing trips ever.

Ten minutes later they reached Cahuilla Park Road, and followed that around the edge of the lake to W Access Road. William pulled the truck over and stopped at a little clearing about forty yards from the water's edge.

Tommy jumped out of the truck before it had had a chance to come to a complete stop. King bounded out after him.

When William joined them at the back of the truck, Tommy was struggling with the tailgate. William reminded him, "Remember, it sticks a little sometimes. You have to push it in while you lift the handle." He then demonstrated the trick and dropped the tailgate down.

It took a couple of trips for them to carry all of their gear down to the bank. Dusk was giving way to night, which prompted William to turn on the battery-operated lantern so they could see what they were doing. A soft yellow glow spread out over the small area.

For all of his eagerness to catch fish, he was still squeamish when it came to baiting his hook with chicken liver. "God, I hate this stuff," he exclaimed.

"I know, pretty gross, huh?" William replied. "But it's the best bait to catch catfish with."

"I just wish it didn't smell so bad."

"What's with that nose of yours? It seems like everything smells bad to you."

"Hey! I can't help it if my nose is sensitive."

"Fair enough. Let's get these lines out there and see if we can hook onto Big Bertha?"

Tommy asked, "That's just a story. She's not real, is she?"

William replied, "Oh, she's real, alright. I saw her once. Must have been nearly five feet long and a hundred pounds."

Tommy was shocked, "Wow! I bet it'd be awesome to hook onto something like that."

William agreed, "I'm sure it would. Maybe tonight's our lucky night?"

William got up from his camping chair after he finished baiting his hook and cast his line out toward the center of the lake. The bait plunked into the water about forty yards out. He let it sink to the bottom and then turned the crank a couple of times to remove any slack. When he was satisfied, he propped the rod up on a y-shaped stick he had pushed into the ground.

Tommy went after him. His effort wasn't as good as his dad's, but was still impressive for a boy his age, landing about ten yards in front of his dad's.

William said, "Nice cast, Tommy."

"But it didn't go out as far as yours."

"It doesn't matter how far it goes out, Tommy. The important thing is to find where the fish are."

King decided at that moment to knock over the bucket filled with bait, sending chicken guts spilling across the ground in a grotesque cascade. Though it seemed like an accident, the sight and scent of the raw meat triggered his instincts, and he immediately lunged for a mouthful.

"King, no!" William's shout pierced the air.

King froze, his ears drooping as he laid down, still chewing his prize. Seeing the look of hurt in his eyes filled William instantly with regret.

Tommy's face turned green at the mess. "Thanks, King,"

he muttered, barely suppressing his urge to vomit.

William sighed, regretting his outburst. "It was an accident," he said, shaking his head. "That tail of his is like a wrecking ball sometimes."

"I know, but it's still gross!" Tommy retorted, looking away from the mess.

"Yeah, but the fish won't mind." William bent down, using his pocket knife to scoop the guts back into the bucket. "Help me clean this up before it starts attracting bugs."

Tommy was about to protest when a faint light streaked across the sky. "Look, Dad, a shooting star."

William looked up, his eyes narrowing. "That's not a shooting star."

"How can you tell?" Tommy asked, puzzled.

"Because it's getting bigger. And it's heading this way."

They both watched as the fiery orb hurtled toward them. William's heart pounded as he realized its trajectory would take it right over the lake and into the surrounding woods.

"We need to get this gear into the truck now!" William said urgently. They began reeling in their lines as fast as they could.

As the meteor streaked over the lake, debris splashed into the water, causing it to hiss and steam. The air grew still, as if a vacuum had enveloped them. A tremendous boom followed as the meteor crashed into the woods, the ground shaking violently beneath their feet.

King barked incessantly at the commotion. William grabbed Tommy and shoved him into the truck, with King leaping in after him.

"We need to check it out," William said tensely. "There might be campers out there."

He backed the truck up and drove around the lake toward the woods. Fortunately, because the heat of the desert summer creates a slow season for the park, they had closed the campsites for renovations.

They reached the entrance to the woods and took a narrow trail just wide enough for his truck to squeeze through. After a quarter mile, they reached the edge of a massive crater, about a hundred yards wide and three feet deep. The meteor had landed in a clearing, minimizing damage to the forest and its inhabitants, but still leaving a trail of destruction. Steam rose from the ground, creating an eerie fog.

William left the engine running and the headlights on, illuminating the area as he got out. "Get the flashlight from the glove box," he instructed Tommy.

The air was thick with smoke and the acrid stench of fire and ash. "Smells like burned hamburgers," Tommy said, covering his nose. King jumped down, immediately burying his nose in his paws.

A strong breeze blew through a moment later, making the odor bearable. William and Tommy pulled their shirts over their noses and walked the crater's perimeter. William's flashlight beam revealed a watermelon-shaped rock at the center, crackling like ice cubes thrown into a hot drink.

"That little rock did all this?" Tommy asked, incredulous.

"It was much bigger before it hit the atmosphere," William explained. "Most of it burned up on the way down."

They climbed down into the crater, moving closer to the rock. The crackling grew louder, followed by a hissing sound like the valve on a pressure cooker opening to release its pent-up steam.

"Don't get too close," William warned.

They were about twenty feet away when King growled, his hackles raised as if a threat were nearby.

"It's okay, Boy," Tommy said.

No sooner had he spoken those words, than the meteor

exploded, sending a shower of rocky shrapnel mixed with a black, oily substance flying. The blast, though not lethal, was powerful enough to send stone fragments tearing at Tommy's face and arms. The flashlight flew from William's hand, and King yelped before he scampered away into the woods.

"King!" Tommy shouted urgently, but the dog had already vanished.

William retrieved the flashlight, checking Tommy for serious injuries. "Are you okay?"

Tommy nodded. "Just a few scratches."

William examined a cut on Tommy's cheek. "We need to get you home and cleaned up."

"But what about King? We can't leave him here."

"He'll be okay. He's probably just scared. He knows the way home."

"I hope you're right," Tommy said reluctantly.

They trudged back to the truck, brushing off clumps of grime and debris. Once inside, William maneuvered out of the woods. As he did so, Tommy peered into the darkness, hoping to glimpse his four-legged friend, fearing that he might never see him again.

CHAPTER 2

Justin's eyes were glued to the screen, his fingers flying over the keyboard as he tried to calculate the trajectory of the meteor that had just crashed. The tension in the control room was palpable; the other four meteors that had been clustered with this one had mercifully disintegrated upon entry into Earth's atmosphere. But this fifth one—larger and much more deadly—had broken through. His heart raced as he imagined the potential damage it could have caused on impact.

He was so engrossed in his work that he didn't notice the subtle shift in the room's atmosphere. Suddenly, the pungent odor of cigarettes and stale coffee assaulted his senses, snapping him out of his concentration. He stiffened, realizing too late that the NEOP director, Dr. Patrick Leonard, was now standing right behind him. The man's presence was oppressive, his breath hot on Justin's neck, as if the weight of his scrutiny alone could alter the course of events displayed on the screen. Justin swallowed hard, the taste of dread mingling with the acrid scent that clung to the air.

"What's the status, Justin?" the Director asked.

Justin replied, "Four of the five objects disintegrated upon entry, sir."

"What about the last one?"

"It looks like it came down somewhere in Southern California."

"Can you narrow down the point of impact?"

Justin slid his chair over a few inches and turned to another monitor, and began typing rapidly. "I'm pulling up satellite imagery right now."

After a few seconds, an image filled the screen. He zoomed in tight and peered closely at the screen. "It looks like it went down in a town called La Quinta. The crash happened in a wooded area surrounding Lake Cahuilla."

Dr. Leonard turned his stocky body around quickly and addressed the six other technicians manning stations of their own, "I want a field team mobilized within the hour."

The technicians began feverishly working at their keyboards, and within seconds, the room was filled with a myriad of voices. After a few minutes, Darcey, a young intern fresh out of Berkley, spoke up, "A team is gathering at Ames shortly."

Dr. Leonard said, "Good. Who's heading the team?"

Darcey replied, "Samuel Greenburg."

The Director nodded his approval. Greenburg was a good man in his book. A little intense at times, but he certainly knew his stuff. They had even been roommates for a semester at Caltech. Then, after graduation, he had remained in California, getting a job as a research scientist at NASA's Ames research facility. Now, ten years later, he was head of the Space Biosciences Division.

Leonard was a little disappointed he hadn't stayed in contact with Samuel, especially after Samuel's wife had died in a car accident a few years ago.

"What's their ETA for arrival at the crash site?" he asked.

Darcey replied, "Their plane is currently on standby. It's a thirty-five-minute flight to Palm Springs International, and from there a forty-minute drive to the crash site."

"Good. Tell me when they're ready to be briefed."

"Will do," Darcey stated and then focused her attention back to her computer terminal.

Dr. Leonard turned back around to Justin, "Can you zoom in closer?"

Justin replied, "Sure," and hit a couple of keys so that the image zoomed tighter until they could make out a truck pulling up to the site. The picture was filled with smoke, but they could make out a man and a boy getting out of the truck and walk toward the center of the crash, with a dog trotting beside them.

The Director muttered, "Christ! I hope they don't do anything stupid."

The words had no sooner left his lips, when they watched the meteor explode on the screen, sending the man and boy reeling backward.

"Shit!" Leonard cried. "That can't be good"

He turned back to Darcey, "Call Samuel back. Tell him he needs to step on it."

He turned back to the screen just in time to see the truck pulling out of the area. "See if you can track that vehicle, Justin."

Justin replied, "I'm on it," and began feverishly typing at his keyboard.

For a quick second, as the Director looked closely at the satellite image of the crash scene, he thought he saw something in the woods. But then it was gone.

"I have a bad feeling about this," he mumbled to himself.

***

The fact that Samuel was a chronic insomniac was a blessing in disguise when the phone rang at eleven o'clock. The reason always hovered around thoughts of his wife. This night was no different, and he was silently grateful for the distraction.

At first, he thought about not answering it. When he was in this kind of mood the last thing, he wanted was human contact of any kind. Then the ringing stopped and he breathed a soft sigh of relief. That didn't last long, because a few seconds later, his phone started ringing again.

"Well, at least they're persistent," he muttered as he reached over and grabbed his cell phone off the night stand next to his bed. A quick look at the source of the call caused him to sit up quickly. He knew instantly that something big was going down.

He pressed the accept button on to connect the call and tentatively said, "Hello."

Darcey answered, "Dr. Greenburg?"

"Yes?"

"There is a serious situation that's come up. We need you to gather a team and assemble at the Ames main conference room in thirty minutes. You will be briefed upon arrival." Then the phone went dead.

An exasperated huff issued from Samuel, "You gotta love NASA's directness."

He scrolled through the contact list on his phone quickly, selecting three colleagues that would provide him with the broadest range of skills, given the fact that he didn't have a clue what their actual mission was.

***

The first name he thought of was Andrea Melborne, one of the leading scientists in the Astro-biology Division. She was a spunky woman in her late thirties, whom he had had the pleasure of working with on a number of projects. Her vast knowledge would prove to be invaluable. Plus, there had been a little bit of a spark between them. His fear of intimacy with another woman after his wife's death had prevented him from acting on it, something he still regretted to this day.

Samuel's thumb hesitating over Andrea's number before he pressed it. The phone rang a few times, each ring amplifying his anxiety, until she answered in a groggy voice.

"Hello?"

"Andrea? It's Samuel," he said, his voice wavering slightly. "I'm sorry to call so late, but we have an urgent situation. I just got a call from the NEOP division and they want me to get a group together and meet at the Ames main conference room in thirty minutes. Of course, the first person I thought of was you."

Andrea yawned. "You do realize it's eleven at night, right?"

"Yes, I'm aware. Believe me, I'm not happy about this either."

"What's going on? Is everything okay?"

Samuel took a deep breath, trying to steady his racing heart. It had been a long time since he'd talked to Andrea, yet his stomach was still filled with butterflies, as if he were a kid back in high school. "I don't have all the details yet, just that they said it's serious. We need your expertise, Andrea."

"And my expertise is all you need, Sam?"

Samuel was silent. The conversation had turned precisely the way he hadn't wanted it to go and now he was tongue-tied.

Andrea's tone shifted, as if she could sense Samuel's uneasiness on the other end. "Alright, give me ten minutes to get ready. I'll be there."

"Thanks, Andrea. I knew I could count on you."

"You realize you owe me big time for this, Samuel? You know that, right? I expect to be paid back for this in the very near future."

As he hung up, Samuel felt a slight sense of relief knowing Andrea was on board.

***

Samuel dialed Kelvin Knepler's number next, his hand shaking slightly. Even though Kelvin could be a hot-head at times, there wasn't a better environmental scientist alive. The phone rang several times before a gruff voice answered.

"Who the hell is calling at this hour?"

"Kelvin, it's Samuel," he said, trying to keep his voice steady. "We have a situation. I need you at Ames main conference room in thirty minutes."

Kelvin groaned, his frustration evident through the phone. "Do you have any idea what time it is? This better be important."

"It is," Samuel insisted, his voice urgent. "NEOP called. It's something big, and I need your environmental expertise. Please, Kelvin."

Kelvin sighed heavily. "You know I hate being dragged out of bed for these things, Samuel."

"I know, but I wouldn't ask if it wasn't critical. You're the best at what you do, Kelvin," Samuel pleaded, his desperation evident in his voice.

There was a pause before Kelvin spoke again, a clearly agitated tone in his voice. "Fine, I'll be there. But this better be worth it."

"Thanks, Kelvin. We'll meet at the Ames main conference room in thirty minutes," Samuel said in relief.

"Yeah, yeah. See you soon," Kelvin replied, hanging up with a grumble.

***

Last on the list was Simon Wright. Formerly a brilliant neurobiologist, Simon had shifted his passion to the camera and had become quite an accomplished videographer. His camera skills would come in handy as they documented their findings, whatever they may be. Plus, he was also Samuel's best friend.

Simon picked up almost immediately, answering in his usual cheerful voice.

"Sam! What's up, buddy?"

"Hey, Simon," Samuel said, trying to mask the urgency in his voice. "I need your help. We have an urgent mission. Can you be at Ames main conference room in thirty minutes?"

"Wow, middle-of-the-night call, huh? Must be serious," Simon replied, his tone turning more serious.

"It is," Samuel confirmed, his voice wavering. "NEOP called, and we need to document whatever we find. Your camera skills are essential."

Simon chuckled, trying to lighten the mood. "You know I love a good adventure. I'm in. Anything else I need to know?"

"Not yet. I know as much as you do," Samuel replied. "We'll be briefed when we get there. Just bring your gear. I really need you on this one, Simon."

"Got it. See you in thirty, Sam," Simon said.

"Thanks, Simon. You're a lifesaver."

"Always here for you, buddy. See you soon."

***

As he hung up, Samuel took a deep breath, feeling a sense of calm amidst the chaos. His team had come together a little better than anticipated. He hoped it would stay that way.

Quickly, he jumped into the shower and got ready for what he knew was going to be a long night. After throwing on some clothes and grabbing a slice of cold pizza from the fridge, he was out the door and on his way.

The drive to the facility was almost exactly fifteen minutes, giving his mind a chance to make up all sorts of weird scenarios that he was about to walk into. An urgent call late at night usually signaled either an approaching disaster, or that one had already happened, and he certainly hoped that the latter wasn't the case.

Thirty minutes later he was walking down the hall, heading toward the Ames main conference room. When he entered the room, he saw that Kelvin and Simon were already there. Kelvin glared at him for a moment, while Simon merely nodded and went back to sipping his cup of coffee.

Samuel took a seat next to Simon at the table. "Thanks again, guys," he said.

Simon replied, "Any word yet on what's going on?"

Samuel shook his head. "Not yet."

Kelvin muttered, "Figures."

A minute later, Andrea entered the room, followed by the Deputy Director of the center, Ashton Brown, an older man in his fifties with white hair who looked like a cross between Albert Einstein and Colonel Sanders. Behind him walked a young man in his thirties, who was dressed more like a mafia hit man than a scientist. The stranger took a seat at the table opposite everyone else, and just sat there silently observing.

Ashton walked to the corner of the room and pressed a button on the wall, which caused a panel to slide open, revealing a large screen. "Gentlemen…and lady," he said in a southern drawl that seemed totally out of place in California. "We have a serious situation that needs our immediate attention." He pointed a small remote at the screen and a second later the image of Dr. Leonard appeared.

The Doctor got right to the point, "Recently, a small cluster of meteors suddenly appeared out of nowhere perilously close to Earth's orbit. We were hoping they wouldn't pose a threat. We were wrong. Approximately forty-two minutes ago, they entered Earth's atmosphere. While most of the meteors disintegrated upon entry, one of them survived and crashed down in a wooded area near Lake Cahuilla, approximately thirty miles southeast of Palm Springs. Local authorities have already been contacted to secure the crash site until you arrive."

Kelvin spoke up, his grumpiness magnified even more, "So, this is nothing more than a simple bag-and-tag expedition?"

"Not quite," Leonard said. "Shortly after impact, the object exhibited some unusual behavior."

The group looked skeptical. "What kind of behavior?" Andrea asked.

Leonard simply said, "It exploded."

Samuel stated, "That's not uncommon, given the extreme temperature the meteor endured during its descent."

"This is true," the Director replied. "But this happened with civilians present, and they were exposed to some kind of substance when the explosion happened. We need to get there and analyze the site A.S.A.P. Once we've identified the civilians, we'll let you know so you can follow up with them."

The screen went blank, and then Ashton addressed them once more, "NASA has placed this mission at the highest level of importance. Clause here has been hired as your driver and guide. He's familiar with the area and will be there to assist you in case there's any trouble."

Kelvin quipped, "What kind of trouble could there possibly be?"

"The biggest problem may come from the media, as they try to get a closer look at the crash site. But you may also run into some wildlife out there."

Andrea asked nervously, "What kind of wildlife are we talking about?"

Clause replied, "Mainly coyotes, but there could also be bobcats running around. Usually they stay away from humans, but something like this could cause them to behave erratically."

Ashton interrupted, "No need to worry everyone needlessly, Clause. I'm sure everything will go as smoothly as possible. Now, we need to get you on the road right away. Your plane is scheduled to depart in twenties minutes. A truck will be waiting for you in Palm Springs with all of your necessary equipment. We'll maintain constant communication during the entire mission."

With that, he turned and left the room. As the rest of them filed down the hallway toward the hangar, Samuel couldn't help but think that there was more to this 'simple' mission than what they were being told.

CHAPTER 3

After William navigated past the deserted camping area, he turned onto Jefferson Street, the tires of his truck crunching over gravel. With the meteor crash looming in his mind like a dark specter, the night turned thick and oppressive, the kind of darkness that seemed to swallow the truck's headlights whole.

As he rounded onto 58th Avenue, a sensation like searing fire ants erupted across his skin, burning and itching as if his flesh were being devoured alive. He looked over at Tommy and saw him squirming in his seat, clawing at his arms.

"What in the world is this stuff?" Tommy exclaimed in a panic. "It itches like crazy!"

William fought to keep his voice steady. "We'll be home in a few minutes, then we can get cleaned up," he said, though his mind was churning with unimaginable possibilities. Whatever it was, it wasn't from this world, and God only knew what that meant.

"It feels like I have bugs crawling all over me!"

"I know. Me too. Just try not to think about it."

Tommy fell silent, as he tried to ignore the immense worry hammering through his heart. After a minute, he said softly,

"I hope King's okay."

"I'm sure he's fine," William replied, though he wasn't entirely convinced. "Remember, this isn't the first time he's run off, only to come crawling back home a few hours later."

"I guess you're right," Tommy said.

The drive home seemed to take forever, but soon enough, they turned onto Salida Del Sol and pulled into their driveway. The truck had barely come to a stop when Tommy sprang from his seat and bolted out of the truck, sprinting into the house with a pained look plastered on his face. William followed behind, his body aching and his mind swirling as he tried to process the events that had just transpired.

Melinda met him on the porch with a worried look on her face. "My God, William!" she gasped. "What on earth happened to you?"

"It's a long story," William said wearily. "I'll tell you all about it after I get cleaned up."

"Where's Tommy? Is he okay?"

"He's fine. He ran in through the back door to get cleaned up too."

Melinda's eyes narrowed when she realized they were missing someone. "Where's King?"

"He ran off," William said. "That's why Tommy's upset."

"Again?"

"Yeah. Something happened at the lake tonight that spooked him."

With the mysterious substance clinging to his skin, William trudged up the steps, the weight of the night pressing down on him hard.

***

Tommy scrubbed feverishly at the tar-like substance smeared across his face and arms. Hand soap, body wash, even shampoo—all proved useless. The black goo clung to his skin, refusing to budge. He opened the medicine cabinet and spotted a bottle of rubbing alcohol. Desperately, he reached for it, just as Kate shuffled into the bathroom, rubbing her eyes.

"What are you doing up?" Tommy snapped.

Kate blinked sleepily. "You were making so much noise you woke me up."

She squinted at him, looking closely in the grime smeared over his skin. "Ewe, what happened to you? You look disgusting! And you smell bad too!"

"I don't know what this stuff is," Tommy replied. "It came from some rock that crashed down in the woods."

Kate's eyes widened. "Wow! You mean it crashed down from outer space?"

"Yep. I bet it came from Mars, or maybe even farther away, like Jupiter or something."

Kate's expression changed to doubt. "Nuh-uh."

"I bet it did," Tommy insisted, his voice rising.

Kate just rolled her eyes. "Whatever. Just finish cleaning up so I can go back to sleep."

Tommy shot her an irritated look and turned back to the sink. He was about to splash the rubbing alcohol on his arms when the black, oily stuff began to disappear, almost as if being absorbed into his skin. A few seconds later, he was clear of the mysterious substance.

"What in the world just happened?" Kate asked nervously.

Tommy shrugged, bewildered. "Beats me. At least it's gone. Now you can go back to bed and quit bugging me."

Kate stuck her tongue out at Tommy and flounced back

toward her room. Tommy decided he was clean enough for now, turned off the bathroom light, and followed her into the hall. Suddenly, he cried out in agony as a crippling pain shot through his stomach, bringing him to his knees.

Kate rushed back, her eyes wide with worry. "Tommy, what's wrong?"

"It's my stomach," Tommy gasped through clenched teeth. "It hurts bad. Hurry and get Mom."

Kate dashed toward the living room, finding it empty. Panic rising, she sprinted to her parents' bedroom and burst through the door.

Melinda looked up, startled. "What are you doing out of bed, young lady?"

"It's Tommy! He's really sick," Kate blurted out.

Melinda jumped from the bed and followed Kate out of the room, leaving William alone in the shower. She reached the bathroom just as Tommy finished emptying the contents of his stomach into the toilet.

"My God, Tommy!" she exclaimed, rushing to his side. She grabbed a towel from the rack and began wiping up the black mucus that had splattered onto the floor.

Tommy looked up, his face pale. "I don't feel too well."

Melinda pressed a hand to his forehead, her worry deepening. "Oh, you poor thing. You look terrible."

Kate stood nearby, her eyes wide. "I bet it was the space rock."

"Space rock?" Melinda asked, confusion mixing with fear. "What in the world are you talking about?"

"Tommy said it crashed down into the woods and exploded. That's where all of that black junk came from. It was over his skin and then it just disappeared."

Melinda glanced at the towel in her hands and gasped. The black substance was moving. She quickly flushed the toilet and threw the towel into the bathtub, her heart pounding.

"Here, let's get you to bed," she said, her voice trembling as she helped Tommy to his feet. "A good night's sleep should get you feeling better by morning." But inside, she wasn't so sure. She had no idea what was going on, and was afraid to find out.

Tommy was asleep almost instantly when his head hit the pillow. Melinda bent down to kiss his forehead and recoiled in alarm. He was burning up.

She rushed back to the bathroom and returned with a cold, wet washcloth, placing it gently on Tommy's forehead. She tucked his blanket up to his chin, hoping to battle the chills wracking his small body.

Then she turned to Kate, "Okay, little lady, time for you to get back to bed."

Even though Kate usually acted like she hated her big brother, at this moment, seeing him in agony, she couldn't help but feel bad. "Is Tommy going to be okay?" she asked.

"He'll be fine, dear. He just caught a flu bug or something." But Melinda wasn't quite so convinced.

Quietly, Melinda ushered Kate out of the room, closing the door behind her with a soft click. A minute later, she was tucking Kate back into her own bed, smoothing the blankets over her daughter's small frame.

"Try to sleep, sweetheart," she whispered, brushing a stray lock of hair from Kate's forehead, before she kissed her goodnight.

As Melinda walked back toward her bedroom, a sense of unease gnawed at her. The uneasy feeling morphed into cold, hard fear when she heard a loud thud echo from the shower. Her heart leaped into her throat.

She rushed to the bathroom, her breath coming in shallow gasps. The sight that met her eyes was a waking nightmare:

William lay sprawled on the shower floor, twitching uncontrollably. Water still beat down on him from the shower-head, mingling with the wriggling, black mucus being sucked down the drain. Melinda's stomach churned when she saw the smear of blood on the wall where the back of William's head had struck the ceramic tile.

Panic threatened to overwhelm her, but she forced herself to act. She reached in and turned off the water, then grabbed a towel and gently placed it under William's head. His skin was clammy, his eyes vacant. She found another towel in the cabinet and draped it over his shivering body, her hands trembling nearly as much.

The shaking stopped after a minute, and Melinda knelt beside him, her voice wavering. "Hold on, Hun. You're going to be okay. I'm just going to call an ambulance really quick, and I'll be right back."

She sprinted into the bedroom, her fingers fumbling as she dialed 911. The operator's voice was a lifeline. "911 emergency. How can I help you?"

Melinda cried into the phone, "It's my husband! He fell in the shower and hit his head!"

The calm, male voice responded, "Just try to stay calm, Ma'am. We're sending help right away. What's your location?"

"I'm at 1215 Salida Del Sol. Please hurry!"

"We'll be there as soon as we can. Don't attempt to move him until the paramedics arrive." The line went dead, leaving Melinda in a tense, agonizing silence.

She rushed back to the bathroom, relief flooding her as she saw William's eyes flutter open. His mouth moved slightly as he regained consciousness. A streak of black ran from the corner of his mouth and down the side of his cheek—the same vile substance Melinda had seen on the towel earlier.

She watched in horror as the ooze dripped from his face and disappeared down the drain.

Suddenly, William's hand shot out, grabbing her arm with surprising strength. "A meteor," he stuttered. "Something's wrong—"

Melinda hushed him, her voice soothing. "Shhh. It'll be alright. I've already called for help. They should be here soon."

William's eyes closed, and he drifted back into unconsciousness. As Melinda looked down at him, a shiver ran down her spine. She had a strong feeling that the worst was yet to come.

CHAPTER 4

Normally, the block surrounding the La Quinta Police Station —tucked in the corner between City Hall and the La Quinta Community Services Building—was bustling with activity, as assorted charities, businessmen, and entrepreneurs filtered in and out in a consistent parade of bureaucracy. But at this late hour, after the establishments had closed for the day, only the police station buzzed with activity: officers answering phones, typing reports, and chatting over cups of coffee. The walls were adorned with community service awards and photographs of local events, giving the place a homey, albeit busy, atmosphere.

Captain Gerald Harrison, a tall, muscular black man in his fifties, was in his office reviewing reports, wishing he had listened to that little voice in his head earlier that had told him to go home for the day. Instead, he had glanced at the mountain of paperwork on his desk that had seemed to be mysteriously growing by the minute. With a deep sigh, he grabbed the file off the top of the stack and flipped it open.

As he finished signing off on the report a minute later, the phone on his desk rang. "Captain Harrison speaking," he answered.

290

Dr. Leonard's voice came through urgently, "Captain Harrison, this is Dr. Leonard from NASA. We have an emergency situation that requires immediate attention."

Captain Harrison sat up a little straighter. "NASA? What's going on?"

Dr. Leonard didn't waste any time. "A meteor cluster entered Earth's atmosphere about forty-five minutes ago. Most disintegrated, but one crashed down near Lake Cahuilla. It exploded upon impact, releasing an unknown substance. We need you to secure the area immediately while we mobilize a team of scientists to investigate the site."

Captain Harrison's eyes widened. "An unknown substance? Is it dangerous?"

"We're not sure yet, but we can't take any chances. We need you to keep everyone away from the site until our team arrives. This is critical."

Harrison nodded. "Understood, Doctor. I'll secure the area right away."

He hung up the phone and stood, his imposing figure commanding attention as he stepped out of his office. He spotted Officer Drew Hanson at his desk, sorting through a pile of paperwork.

"Hanson, get a couple of officers on the phone ASAP. We have an emergency situation at Lake Cahuilla. A meteor crashed and exploded. NASA needs us to secure the area immediately. Sanchez lives close by. Let her know she's on overtime effective immediately. And radio Rodriguez to join her."

Hanson's eyes widened. "Yes, Captain. I'll get on it right away."

***

Officer Maria Sanchez was enjoying a rare, quiet evening at home. After a long day at work, she had just settled onto her couch with a bowl of popcorn and a movie she'd been looking forward to for weeks. Then, her phone buzzed. She groaned as she reached for it reluctantly.

"Officer Sanchez, this is Hanson."

A deep sigh issued from her lips. She knew before she even heard what was coming next that her rare night off was about to be shot to hell. "Hey, Hanson. What's up?"

"We need you to head to the Lake Cahuilla park entrance immediately. Secure it and ensure no one gets in, especially the media. It's urgent."

"Now?" she asked, her disappointment evident in her voice. "What's going on?"

The sergeant's voice came on, sharp and urgent. "No time for questions, Sanchez. Get moving. Now!"

She glanced longingly at the TV, the opening credits of the movie rolling along in a mocking rhythm. "Copy that," she said, her tone resigned, as she pressed the button on the remote to turn the TV off.

"God, this job fucking sucks sometimes," she said as she grabbed a large handful of popcorn from the bowl before she sat it on the coffee table.

Luckily, she'd been too tired to change out of her uniform when she got home, so she was ready in a matter of minutes. As she grabbed her keys and headed out the door, she couldn't shake the feeling that something was wrong, and the unknown was far worse than any movie could portray. She jumped into her squad car and sped down the quiet streets, her mind filled with all sorts of horrifying scenarios.

***

Officer Juan Rodriguez sat in his patrol car, parked under a flickering streetlight at the edge of town. He was halfway through his nightly routine of filling out paperwork and sipping on a lukewarm coffee when his radio crackled to life.

"Unit 54, this is Dispatch. Over."

Juan set his coffee aside and grabbed the radio. "Unit 54, go ahead, Dispatch."

"We need you to secure the entrance to Lake Cahuilla park immediately. Officer Sanchez is en route to meet you there shortly. No one is to be allowed in, especially the media. It's urgent."

Juan sighed, glancing at the half-finished report on his clipboard. "Copy that, Dispatch. What's going on?"

There was a brief pause, followed by the sergeant's gruff voice. "Just get there, Rodriguez. Now!"

Juan felt a pang of frustration. He hated being kept in the dark, but orders were orders. He quickly gathered his things, tossing the paperwork onto the passenger's seat. *At least it gives me an excuse not to finish this stupid report*, he thought before he started the car, the engine rumbling to life as he peeled away from the curb.

He couldn't shake the feeling that something big had happened. The sergeant's tone had been unusually serious, and Juan's mind raced with possibilities. Maybe it had something to do with the strange tremor he had felt earlier.

The sky was blacker than normal as he navigated his patrol car down Jefferson Street, the oppressive darkness swallowing the road ahead, which was eerily deserted at this hour.

Glancing in his rear-view mirror, he saw a second squad car trailing close behind. He hoped it was Sanchez, the petite, brunette officer whose desk was in the opposite corner from his. He had never mustered the courage to ask her out, but tonight he wished he had.

Just as he refocused on the road, a large dog darted in front of him. "Holy shit!" he cried, swerving to avoid the animal. His headlights illuminated the beast, revealing a grotesque sight. Half of its face had been torn away, leaving raw flesh and bone exposed. The remaining fur was matted with blood, and it snarled at him through a fleshless mouth.

His heart was pounding rapidly as he continued to the park entrance, pulling over just inside and stepping out of his car. Officer Sanchez joined him a minute later, and despite the dread pooling in his stomach, he couldn't help but smile as he watched her approach.

"Nice move back there, Rodriguez," she said sarcastically.

"Hey, a dog ran out in front of me," Rodriguez replied defensively.

"Sure, it did."

"You should have seen it. Its face was all mangled and ripped apart."

"That sounds really disgusting! Let's just hope we don't run into whatever attacked it."

"I couldn't agree more."

Juan's nerves were already on edge, so when he heard a low growl behind him, he whipped his gun from its holster and spun around.

"What the hell was that?" Sanchez asked nervously.

"I don't know. Just stay close," Juan replied.

Sanchez pulled out her flashlight, the beam cutting through the darkness as she drew her own gun. The light stopped on a gruesome scene, making her stomach lurch. A large Bighorn Sheep lay on its side about twenty yards away. The huge animal snarled angrily as it tried to paw its way toward them, its body gruesomely severed in half. A pair of coyotes chomped hungrily on the sheep's stomach, their eyes reflecting the flashlight's beam with an eerie glow.

The two officers backed away slowly until they were right next to Juan's car. He was about to go around to the driver's side when a third coyote emerged from the shadows, blocking his path. This one had a dark, empty socket where one of its eyes should have been, and its right front leg was chewed off up to the joint, causing it to lurch awkwardly. Thick, black blood dripped from its mouth as it growled.

Juan squeezed his gun tighter, preparing himself. The beast lunged, and he jumped sideways, barely avoiding its gnashing fangs. He spun around and pumped a round directly into the coyote's stomach, sending it crashing to the ground.

He was about to turn to Sanchez when, to his horror, the wounded animal got up and started coming for him again. He shot it directly in the chest this time, and it dropped with a thud.

At that moment, he heard Sanchez fire two shots of her own. He spun around to find that the other two coyotes had turned on her. Both were down, one with a bullet in the head and the other through the chest. The one with its brains splattered on the ground stayed down, but the other one got back up and came at her again. Quickly, she shot it between the eyes, and this time it stayed dead.

Juan was so distracted by Sanchez that he failed to notice the coyote that he thought was dead had gotten halfway up and was shuffling toward him. He cried out in agony as the creature's jaws clamped down on his left leg, tearing his calf muscle in half. His gun slid under the squad car as he fell to the ground.

The mangled canine released its grip and lunged for his

throat. Its jaws were inches from his flesh when another shot rang out, hitting it in the side of the head.

Sanchez rushed over to Juan, her face a mask of fear. She set her gun on the ground and quickly ripped off his pant leg to inspect the wound. Even though the sight sickened her, she still had the presence of mind to remove her belt and secure it around Juan's leg as a tourniquet. A sharp cry flew from his mouth as she tightened the belt as much as she could. Then, his body started to shake as the first stages of shock set in. He looked at her in terror for a second before his eyes started rolling back in his head.

"Stay with me, Rodriguez!" she commanded.

As blood poured profusely from the wound and created a large pool around him, the sound of her voice snapped him back to the present. "I don't think—"

"Don't start talking crazy now, okay? I'm gonna get you into the squad car and we're getting the hell out of here," she said as she opened the rear door to the squad car and fought to lift Juan's blood-soaked body into the back seat.

Suddenly, a low, guttural growl filled the air. She looked up to see a big, black mangled German Shepherd bearing down on her. She reached for her gun but it was out of reach.

Juan looked at her and smiled weakly. It was an easy choice, deciding in that moment to sacrifice his life for her. He just prayed that his last act would give her the chance she needed to survive. As the dog drew closer, he picked up a rock and hurled it with the last of his strength, hitting the animal hard enough to divert its attention. The beast turned and lunged at Juan. "Run!" he cried.

He fended the beast off for a few desperate moments, but his injury had sapped his strength. Finally, the dog's jaws clamped down on his neck, ripping his windpipe out in a spray of blood.

Everything had happened so fast that Sanchez was paralyzed with terror as she watched the gruesome scene unfold. She didn't notice the blood-soaked bobcat creeping up behind her until its claws raked down her back, sending her falling forward under the weight of the maddened feline. A brief scream erupted from her mouth before its sharp teeth sank deep into her skull, silencing her forever.

AUTHOR BIO

Growing up in the shadow of Notre Dame's Golden Dome, Scott Dokey developed a strong affinity for the arts, learning at a young age the joy of transforming an empty page into something magical. Eventually, as an adult, his creative endeavors expanded to include writing and filmmaking. Focusing primarily on subjects with horror and supernatural aspects, he became an award-winning screenwriter, and has produced and directed several short films and a no-budget feature film.

Scott currently lives in Southern California with his wife, Jennifer, and their daughter, Kaylee, enjoying the sweltering 120° summer heat. Of course, 85° in January more than makes up for it.

To find out more about his work visit his website at www.scottdokey.com

Be sure to check out the Hellish series:
Hellish Book One: Tortured Souls
Hellish Book Two: The Chosen
Hellish Book Three: Unholy Religion

Hellish Book Four: Vizibir

* 9 7 9 8 9 9 0 8 6 9 6 1 5 *